# JENNIFER ANNE DAVIS

# RISE

## ORDER OF THE KRIGERS
## BOOK ONE

**Month9Books**

RISE by Jennifer Anne Davis
All rights reserved. Published in the United States of America by Month9Books, LLC.

ISBN: 978-1-942664-89-5

Published by Month9Books, Raleigh, NC 27609
Cover designed by www.derangeddoctordesigns.com

Month9Books

*For Jessica*

# Krigers

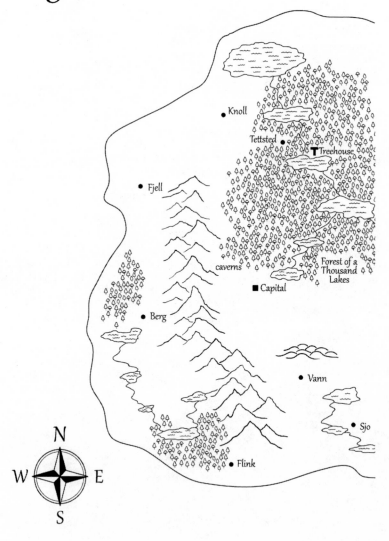

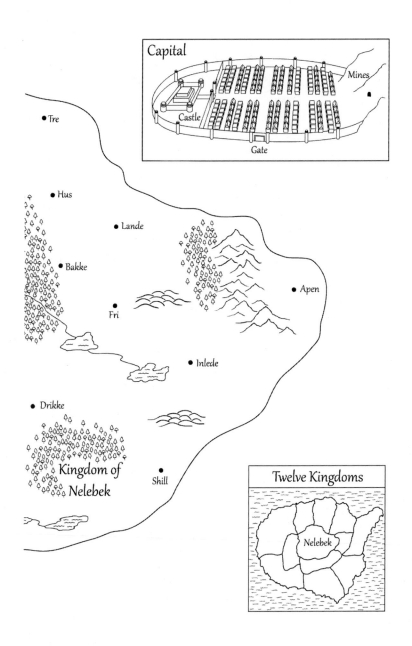

Capital

Mines

Castle

Gate

Tre

Hus

Lande

Bakke

Fri

Apen

Inlede

Drikke

Kingdom of
Nelebek

Shill

Twelve Kingdoms

Nelebek

# RISE

ORDER OF THE KRIGERS
BOOK ONE

# Prologue: *Fortid*

In a hut on the outskirts of a small village, the old woman tied the girl's wrists and ankles to the table. Dawn's first light shone on the horizon, and the moons still hung in the sky to the west—the best time to perform powerful magic. At the ripe age of sixteen, the naive girl had no idea what was about to happen.

"Why are you willing to help me?" she asked.

The old woman's lips curled into a smile. "My kind is fading away. By giving you my magic, I am creating something far more powerful than me to save all the *Heks*."

"Isn't that what Skog Heks is trying to do in the mines?"

"If she finds the power source, there's no guarantee new *Heks* will be born. Now that the balance of power is off, I know what to do. By using you, I can guarantee *Heks* don't become extinct."

The old woman clasped her hands together. When she pulled them apart, a blue light appeared. The small ball of magic glowed, waiting to be molded and used. "Our land is divided into twelve kingdoms," she murmured. "I will create twelve warriors who will not only save Nelebek, but all our land." She drew her hands farther apart, and the blue orb grew larger. "They shall be bound to my magic and will have no choice but to do my will."

"Twelve warriors? Bound to your magic? What are you talking about? You didn't tell me any of this!" The girl's pretty brown eyes widened. "You said you would help undo what Skog Heks did! That I would be reunited with the man I love."

"If I told you the truth, you never would have agreed."

"Why me?" The girl struggled against her bindings to no avail.

"I'm sorry, child, but it has to be you. The king is protected under the treaty. However, you are simply a mere human, and the terms of the treaty don't apply to you the same way they do to those who govern. You are the only one who can undo it all. You are his weakness." She pointed to the twelve weapons lying on the ground. A piece of the blue orb broke off, splitting into a dozen smaller balls, each one plunging into one of the weapons and filling it with a bit of magic.

"The next eleven male births will start this." Another chunk of the orb broke off and formed eleven smaller pieces that darted out of the room and disappeared. "Now, it's your turn." Her hands moved over the girl's chest, and the blue light hovered there.

"Please don't hurt me!" the girl begged, thrashing against her bindings.

"Yours will be the first one, the strongest one, and will save all the *Heks*." She said the next part of the spell in a language rarely spoken—words from the old days—sealing the kingdom of Nelebek's fate.

The light flashed and then plummeted into the girl's chest.

She screamed; flailing her body as the magic filled her. A moment later, the blue light faded away. The girl stilled and passed out.

"It's done." The old woman leaned down and kissed her forehead. "Once the twelve have risen, a new era will dawn. One in which *Heks* and humans are one, and *Heks* will finally have a choice."

# Chapter One

I staggered into my apartment. The bed, tucked in the corner of the room, begged me to lie down, if only for a moment. But my sore feet, raw hands, and aching back—the result of washing clothes for twelve hours straight—would have to wait for a reprieve because hunger overruled the need for sleep. Opening the kitchen cupboard blackened with dirt and grime, I found only a few crumbs scattered on the shelves. How were we going to survive? Stomping from above shook the ceiling, causing dust to rain down. A baby cried and a couple argued on the other side of the wall.

"Kaia," my father said as he entered the room. "I didn't hear you come in."

"Why are you home so early?" I asked, kissing his cheek. His face was paler than usual, his hair disheveled, and his eyes had dark circles under them.

Instead of answering, he swung his arms, loosening them up.

"Let's get to it."

Hopefully, he hadn't lost his job from being too sick to work. If he did, we would not only be out of food, but we'd be out of this apartment as well. It might not be much, but it was all we had. I'd grown up in these two rooms, and, most likely, would be where I lived the rest of my life.

"Sure," I said, too tired to train. "What do you want to work on first?"

"Hand to hand combat," he said. Besides the kitchen cupboards and my straw mattress covered with a few dingy blankets, the only other furniture in the room was a wooden table, two chairs, and a box for my clothes.

As I stood across from Papa in the middle of the room, my stomach growled. His hand barreled down toward me. Raising my left arm, I blocked the strike and punched his gut. When he hunched forward, I latched onto his shoulders, pulling him down and slamming my knee into his head. He toppled to the ground.

After a minute, my father raised his eyebrows. "Aren't you going to finish me off?" he asked, leaping to his feet. "You had me. Why'd you stop?"

"When my attacker is on the ground, there's no reason to render him unconscious or murder him. Fleeing is easy at that point."

He shook his head. "Honey, when the time comes, you won't have the opportunity to consider whether a person should be killed or not. We train so you can act without thinking."

"I'd rather train so that when the time comes, if it ever does, I can defend myself and make the right choice. If there's another way to escape, why should I murder the person?" It was difficult to argue with my father since he always insisted he was right. As much as I loved him, I didn't necessarily agree with him.

"Your mother would be proud of the woman you've become," he said, changing the subject.

"Why don't you ever talk about her?" I asked. "Do we look alike? How'd she spend her time?" If only he would tell me something, anything, so I could feel a connection to her.

"Not right now," Papa said, staring at his feet. "You're not done with your lesson."

Of course. Training always came first—it was the most important aspect of my life. Since my mother had died delivering me, my father felt it was his duty to make sure I could take care of myself. Inconsequential things such as knowing anything about my own mother would have to wait. Survival was the one, and only, goal in this desolate kingdom.

Even though my arms shook from hunger, I smiled. "What do you want to work on now?"

"Let's practice what to do if someone comes up behind you."

Turning my back to my father, I patiently waited for him to attack. When he didn't, I glanced behind me. Papa bent over clutching his chest. Running to where he kept his medicine, I grabbed the bottle off the moldy shelf and uncorked it. It was empty, and my heart sank. There should be at least another week's worth. Papa had to be taking more than he should, which could only mean one thing: he wasn't getting any better.

"I'm sorry," he said, wheezing. "I didn't want to worry you." He coughed, and little droplets of blood spattered on the floor.

Tears filled my eyes, and I hastily blinked them away. "I'll go to the apothecary's and get more medicine." I wrapped my arm around his torso and helped him hobble to the wooden chair at the table.

"It's almost curfew," he said, sitting down. "It's too dangerous for you to be out at this hour."

Without the medicine, my father's condition would only worsen. "Let me do this for you." It was nothing I couldn't handle. He worked hard to ensure I was taken care of—it was my turn to see to his needs.

Papa pulled out his handkerchief and wiped off the blood covering is lips. "There's no money left."

He started coughing again, and I struggled to hold back my rage. He was forced to work as a *soldat* in the mines for the king, yet he wasn't paid nearly enough to feed us, let alone to have extra money for expensive items such as medicine. It wasn't fair.

"Don't worry," I replied. "There's a little bit of money left over from my job." Reaching under my mattress, my fingers fumbled around until they came across my one and only coin. It wouldn't be enough, but it was better than nothing.

"Kaia," my father said. "Go tomorrow instead. It'll be safer." The handkerchief clutched in his hand was moist with blood, and a foul, metallic smell permeated the air.

"You might not be alive come morning. I'm going—and there's nothing you can say to stop me." I leaned down and kissed his cheek.

"Remember everything I've taught you, everything we've practiced." He patted my shoulder. "And when you return, we need to talk. There's something I must tell you."

With curfew going into effect in a few short hours, I needed to leave instead of dwelling on what Papa had to say. Wrapping a knit scarf around my neck, I closed the door to our apartment and ran down the rickety, wooden steps to the first floor. The repulsive smell of body odor and waste hung heavy in the stale air. Holding my breath, I hurried along the dark corridor and shoved the door open, stepping outside and inhaling the fresh air.

The chilly wind whipped around my body. Thankfully, I had on sturdy pants, a plain shirt, and a thick leather vest instead of a dress. For as long as I could remember, Papa insisted I wear trousers because they were easier to move and fight in. Pulling the scarf around my mouth, I made sure my long, brown hair was tucked under my shirt. The key to making it through the capital without attracting the *soldats'* attention was to keep my head down and walk quickly.

Since most people hurried home from work at this hour, I easily vanished into the crowd. *Soldats* stood posted at each street corner watching everyone. Across the way, a young man joked with his friend—he should have known better. In less than a minute, half a dozen men dressed in red uniforms descended upon him.

"I didn't do anything!" the young man screamed. A *soldat* punched him in the stomach, yanked his hands back, and tied his wrists together. He dragged the young man down the street, presumably to the dungeon. It took all my willpower to keep walking the other way. Papa had drilled it in me to pick my battles. Unless my life was in danger, I had to stand down, regardless of the injustice of the situation. Curling my fingers, I made two fists, keeping my anger under control. This was no way to live.

Passing between the tall, gray, windowless buildings lining the street, an oppressive feeling overwhelmed me. Each structure was jam-packed with apartments housing multiple families similar to the one I lived in. The sound of people speaking, children crying, and soldiers yelling was constant. The smell of decaying rats, trash, and vomit coated the air like a wool blanket.

Rounding a corner, I spied the king's castle in the distance. Its imposing black stone walls and bleak towers mirrored the capital and my future. Legend said it was once a shining, gleaming, white castle filled with lively parties and a ruler who cared about his subjects. I didn't believe any part of that. It was probably just wishful thinking—a fairy tale to lull children to sleep at night. The only people who entered or left the castle were *soldats* from the King's Army. The king didn't care about his subjects—he obsessed over hunting down and capturing the Krigers.

Turning onto another street, I quickly took note of where each *soldat* stood and avoided passing near them. Men covered with dirt from laboring in the mines stopped at the taverns on their way home from work. Women carried baskets, desperately trying to sell knitted scarves, socks, and gloves. There were two hours until curfew, just enough time for me to buy my father's medicine and make it home.

After passing the baker and blacksmith, both closing up for the night, I finally arrived at my destination. I entered the apothecary's store; a gray cat darted in front of me, but otherwise the place seemed empty. Shelves containing all sorts of glass jars, most of them no larger than my hand, lined the walls of the small room from the scarred wooden floor to the cracked plaster ceiling. At the counter, I cleared my throat. A moment later, the apothecary entered through the back curtain, his dark eyes darting around the store nervously.

"Kaia." He smiled, relieved. "How is your father doing?" he asked, wiping his hands on a small towel.

"He hasn't improved." Placing my money on the counter, I hoped we could strike a deal. "He needs more breathing medicine."

"Maybe it's time to let your father go." The apothecary slid the coin back toward me.

Papa was all I had left, and just the thought of losing him

made it hard to breathe. I pushed my coin back toward the apothecary and folded my arms.

The apothecary rubbed his tired face. "Medicine is expensive. Didn't you just turn sixteen?"

I nodded.

"Then you can legally work."

"Are you offering me a job?" A woman in my apartment building already employed me at helping her wash clothes. It didn't pay much, but it afforded me the flexibility to go home and take care of my father if needed.

"I can't hire you," he said. "An apprentice is already assigned to me." He turned around and took a jar off the shelf behind him. "This is one week's worth of medicine."

"Thank you." As I reached for it, he snatched it away with his long, bony fingers.

"This isn't free," he scolded me.

"I promise to pay you."

"I have mouths to feed, too." The cat jumped onto the counter and lay down so the apothecary could scratch its plump belly.

"What about cleaning your store or making deliveries?" There had to be something he needed.

He held the jar in his free hand, taunting me. "There is an errand that must be taken care of." He leaned forward on the counter, placing the glass bottle before me and shooing the cat away. "Do this favor for me, and I'll give you one day's worth of medicine."

Clenching my hands, I muttered, "Only one day?"

"That's what I'm offering." He smiled.

The gray cat slunk up next to me, rubbing its body against my legs. Seeing no other feasible option at this late hour, I agreed. The apothecary reached under the counter and pulled out a small jar, setting it on the wooden surface. After pouring a tiny amount of medicine inside, he corked it and held the bottle in front of my face. "I need you to go to the Town Square."

The Town Square always crawled with men from the King's Army looking for young, able-bodied people to recruit. They would arrest the person and tell him that he could go free if he willingly joined the army. Other times, they would put the person to work in the mines, digging for the *Heks* power source. Many steered clear of the Town Square in order to avoid being forced into the king's service. I would rather die than become a slave.

"Still want the medicine?" the apothecary asked.

"Yes," I snapped. "Tell me what to do."

"Look for a man wearing a fur-trimmed jacket," he instructed. "He's … well, not from around here. And he's someone you never want to cross."

Most likely, this man was a criminal. I swallowed, contemplating my options. Doing this errand meant receiving my father's medicine. Papa would be upset with the risks involved. However, he'd also told me to pick my battles—and this battle I was willing to fight.

I reached for the jar, and the apothecary nicked it away. "I'll give it to you when you return. I need some form of insurance you'll make the delivery."

"It'll be curfew by then," I said, clutching the counter so tightly, my knuckles turned white.

"Then I suggest you hurry." The apothecary went to a wooden cabinet concealed in the corner of the room between two large shelves. Slipping his hand into his pocket, he produced a long, thin key. He unlocked the door, reached inside, and pulled out a black bottle the size of my pinkie finger. After locking the door, he came over and carefully placed the bottle on the palm of my hand.

"I have some advice for you," he said, drumming his fingers on the counter. "This man disposes of people for a living. Try to avoid asking him any questions, and don't make eye contact."

My heart pounded just thinking about the task before me. "I understand."

"You better be on your way. He's expecting someone to deliver it at any minute."

With shaking hands, I hid the bottle under my leather vest. The apothecary crept out from behind the counter, shoving me out of his shop and onto the street, closing and bolting the door behind me.

I shivered, wanting to forget the feel of his fingers digging into my shoulders. Folding my hands under my arms, I took the main road that led straight to the center of town. Nearing the Town Square, the street became unusually packed.

Walking shoulder to shoulder with dozens of people filtering into the Town Square, I tried to listen to the conversations of those around me. Many whispered the word *execution*. I froze, not wanting to witness something so heinous. People bumped into me, pushing me forward into the open cobblestone area.

The Town Square was approximately one hundred feet by one hundred feet wide, surrounded by shops. A wooden platform was situated in the middle. A man dressed in black holding an ax stood atop it. My stomach lurched. I'd never witnessed an execution before. There hadn't been any gossip in my building and, hopefully, it was no one I knew. This was another reason my father insisted the area be avoided at all cost.

Making my way through the crowd of at least three hundred people, I searched for the man dressed in a fur-trimmed jacket, hoping he'd stand out and I'd find him before the prisoner was brought forth.

A hush descended over the crowd as the king's personal guard—men dressed in solid black with the royal crest embroidered on their tunics—marched into the Town Square, clearing a path between the people, directly to the execution platform. A clattering sound arose as a shiny black carriage with its curtains drawn shut rode through the open area the *soldats* had created. When the carriage turned, the painted crest of the king, Morlet Forseve shone. Even though we lived in the capital where the king's primary residence was located, Morlet rarely made public appearances. He spent most of his time scouring the various towns in the kingdom of Nelebek, searching for the Krigers.

The carriage pulled to a stop before the platform, and a footman opened the door. A figure dressed in a black cape that covered his head and body emerged. He glided up the stairs and spoke briefly with the executioner. I stood on my toes, trying to get a better look.

No one in the Town Square spoke.

"What's going on?" I whispered to the man standing next to me.

"The king ordered the execution of the man who aided Kriger Henrik before he was imprisoned two seasons ago."

Legend stated that when Morlet used dark magic and came into power, twelve warriors, known as Krigers, were born. Krigers had special abilities and magical weapons. When all twelve Krigers came together and united their powers, they would be strong enough to defeat Morlet. Papa told me that at first, Morlet hunted down and killed the Krigers. However, every time he killed one, a new one was born. The only way for him to end the

Krigers was to kill all twelve at the same time, when their powers were linked, thus ending the Order of the Krigers forever.

And now, the king had eleven of the twelve imprisoned.

Although I'd never known or met a Kriger before, every night I wished I'd see the day they came together and killed the king. If Morlet was gone, surely the people of Nelebek would have a chance at a better life—one without poverty and fear.

Morlet was so desperate to capture the twelve Krigers that he cast a spell on the borders of the kingdom, one that prohibited anyone from entering or leaving Nelebek. Landlocked and with trade to the other eleven kingdoms cut off, the people of Nelebek sank deeper and deeper into poverty. Of course, we were also the only kingdom ruled by someone consumed with dark magic. The king was human—not a *Heks*—but he didn't age like humans. Some said he'd been ruling Nelebek for over a century. And since he used dark magic, no one could harm him. Except for the Krigers.

A man dressed as a scribe stepped to the edge of the platform, holding a scroll. "Anyone aiding or abetting enemies of His Royal Highness will be prosecuted under the full extent of the law. The charges are as follows: Finn Flanning knowingly housed Kriger Henrik and didn't report it to the authorities. He is hereby found guilty and sentenced to death." The scribe stood tall and stiff.

The king sauntered to the middle of the platform. What was he doing here today? He wouldn't attend simply for a scheduled execution. There had to be something else going on.

The scribe cleared his throat and continued. "If anyone has information regarding the twelfth and final Kriger, you are hereby ordered to report your information immediately. Otherwise, you will be subject to execution." His hands shook, and his voice became high-pitched as he spoke. "We have reason to believe the twelfth Kriger is in the capital."

People around me gasped in astonishment, looking at one another. There was no way to know if someone was a Kriger until he turned eighteen and his latent powers revealed themselves. Could the Kriger be here among us at this very moment? The king glided forward and clapped his hands together, sending a *boom* throughout the Town Square. Cool air brushed against my skin, blowing my scarf into the air. My hair tumbled down my back. The need to get out of there became intense. Inching my way to the side, I slowly moved toward the exit, still looking for a man dressed in a fur-trimmed jacket.

"Does anyone have information on the last Kriger?" the scribe asked before rolling up his scroll.

No one spoke.

"I will find the last filthy Kriger," the king bellowed, his voice harsh and cold. "Even if it means I have to torture every single one of you to do it."

More *soldats* entered the courtyard, surrounding the crowd. They held their swords before them, ready to fight. Was the king intending to kill all of us right now? The exit was still too far away for me to make a run for it. Sweat coated my forehead, and my heart beat frantically.

The king pointed a black-gloved finger toward the crowd. A woman screamed as an invisible force ripped her toddler from her arms. The king pointed to his own feet, and the child moved through the air, landing on the ground in front of him. The toddler sat on the platform, crying for her mother. I watched, horrified at the prospect of what the king would do to the child. Morlet clapped his hands, and thunder rumbled. He rubbed his hands together and then pulled them six inches apart. A single blue flame appeared.

I wanted to rescue the child. However, I was no match for

Morlet and his evil magic. All that would result would be my own death, and then who would save my father? I bit my lip, trying to keep my anger and fear hidden, instead of doing something I'd regret.

As Morlet spread his arms wider, the flame grew. His hands extended toward the toddler. "Does anyone have information regarding the twelfth Kriger?" Morlet asked, his voice dark and menacing.

The child's mother ran to the platform. A *soldat* standing on top of a nearby building released an arrow, hitting her thigh. She screamed and fell to the ground, clutching her leg. Everyone stood frozen, afraid to move and be shot.

"Anyone?" Morlet asked again. The flame fluttered above the child's head while she cried. The child tried crawling to her mother, but was unable to do so because of the magical force holding her in place. The mother dug her nails into the cobblestones, dragging herself forward. A *soldat* ran over and put his foot on her back, preventing her from going anywhere.

Anger filled my body. My hands tingled, and a rush of heat coursed through me. The sudden desire to kill the king in order to protect the child overwhelmed me. Against my better judgment, I stared at Morlet, wanting to see the monster hiding under the black cape. His head jerked back, and the flame disappeared. It felt as if something extended from my core to his, and I couldn't look away from him. A single beam of sunlight broke through the thick clouds, shining on the face formerly hooded underneath.

To my great shock, the king was a young man around twenty, with an appealing face, strong jawline, and short, dark hair. His penetrating blue eyes met mine. He cocked his head, studying me. As he waved his hand in an arc, a blast of heat hit me. I cried out and fell to my knees—our eyes still locked on each other.

Was the king using his dark magic on me? My arms and legs shook. I couldn't stand or tear my eyes away from Morlet's.

The word *Kriger* formed in my head, gently, like a soft whisper of smoke curling around a branch.

*Kriger.* This time louder, more forceful, almost accusing.

My palms tingled. Something swelled in them below the surface. What was happening? A hand clamped down on my arm, and I was finally able to break eye contact with the king.

"Look at me and focus," a gruff voice whispered. I glanced at the man holding me. "We don't have much time." He released my arm. "Can you touch this?" He pulled out a silver necklace from under his shirt. A large, round medallion dangled from it.

I hesitated, since I had no idea who this man was or why he was helping me. "Unless you want to be arrested, do as I say."

"Move!" Morlet roared. He descended from the platform and made his way toward me.

I reached out and touched the medallion. The man cursed.

"Where did she go?" the king shouted frantically, unable to see me through the dense crowd.

"Morlet is coming for you." The man slipped off his large, fur-trimmed jacket and handed it to me. "Put this on."

I shoved my arms into the warm coat, realizing this was the man I was looking for. Pulling out the black jar, I handed it to him.

He rocked back on his heels, startled, but quickly put the bottle in his pocket. "I have to get you out of here," he said, his brown eyes intense.

The apothecary had said this man was dangerous and that I shouldn't speak or look at him. I quickly averted my eyes to the ground. Yet, something in my gut urged me to trust the assassin.

"Rise to your feet very slowly," he instructed.

I got up, and he moved in front of me, his large frame

blocking me from the king's line of sight. The assassin was a good foot taller than I was. He appeared to be around eighteen, but there was something about his demeanor—the way he stood, the intensity in his brown eyes—that indicated he'd been around much longer. Unlike most men, his brown hair was shorn close to his head, and he had the muscular build of a man from the King's Army instead of the scrawny, malnourished body of a commoner.

"Can you ride a horse?" he asked in a low voice.

"No." I'd never even been near a farm of any sort.

He cursed. "Are you a fast runner?" His eyes darted around the Town Square.

"Sort of." Panic engulfed me. I couldn't afford to be captured by the king. Papa needed me.

"Take my hand. Whatever you do, don't let go. Understand?" I nodded, and his fingers curled around mine. He dropped his free arm to his side, and a long dagger slid out from his sleeve. Lifting his arm, he threw the dagger behind me. It embedded in a *soldat's* chest.

"Run," the assassin commanded, "straight to the tailor's store."

Morlet, once again hidden under his cape, pointed a finger at me as he'd done to the child. I stayed rooted in place. He began walking my direction, tossing people out of his way as he shouted at his men to capture me.

The assassin pulled me forward, and we sprinted for the store located twenty feet away. Screams echoed through the Town Square, and chaos erupted. People ran every which way. The *soldats* advanced on us. We bumped into several citizens as we headed for the door with a Closed sign hanging on it. Without stopping, I grabbed the handle and threw the door open, relieved it wasn't locked.

He shoved me inside and slammed the door shut behind us,

holding it closed with his body. "Move that piece of furniture over here," he yelled, pointing to a table in the room. "Hurry, before they break the door in."

Squinting in the dim light, I found a large table covered with fabric swatches. I shoved it toward the entrance and turned the table on its side. The assassin thrust it against the door, holding it in place.

"Hurry and get two wooden dowels."

*Soldats* pounded on the other side of the door. The assassin's face reddened from straining to hold it closed. I grabbed the dowels. Handing one to him, I put the other one on the ground and then angled it toward the table, wedging it in place. Once it was sturdy, I did the same with the other dowel.

"Now lift up the rug in the corner," he demanded, still leaning his body against the table.

I followed the man's line of sight and ran to the corner, then pulled up the edge of the area rug, revealing a small, rectangular door.

"Open it and get inside."

As I lifted the wooden door, the assassin slowly released the table, ensuring the dowels held it in place. He ran to the back of the store and broke a window. Was he leaving me?

Shouts came from the front of the shop. The table and dowels shook as *soldats* banged against the door. I lowered my feet into the black hole and dropped onto the ground. The assassin came into view above me. He lowered himself, reached out and flipped the rug on top of the door, and then finished closing it all the way. I heard metal clang and then the sound of a bolt sliding into place.

Darkness swallowed us. A hand clamped over my mouth, and the assassin held me against his body. I yelped, but the sound was muffled by his hand. "Don't speak," he whispered. "They'll be inside any minute. They have to believe we left out the back window."

Realizing he wasn't going to hurt me, I nodded, and he released me.

There was a rustling sound, and the assassin lit a small fire. He raised the flint to the torch hanging on the wall. Once it took, he grabbed the torch and motioned for me to follow him. We headed down a long, dark tunnel, dirt crunching under our boots. After about thirty feet, he turned to face me. "We need to put as much distance between them and us as possible."

He started running, and I took off after him. Our elongated shadows bounced on the walls as we sprinted. The heavy, fur-trimmed jacket weighed me down. After ten minutes, my legs ached and my lungs burned. Unable to run another step, I stopped and bent over, heaving deep breaths.

The man jogged back to me. "The exit is near." He grabbed my arm and dragged me down the tunnel.

Thinking only of getting to my father, I forced my legs to move. Not only did Papa desperately need his medicine, but if someone from the Town Square managed to identify me, *soldats* could go to my home. My father would be taken to prison and tortured. I needed to get to him before they did.

We finally arrived at a dead end. "There's a ladder," the man whispered. "I'll go first to make sure the exit is clear. If it is, I'll wave you up."

He handed me the torch and swiftly scaled the ladder, not making a sound. Once he was at the top, a crack of light pierced the darkness. Opening the door in the ceiling farther, the assassin exited, closing it behind him.

Standing there, holding an almost-burned-out torch, I had no idea what I'd gotten myself into.

# Chapter Two

The last of the torch burned out, and complete darkness engulfed me. Neither voices nor the sound of commotion came from above. Throwing the useless torch on the ground, I felt around for the ladder. When my hands came across the rungs, I grabbed on and climbed up until my head hit a wooden door.

It flew halfway open, and two startled, brown eyes were right in front of me. "What are you doing?" the assassin asked. "I told you I'd wave you up when it was clear."

"I got tired of waiting."

He threw the door the rest of the way open, and I climbed out into a small, dimly lit room. Three older men wearing mining uniforms stood staring at me.

I wanted to ask where we were, but decided to keep my mouth shut. Did these men intend to harm me? Would they take me to Morlet for a reward?

"Are you certain?" one of them asked, squinting at me as if I were an insect.

The assassin nodded. "She can touch the medallion."

"And only Krigers can do that?"

"Krigers or those cursed by a *Heks*," the assassin answered. "Regardless, I'll take her to him for confirmation."

"I don't understand," another said. "She's a girl. And tiny. Just look at your coat—it's so long that it hangs past her knees. There's no way she's a warrior."

Sliding off the jacket, I tossed it on the ground. These men didn't appear to be adversaries—but that didn't mean I had to stand there and listen to them insult me. Crossing my arms, I asked, "Who are you, and why did you bring me here?"

The three men looked to the assassin. "I'll explain everything later," he said. "For now, we need to get to a safe location. Morlet is searching for you."

"Am I a Kriger?" It didn't seem possible—I was a girl and only sixteen. Krigers were men who didn't come into their powers until the age of eighteen. Yet, when the word was whispered in my head, something inside of me had responded.

No one spoke. I didn't have time for this. "I need to get to the apothecary's. He has my father's medicine." When I turned to leave, the assassin blocked my path. "Get out of my way."

"You have to come with me," he insisted.

"I don't have to do anything."

"You don't understand the enormity of your situation," he whispered. "Morlet knows you're the twelfth Kriger."

Cold fear gushed through me. If the king believed I was a Kriger, he'd stop at nothing to capture me. My hands tingled, and I curled my fingers, making two fists. "My father needs me."

A scratching noise came from a narrow door I hadn't noticed before. One of the men went over, opened it a crack, and briefly spoke to someone on the other side. After he closed it, he turned and gravely said, "The *soldats* are already here."

"Where is your father now?" The assassin clutched my arm.

"He's at home." How was I supposed to make my way to the apothecary's and then to the apartment when not only was curfew going into effect at any minute, but the army was now after me? I turned and kicked the wall. This was an impossible situation.

Grabbing my hair, I twisted it over my right shoulder, trying to think of how to accomplish everything. There had to be a way. My hands started shaking, and my stomach churned. The horror of today's events took its toll on me.

"The apothecary you made the delivery for, does he have your father's medicine?" the assassin asked. He pulled my hands from my hair, forcing me to focus on him.

"Yes."

"I know the apothecary you speak of," one of the men said. "I will go and get the medicine for your father."

Another one added, "And I'll fetch your father. He'll be safe at my home. He can stay with us for the time being, and my wife will tend to him."

Why were these strangers willing to help me? Could I entrust them with Papa?

"Excellent," the assassin said. "Let's go." He grabbed my arm and dragged me to the door.

"Not until you tell me where we're going and why you're helping me." I tried yanking free.

The assassin cursed. "I need to get you out of the capital and physically away from Morlet. Once you're safe, we can talk."

"But my father—"

"These are good men." The assassin's face hardened. "They will see to his safety." There was a sharp edge to his voice, his patience wearing thin. "We must leave before you're discovered." He threw open the door and hauled me out into a dark hallway. At the end of the corridor, he opened another door and shoved me inside. Clothes littered the ground, and the bed was unmade.

"What's your name?" he asked.

"What's yours?" I countered. Why had he brought me to this bedchamber?

He sighed, staring at the ceiling. "Anders," he replied, not looking at me.

The door flew open, causing me to jump. A well-endowed woman entered. "There are half a dozen *soldats* downstairs rifling through the place," she informed us. "They're searching for a girl with long, brown hair who is wearing pants." She looked pointedly at me.

Anders's eyes raked over my body, making me feel uncomfortable. I took a step back, hitting the bed. "Can you cut her hair?" he asked. "And put her in a dress?"

"It won't be pretty since we're rushing, but I can do it."

"I don't care whether she looks pretty or not," he said. "Just make her look different." He turned and left.

The woman, whose breasts were barely contained in her dress, opened a drawer and pulled out a short knife. "Don't move," she said.

"What are you doing?" I demanded, dashing to the other side of the bed.

"Chopping off your hair," she replied, exasperated. A loud bang came from below. "We need to hurry."

Reluctantly, I scurried over to the woman, and she began sawing off my long strands. Hair dropped to the floor, scattering around my feet while I bit my thumbnail, wishing she would move faster.

"There," she said, examining her work. "Not bad." She went to the large armoire in the corner of the room. "Now for your clothing." She rummaged around inside. "Here we go." The woman pulled out a dark green dress made of lamb's wool and threw it to me.

After quickly changing, I glanced at the only mirror in the room, praying the disguise would work. My choppy, shorn hair hit my shoulders, making me look even younger than before. The dress was laughably large since I didn't have a chest to fill it out. When was the last time I'd worn something so … feminine?

"Stop scowling," the woman chided. She cinched up the back of the dress, but it still hung loose on me. "That's the best that can be done," she mumbled. "You need to be on your way."

Anders opened the door and poked his head in. "Let's go." He now wore a gray knit cap and a black sweater that complemented his eyes. I hurried down the hallway after him. He paused before a door. "I sincerely hope you're a good actress," he said, "because if you're not, we're both dead."

What had I gotten myself into now? He opened the door, and we stepped onto the landing of the second floor. On the level below, a *soldat* stood guard by the door while half a dozen others roamed about the room. It was easy to pick them out since they wore the standard red uniform of the army. Several tables were occupied by men drinking, while a dozen women meandered around, all scantily clad and not at all bothered by the presence of the king's men.

My eyes bulged. "Is this a brothel?" I asked, horrified.

Anders leaned down close to me. "It is," he whispered in my ear, sending shivers down my spine. "And we just bedded. So I suggest you start playing the part, and lead me downstairs, woman." He swatted my bottom.

My entire body heated up from utter and complete embarrassment. There was no way I, a sixteen-year-old girl who had nothing to entice a man with, could pull this off. My free time was spent learning to fight, not wooing men. The girls my age who did this sort of thing didn't look or act like me. Then again, it wasn't as if I was a harlot—I just had to pretend to be one.

Rolling my shoulders back and standing tall, I held onto my green dress, trying to still my sweaty hands as we headed down the stairs. A couple of tables had been flipped upside down, and two *soldats* stood at the bar questioning patrons about me. The only way out of this alive was to play the part. Reaching back, I grabbed Anders's hand and batted my eyelashes at him like girls my age did when flirting. Luckily, the king's rules about not laughing or showing public affection were only enforced outside. The corners of Anders's lips rose as he fought a smile. My face went flaming red.

At the bottom of the stairs, he slid his hands around my waist and nuzzled his head to my neck. "Sit in a dark corner," he whispered. "Don't let them see your face. As soon as they leave, we'll exit through the kitchen."

There were many dark corners to choose from. Heading to the nearest one, Anders sat on a chair and pulled me onto his lap. There had better not be anyone here from my apartment building.

"This isn't going to work if you keep acting like a stiff board," Anders mumbled. "At least pretend you're an alluring woman who has bedded dozens of men."

If there hadn't been *soldats* crawling all over the place right now, I'd have punched Anders right across his face. What infuriated me the most was that he was right. Not having any idea how to act, I observed the people around me. At the table next to us, a man sat on a chair drinking from a pewter mug, while a woman straddled him, playing with his shoulder-length hair.

Anders didn't have enough hair to run my fingers through, and there was no way I was going to sit astride him while wearing a dress. Anders laughed, throwing his head back.

"What?" I asked, appalled he'd been able to read my mind.

His hands slid on either side of my face. I tried pulling away, but he drew me closer. "Stop scrunching your nose as if you're disgusted." He moved his lips to my right ear. "And if you're not going to play the part, then I will for the both of us. There's no way I'm going to be taken before Morlet to be executed like a dog." He kissed my neck.

I froze. I'd never been kissed by a man before. There wasn't time for such trivial activities or things like courting. Work, training, and taking care of my father were all I did. Anders's lips left a hot trail along my skin. "What are you doing?" I hissed. There was no need for him to go that far. He could pretend to woo me without actually pressing his soft, tender lips to my neck. My eyes fluttered closed as warmth spread through me.

"Believe me," he murmured against my skin, "I'd prefer not to have to do this either."

My eyes flew open, and common sense returned.

"Sorry to disturb you," a man said from behind me. "But we're looking for a girl, about sixteen years old, wearing pants and a vest, maybe a jacket. She has long, brown hair. Have you seen anyone matching this description?"

Anders peered up at the *soldat*. I used the opportunity to snuggle closer to him, hiding my face against his neck.

"Been here all night," Anders lazily replied. "Haven't been

paying attention to those wearing pants, if you know what I mean."

The man chuckled. "I do."

"And that sounds like a boy," Anders commented. "Are you sure it's a girl you seek?"

"Yes, because of the long hair. She was probably dressed as a boy to disguise her identity. We've been rounding up all the sixteen-year-old girls matching that description. Got over twenty already."

My hands tingled as fear radiated through me. What would Morlet do to all those innocent people? Would he kill them?

"Well," Anders said, "if I see any girls that age out and about, I'll be sure to report them."

There was a shuffling noise as the *soldat* left. I exhaled. That was close.

"Let go," Anders growled. I jerked back, staring at him. "Your hands." His eyes darted to where I clutched his shoulders. "I can feel your power trying to connect with your weapon. You need to learn to control that. Luckily, I'm wearing the medallion. Otherwise, you would have severely injured me."

The necklace was tucked under his shirt, hidden from sight. "I don't understand," I said, letting go. "How does it protect you?"

His fingers wound in my hair, pulling my head against his, our foreheads touching. "The medallion shields the bearer from magic," he whispered. "In the Town Square, when we held hands, it protected you, too."

He released me. My palms looked the same as they always did. It was hard to believe they could wield any sort of power.

"They're gone," Anders said. He stood, and I fell from his lap. "Let's go."

Scrambling to my feet, I tucked my newly shorn hair behind my ears and spotted Anders already halfway across the room, heading toward a swinging door. As I hurried after him, the dress swished around my legs, scratching them, making me want to tear the thing off.

"Hey, purty girl," a man said. He reached out and grabbed my arm. "How about we go upstairs?" His breath reeked of strong ale.

I tried yanking free, and he laughed, tugging me against his body. Anders stalked up behind him. "Let her go," he calmly said, his voice cold and deadly.

"She has spirit," the man said. "I'd like a tumble with this feisty one."

In one swift motion, Anders reached out and punched the man's arm. When he released me, Anders grabbed him by the throat, throwing him on the nearest table. He leaned down over the top of him. "I hate when people don't listen." He pulled out a small pocketknife and slammed it down, pinning the man's right hand to the table. The guy screamed in pain. "Are we clear?" Anders asked.

"You're crazy," the man cried.

Anders shoved the knife deeper, waiting for an answer.

"We're clear!" the man hollered.

"Good." Anders yanked out his knife, wiping the blood off on the man's shirt. He walked over to me and snatched my arm, dragging me the rest of the way across the room. I couldn't believe he had just put a knife through a man's hand.

We entered the stifling hot kitchen, the cook not paying us any heed as he continued to chop potatoes and cabbage. Exiting through the back door, we stepped into a dark alleyway. Cold air engulfed me. Night had descended and no moons shone in the sky. I shivered, wishing I still had the warm, fur-trimmed jacket.

"Now what?" I asked. No one was out. "Is it past curfew?" If so, we needed to go inside before we were discovered and thrown in the dungeon or had our feet chopped off.

"Not yet," he replied. "I haven't heard the clock tower." He started walking. "We need to get out of the capital. We'll have better luck evading Morlet in the forest or a smaller town."

I'd never been anywhere else in the kingdom of Nelebek. "Don't we need traveling papers?" I asked, trying to keep up with him. I didn't like the idea of leaving my father behind and hiding with an assassin. Especially in the forest.

"Do exactly what I say, when I say it," Anders commanded, his voice low and urgent, sending a chill down my spine. "Understand?"

I nodded, wondering what threat he detected. We turned down a side street, sticking close to the buildings. The stupid dress kept swishing, making noise. Anders shot me a look of annoyance, but there was nothing I could do to make it any quieter.

At the end of the street, we stopped, leaning against the wall. Anders poked his head around the corner, observing the main road. "It's clear," he whispered. "Let's go."

We stayed on the sidewalk, carefully not touching, as we headed to the edge of the capital.

A pair of *soldats* stepped out of the shadows in front of us. "Little late to be out for a walk," one said, sliding his hand to the hilt of his sword.

Anders chuckled. "We're not really out for a stroll," he said with a drawl to his words, as if he were drunk. "I'm just taking this one home."

The men looked at me. "She doesn't match the description,

but we should take her in anyway." One reached for my arm.

Quick as lightning, Anders grabbed him, flipping him onto his back. Spinning, he kicked the other one in the head, knocking him over. Anders glanced around, and then pulled a dagger from his back pocket.

A loud bell tolled over the capital, indicating curfew was now in effect. We had to get off the streets.

"Let's go," I said. There was no need to kill these men. They were both on the ground, and we could easily outrun them.

Ignoring me, Anders bent over one of them and slit his throat. Blood flowed from the cut, and the man's eyes widened with shock. My hands flew to my mouth, smothering my scream. Anders moved to the other one, doing the same. Vomit rose in the back of my throat. Repelled by Anders's total disregard for human life, I turned and ran.

I hadn't even made it a block when a hand clamped down on my shoulder.

"Let go!" I hollered, struggling to break free from the heartless assassin. "Why did you kill them?"

"Run," was all he said as his hand slid down to my wrist, firmly clutching it.

We sprinted toward the wall surrounding the capital, my eyes filling with tears. "You're crazy," I accused him. "Leave me alone. I'll take my chances on my own."

"I can't do that," he coldly responded. "I'm responsible for your safety."

"No, you're not. You don't owe me anything—and I don't owe you either. Let's just part ways now."

"You'll never make it without me," he said, squeezing my wrist tighter. We were almost to the wall.

"Let go," I demanded, yanking out of his grasp.

Leaving the assassin meant I could go to my father. We'd have to find a safe place to hide from Morlet. Only, this plan presented some issues. In an attempt to keep track of all citizens, we were required to have papers authorizing travel between cities within the kingdom of Nelebek. Neither my father nor I had the required paperwork to leave the capital. Even if we did manage to get out, with the spell on Nelebek's borders, we couldn't leave the kingdom. Since Papa was sick, he couldn't move quickly, and the cold air would only make his condition worse.

"Easy," Anders growled. "Morlet will be able to find you in a heartbeat."

"Only if I'm truly a Kriger." I shivered, not from fear but from the idea of Morlet being able to sense me.

Anders laughed. "Don't be so naive. You know you're a Kriger. Even I can feel it. Once Morlet has all twelve of you, he'll kill you. Your power won't be enough to save you—not until you learn to control and master it. To do that, you need your weapon." My body pulsed at the mention of my weapon. It was as if a flame was lit in me, slowly growing. I wanted to understand what it meant to be a Kriger.

We reached the twenty-foot-high wall surrounding the capital. Anders started feeling around the stone blocks, looking for something. There was only one gate in the wall where citizens could enter or exit, and *soldats* checked everyone's paperwork. We were nowhere near there.

Shouts rose behind us. The bodies must have been discovered. My heartbeat quickened, and I frantically looked around for a hiding place.

The assassin cursed and pulled me against the nearby building. "Wait here," he instructed.

"What are you going to do?" I demanded, fearing he'd murder

more people. Instead of answering, he sprinted away, leaving me all alone in the dark.

I needed to know if Papa was in our apartment or if the man from the brothel had taken him to his home. Pressing against the building, I moved to the other end of the street and glanced around the corner. Not a soul lingered and no lights shone. Most people put fabric over their apartment windows to prevent others from seeing inside. Taking a deep breath, I steeled my resolve. Staying close to the towering apartment buildings, I jogged several blocks, eventually passing the familiar blacksmith and bakery.

When I reached my street, a group of men from the King's Army exited my building. Ducking into a nearby doorway, my breathing became unsteady. Had they discovered my identity already? Thankfully, my father wasn't being dragged out as they left. When all of them had passed, I ran inside, sprinting up the dark stairs and throwing open the door to my apartment.

"Papa?" I frantically whispered. He didn't respond. His bedchamber was empty. Relief and dread filled me. If the man from the brothel had him, that meant he was an honest man who truly wanted to help me. However, what if the *soldats* had already taken Papa and the ones I saw leaving the building were simply the tail end of the raid? The only way to know for certain was to question the apothecary to see if someone had come for my father's medication.

Ripping off the scratchy dress, I pulled on a pair of trousers, a long-sleeved shirt, and a leather vest. My father's jacket hung on a peg near the door, so I grabbed it, along with a knit hat. The apothecary probably wasn't at his shop. I'd have to wait nearby until he opened in the morning. After lacing up my boots, I slipped out of the apartment building, surveying the street. Not seeing any movement, I ran. The temperature continued to drop rapidly, and my breath came out in white puffs. I pulled my sleeves down under the jacket and over my fingers, trying to stay warm.

When I reached the apothecary's street, three *soldats* were dragging a girl about my age northward, away from me. Sprinting to the nearest doorway, I pressed my body flat against it, hoping they didn't see me. A whistle sounded from somewhere above, and footsteps pounded on the ground as someone neared.

"You there," a man shouted, pointing at me.

Stepping away from the door, I raised my hands in surrender.

"You're out past curfew," he stated. "We're taking you in for insubordination."

He had a sword strapped to his waist, no other weapons visible. He was at least a foot taller than I was, but his red uniform was loose, his cheeks sunken in. The two others stood a good thirty feet away, holding the girl. There was no way they were going to imprison me. Spinning around, I kicked high, hitting the man's head and easily knocking him over. My father's instructions to "finish him" came back to me. Yet, I couldn't viciously kill like the assassin, so I took off running.

A moment later, boots stomped on the ground behind me. I sprinted faster, hoping to put enough distance between us to afford me the opportunity to hide. Nearing the next street, the man shoved me and I fell forward. He jumped on top of me, pinning me to the ground. He forcefully yanked my hands back, tying my wrists together.

"You stupid idiot," he said, seething with rage. "You're going to the executioner for this." He grabbed my arms and hoisted me to my feet, dragging me to where the other *soldats* stood waiting.

The men pushed me and the girl forward, and we started

walking down the street. The girl cried and pleaded with them to release her while I fumbled with the rope around my wrists, trying to untie it. There was no way I was going down without a fight.

A body suddenly fell from the rooftop, landing in front of us with a bone-chilling *thud*. The girl screamed and tried running away, but the men held her in place while they withdrew their swords. The man who had fallen was dressed in a red *soldat* uniform. He held a bow in one hand and wore a quiver filled with arrows on his back. Blood pooled around his head, seeping onto the street.

The three *soldats* looked at the rooftops of the surrounding buildings. One of the men grabbed his neck and then crumbled to the ground. Another did the same. The last man took off running and then he, too, collapsed to the ground, a small dart protruding from his neck.

# Chapter Three

Anders rounded the corner and strode toward me, as if stalking an animal. The girl screamed and ran away. I stumbled backward. With my hands still bound behind my back, I sprinted awkwardly down the street. A moment later, strong arms snaked around my waist, and Anders pulled me into a narrow alleyway between two buildings.

"Why are you running away?" He slid a knife from his boot and cut my bindings.

"Why?" I shrieked, shoving him away from me. "You've killed at least six men tonight. Six. You're crazy."

His eyes narrowed. "I saved you."

"By killing people. You're no better than the king."

Anders growled and took a step toward me, making my back hit the wall. "We need to get out of here."

"I'm not going anywhere with you."

"You need to meet Vidar. He can protect you, and he'll

explain what's going on."

I crossed my arms, wishing he'd back up.

He leaned forward, invading my space even more. "Would it make you feel better if I told you Vidar wasn't an assassin?"

My eyes narrowed. "What makes him so special?" Vidar obviously wasn't a Kriger since eleven of the twelve sat in prison. So who was he and how was he connected to all of this? Why did Anders claim Vidar could protect me—especially if I was a Kriger endowed with powers?

His eyes flickered, but his face remained blank, unreadable. "Nothing. Nothing at all."

He was hiding something from me. "Why are you helping me? What's in it for you?"

"Vidar and I have been helping Krigers for years." He put his hands on either side of me, pinning me against the wall, our faces only inches apart. "We need you," Anders whispered, his penetrating eyes staring into mine.

"Why?" I demanded, feeling vulnerable. He could whip out a dagger and slice me open from navel to throat, or kiss me. His hardened features revealed nothing.

His intense eyes remained focused on me. "We want to train you so you can join the other Krigers and save the kingdom of Nelebek."

Right now, I needed to save my father; I'd worry about the kingdom later.

"We don't have time to discuss this," he said. "Every moment we stand here, Morlet is strengthening his ability to sense your location." Cold fear slithered down my spine, and my hands tingled. "I'm not sure how far his reach extends, but I believe it's two or three miles." His hands dropped to his sides. "We need to hurry."

"But my father—"

"Is safe and taken care of."

"How can I be certain Morlet doesn't have him?"

"The men from the brothel are part of a secret organization whose sole purpose is to aid the Krigers. They will make sure your father is safe."

I hoped all he said was true. Looking again into his brown eyes, an odd sensation filled my body, and something inside me whispered to trust this man. A fierce strength radiated from within him.

"Let me get you to safety," Anders gently said, his face softening. "Afterward, I'll come back here and check on your father. I will ensure his well-being and bring you proof." He closed his fist and placed it over his heart, sealing his promise.

That odd feeling washed over me again—urging me to trust him. "Fine. I'll go with you."

Anders's shoulders relaxed, and he gave a curt nod. "Stay right behind me."

Moving to the end of the building, he observed the street before waving me forward. We took several smaller streets, careful to avoid areas heavily populated with *soldats*. At one point, we saw a few men exiting a building two blocks away. Anders flattened his body against the wall and froze. I did the same, trying not to make a sound. Luckily, they didn't notice us and moved on to another street.

We made it to the wall surrounding the capital without incident. I had an eerie sensation someone was watching me. My body tingled as Morlet's power reached out, penetrating into me.

Anders felt along the wall, pushing several stones in a particular area until he found one that wiggled loose. Thrusting it forward, it fell to the other side. He did the same to the surrounding blocks, opening a space large enough to crawl through.

"You go first," he said, pointing at the hole.

My hands throbbed with pain. I expected to see something wrong with them, but they appeared normal. My vision blurred, my head felt like it was floating in water, and I swayed on my feet.

"Hurry," Anders urged. "Morlet probably knows where you are and has *soldats* on their way."

I heaved my body through the opening, tumbling down the other side. My head cleared, and the pain in my hands vanished.

The assassin came through the gap and picked up the blocks, jostling them back into place. "We need to make it to the cover of the trees before Morlet sends archers to the wall to shoot us."

In the darkness, I could just make out the land before me. About a mile away, the Forest of a Thousand Lakes ominously stood. Anders started running, and I took off after him, trying to comprehend that for the first time in my life, I was on the other side of the capital's wall. When we reached the edge of the foreboding forest, I stopped to observe the thick trees, taller than any building I'd ever seen. The heady smell of pine filled the air.

"Keep moving," Anders insisted.

I followed him into the forest. We traveled single file, our pace only slightly slower than before. "I can barely see," I said, but he ignored me.

An owl hooted, and something howled in the distance. I'd heard stories growing up about travelers who strayed from the road never to be seen again. The forest was said to crawl with *brunbjorn*—large, bear-like creatures that fed on human flesh. There were also rumors of *fugls*—enormous birds that could eat a person in one gulp. I shivered, trying to convince myself that was all they were—stories.

"Do you think the King's Army will come into the forest searching for me?"

"Morlet will send them to hunt you down."

"Why do you think you can keep me safe? Because of the medallion?"

The assassin stopped, and I almost smashed into him. He spun around to face me. "I have been assisting Krigers for years. In all my time, not *one* has questioned me like you." Fury simmered in his low voice. "If you don't keep your mouth shut and do as I say, I'll leave you here to be eaten by a *fugl.*"

He turned and jogged away, heading deeper into the woods.

I hurried after him, not wanting to be alone in this strange place. Leaves crunched under my feet, yet Anders managed to move silently, gliding over the land. After an hour of traveling, my breathing became labored and my legs grew heavy. The events of the day started to crush me and tears threatened. I refused to let Anders see me cry. I couldn't think about my father, Morlet, or being a Kriger. All my focus was on staying upright—one foot in front of the other. *Never give up.*

"Just a little farther," the assassin whispered. "There's a place ahead where we can rest for a bit."

My foot connected with something hard, and I flew forward onto my stomach, my head smashing against a rock. Warm liquid oozed down the side of my face. My head collapsed onto the forest floor. Everything went black.

\*\*\*

My forehead throbbed as if someone had smashed a hammer against it. I sat up and found myself on the rocky floor of a small cave, a low-burning fire next to me. The assassin sat on the other side of the fire, staring at me.

"What happened?" I asked, my voice raspy.

"You tripped and knocked yourself out," he replied, his tone condescending. "I suggest you sleep some more. As soon as the sun rises and you're able to see the ground, we'll be on our way."

We had been traveling at night through a forest littered with fallen branches and rocks. Of course it would be difficult to see—especially considering I'd never even been in a forest before. He was lucky that I hadn't fallen to my death.

Gently touching my forehead, I felt some sort of thick paste that smelled of bracken fern covering it. A horrible thought occurred to me. "How did I get here?"

"I carried you. Now stop talking and go back to sleep." Anders shifted his body, his back to me, so he had a view of the cave's opening.

Lying down, I faced away from him. He must have thought I was an incompetent fool who had to be taken care of. Not that it mattered what he thought of me. My eyes grew heavy and I drifted off to sleep.

*I stood in the middle of the deserted Town Square next to the execution platform. A thick fog coated the area, making it hard to see the nearby shops and buildings in the early morning light. A harsh wind blew through the square, tossing my hair in my face. The fog parted around the platform, revealing a lone figure wearing a black cape.*

*Morlet.*

*"Come here," he commanded, his voice smooth and seductive.*

*Where did Anders go, and how did I get here? The fog swirled around my feet, sliding up my legs.*

*"I won't hurt you," Morlet purred. "I just want to talk."*

*The fog reached my shoulders, slinking around my neck. A sense of calm spread through me and, without thinking, I climbed the stairs and stood before the king.*

*"You cut your hair," he mused, his voice friendly. "And hurt your head." I touched my forehead, feeling the gooey substance still there. "You're different from the others." Cocking his head, his face remained hidden beneath the cover of the black hood. "Where are you hiding?"*

*My palms throbbed with pain. "Isn't this the Town Square?" I balled my hands into fists, willing them to stop hurting. Where were the* soldats *and all the people?*

*"You're in a dream," he explained. "When you wake up, where will you be? Are you in the capital somewhere?" He shook his head, frustrated. "I can't feel your presence. You must have managed to get outside the capital's walls."*

*My hands flared with intense pain, as if they were on fire. Morlet reached toward me. When his gloved hand neared my face, a feeling rose inside of me that begged me not to tell the king about the cave or the assassin.*

*I jerked back. "Don't touch me!"*

*He laughed, a deep, throaty sound, making my skin crawl. "I'll get what I want from you," he snarled.*

My eyes flew open, and I gasped. My entire body shook, even though the dying fire burned right next to me. Anders tossed a log into the fire, his eyes dissecting my every move. The flames swayed around the wood, making it crackle.

"You don't look good," he observed, his voice rumbling off the walls of the cave.

Too bad there wasn't a small rock to hurl at him. Of course my forehead must look bad, but that didn't mean he had to point it out to me.

"Is it morning?" I asked, wanting to change the subject.

"Yes," he replied, shifting uncomfortably. "I, uh, just went out to gather some food for breakfast. When I returned, you were tossing and mumbling something unintelligible. Were you dreaming?"

Trembling from the memory still fresh in my mind, I said, "It was more like a nightmare." The thought of Morlet's magic slithering around me made me recoil.

"Tell me about it," Anders said, his words laced with a sense of urgency.

I scooted closer to the fire, and the growing flames warmed me. "I dreamed about Morlet. He wanted to know where I was."

The assassin stilled. "You dreamed of the king?"

"As I said before, it wasn't pleasant." Wrapping my arms around my legs, I rested my head on my knees, gazing into the fire. Images of Morlet danced in the flames—the cloaked figure rising in the inferno, feeding off it, growing in strength. The image blurred and disappeared.

"Is there anything specific you recall?"

Closing my eyes, I remembered the figure standing on the platform and the fog swirling around me. "He told me I was dreaming, and he wanted to know where I would be when I woke up."

Anders huffed. "I'm sure that's all it was. Just a dream." Turning, he grabbed a skinned squirrel lying behind him. He shoved a green stick through its body from its tail to its head and placed it over the fire to cook. "I've never heard of Morlet communicating with a Kriger through a dream."

"I didn't say he was communicating with me," I snapped. Why did he automatically want to discredit me? "It was simply a nightmare."

"This is going to be a long journey if you take everything so personally," he mumbled, turning the squirrel over. "Fortunately, I haven't had to deal with any other female Krigers, or I would have killed myself by now."

If the assassin didn't learn to keep his mouth shut, I'd end up murdering him while he slept. Looking directly at me, he raised his eyebrows as if sensing my thoughts. I focused on the fire, trying to ignore him.

We ate the squirrel in silence. When we finished, Anders kicked dirt on the fire, putting it out. The only light came from the cave's small opening, and I headed toward it, eager to be outside in the fresh air.

I walked out of the cave and froze, stunned by the sight before me. There were hundreds and hundreds of trees so tall, the tops weren't visible. I went over to the nearest one and ran my hand along the reddish-brown bark.

"You act as if you've never seen a tree before," Anders said as he ducked out of the cave.

"I've never been outside of the capital," I replied, surprised by the softness of the trunk. "Last night it had been too dark to appreciate the sheer size and coloring of the trees."

The lines in Anders's forehead creased. We stood in silence a minute before he said, "We're heading this way." He nodded to the left. "Follow my path and don't deviate from it." He started walking, not waiting for me to respond.

I hurried after him, tucking my hands inside my sleeves, trying to stay warm. "Are we two miles from the capital?" I asked, hoping Morlet couldn't sense me.

"We're a good four miles out." Anders moved between the trees as if he knew exactly where he was going even though there weren't any visible paths.

We continued in silence for quite some time, which afforded

me the opportunity to review the events from yesterday. My situation seemed surreal. I was one of twelve Krigers destined to save the kingdom of Nelebek. Right now, I would settle for just saving my father. However, even if he managed to overcome his illness, he'd still be a *soldat* working in the mines, and we'd still be living under the king's oppression. If there was a chance to change that—no matter how small or dangerous that chance—I had to take it.

"Do you think you can attempt to be quiet?" Anders said, interrupting my thoughts.

"I haven't spoken at all."

"No," he retorted, turning around to face me. "You walk as if you're trying to announce our presence."

"Do you think the King's Army is nearby looking for me?"

Anders shook his head. "I meant animals. You're moving through the forest like you're trying to attract every single predator to us."

"No, I'm not," I said in a clipped tone. My father had taught me how to travel furtively. Granted, the assassin was an expert in stealth, but I wasn't the fumbling idiot he implied.

Shaking his head, he turned and continued through the forest.

"So," I whispered, "tell me about yourself."

His shoulders stiffened. "You don't need to know anything about me."

Watching him kill those men yesterday was still fresh in my mind. The idea of not only traveling with, but also trusting a killer, made me uneasy. "How did you become an assassin?" He gave no indication he'd heard me. "Do you enjoy … your job?" I prodded.

Anders flinched, but kept walking. "Let me ask you a

question," he said, his voice barely audible. Quick as a rabbit, he jumped over a fallen tree, not even pausing. "Do you have a job?"

"Yes. I wash clothes." I hoisted myself up onto the fallen trunk, climbed over, and then jogged to catch up.

"So you're a laundress." He gracefully ducked under a low branch. "Is that who you are and what defines your life?"

"No." I barely had to lower my head to clear the branch.

"Exactly," he replied.

Washing clothes didn't harm other people. How could Anders justify murdering for money? Did he feel any sort of remorse for the lives he stole?

"What about the people you murdered yesterday?" I asked. "You weren't hired to kill them, so why did you?"

"I did what needed to be done to escape from the capital," he replied.

"You could have rendered them unconscious," I offered. "You didn't have to kill them."

"I didn't have a choice," Anders responded. "If they lived, they would have been able to identify us."

"It's still wrong to kill."

"I hardly think you're one to judge when you benefited from it." He spun around to face me, his eyes alight with challenge.

Not wanting to make him any more upset, I held up my hands in surrender. "All I'm saying is that there are other options. You didn't have to murder innocent people."

"They were *soldats!*" he exclaimed, his face turning red.

"Maybe they were forced into that position." Like my father, I silently added.

"You're a naive sixteen-year-old girl."

My temper flared. I didn't have to be here with him—especially if he intended to belittle me. "Yes. I am only sixteen, and I am a girl. However, you need me, since I'm a Kriger."

"I don't need you," he said, pointing at me. "The kingdom does. If it were up to me, I'd have left you back in the capital to fend for yourself. But I'm required to assist you."

Now we were getting somewhere. "Did the man you're taking me to, Vidar, hire you to help me?"

"I'm not explaining anything to you right now." He rubbed his hands over his face, sighing. "We have a long journey ahead of us. Let's stop talking and get moving."

There was only one way this was going to work. "I want you to promise me something."

"No."

"Please?"

He didn't respond. Instead, he remained there, staring at me.

I didn't want him to berate me any longer, but there was only so far I could push him. "Promise me you won't kill anyone else unless our lives are in immediate danger."

He laughed and folded his arms across his chest. "So if a *soldat* comes running at you, you want me to let him capture you?"

"No." This man was utterly infuriating. Why didn't he understand what I was saying? "Just don't kill unless it's absolutely necessary. You can wound or injure instead."

"You're delusional," he mumbled. "I don't go around killing everyone I come into contact with. I only take a life when it's unavoidable." Leaning closer to me, his eyes pulled tight, making him look furious. "And just so you know, I don't *enjoy* killing people." He turned and stormed away, not looking back.

"Does that mean you won't kill unless you have to?"

He threw his arms up in the air and kept walking. Chuckling, I bent down to retie my boot. Straightening up, I headed in the direction Anders had gone. Twenty feet in front of me, he stood still as a building, spooked by something.

My hands pulsed with severe pain. A heavy breathing came from my right. I slowly turned and scanned the area, looking for the source of the threat. Between the trees only fifteen feet away, an enormous *brunbjorn* was moving directly toward me. It walked on all fours, smelling the air as it neared. The bear-like creature was easily five times my size.

I gradually started to back up, trying to keep a good amount of space between us. It breathed out, making a strange grunting noise. All of a sudden, it charged at me. I turned and ran. The animal pounded on the forest flooring as it neared, swiftly gaining ground. Its hot breath skimmed my neck. It roared a deafening sound and swiped its paw, slamming me to the ground. I rolled over as the *brunbjorn* went up on its hind feet, smelling the air. It dropped to all four paws, the ground jolting under me from the impact. I lay there, motionless, trying to decide if I should kick the animal and run or play dead.

The *brunbjorn* stood over me and roared, the sound vibrating through my body. I shoved myself forward, between the animal's legs, so it couldn't see me. Trying not to make a sound, I scrambled to stand behind it. It huffed and turned around, foam clinging to its mouth. Its eyes were two black coals that promised death. My hands pulsed, and a sharp, stinging sensation shot through me. I fell to my knees, crying out in pain. The animal circled me, observing its prey.

Out of the corner of my eye, I saw Anders noiselessly stalking up behind the *brunbjorn*. It raised its massive paw, its black nails longer than my foot. I leaned back as it viciously swung, narrowly missing my face.

Anders slid a long dagger from his sleeve, clutching the

weapon in his hand as he moved to the side of the animal. When the *brunbjorn* swiped at me again, the assassin darted in and embedded the knife in the animal's side.

It savagely roared in pain and staggered back. I crawled to the tree behind me, wanting something solid to cling to. The animal whipped its head in Anders's direction. When it caught sight of him, it charged. Instead of running away, Anders stood his ground. The massive *brunbjorn* tackled him to the ground.

Anders grabbed the dagger sticking out of the animal and yanked it free. The *brunbjorn* stood above the assassin and swayed. Without hesitating, he thrust the knife into the animal's stomach. It reared its head back, howling in agony. He grabbed the blade strapped to his thigh and with quick and lethal efficiency plunged it into the animal's neck.

It wobbled and collapsed on top of Anders. The assassin shimmied his body out from under the *brunbjorn* and came to me.

"Are you hurt?" he asked, breathing heavily, fresh blood coating his clothes.

"No." Besides a few scratches, I was unharmed.

He squatted next to me. "I hope you consider that an acceptable murder."

"Yes," I said. "That was definitely an appropriate time to kill."

Standing, he pulled me up. "We need to leave before more *brunbjorns* come."

I nodded and said, "Kaia."

"What?"

"My name," I replied. "It's Kaia."

# Chapter Four

Dropping to my knees alongside the stream, I scooped the frigid water with my hands, drinking it. After traveling hard all day, I was desperate to quench my thirst.

"How much farther?" I asked between gulps.

"At the rate you walk, it'll take us another day to get there."

Ignoring Anders's jab, I rubbed water on my forehead, attempting to clean my wound. "Are you related to Vidar?" I stood and dried my hands on my pants.

"No," he replied, rinsing his bloody hands in the water. "Although he is my closest friend."

It was hard to believe Anders had any friends at all. Stretching my stiff back, I asked, "Is Vidar your age?"

His eyes narrowed. "Why do you care?"

"Just curious to know something about the person you're taking me to." Was he a wise, elderly man? Or young and hotheaded like Anders?

"Let's get moving."

"It's almost dark," I pointed out, not wanting to run into another *brunbjorn*, especially at night. Every time the leaves rustled or a branch snapped, I tensed, anticipating another attack.

"Don't tell me you're afraid of the dark, little girl," Anders taunted.

It would feel so good to punch his jaw. "It's not like you're that much older than me. And no, I'm not scared of the dark. I'd just prefer not to be eaten by some predator I can't see."

He smiled sardonically before turning and walking away. "So if you can *see* the animal, you don't mind being its supper?"

Rolling my eyes at his back, I hurried to catch up with him. "That's not what I meant." After walking in silence for several minutes, I hesitantly asked, "Can you tell me why my hands hurt?"

He stilled. "Do they hurt right now?" His voice was tight with concern.

"No," I answered, almost running into him.

"When's the last time they bothered you?"

"Right before the *brunbjorn* attacked." I thought back to the incident. The pain had become intense during the encounter. However, I'd been so concerned with not being the animal's next meal that there hadn't been time to dwell on it.

The assassin continued walking, not saying another word.

"Are you ignoring me?" I kicked a small rock, sending it flying to a nearby tree.

Anders glanced over his shoulder, raising his eyebrows and pointedly looking from me to the tree before saying, "I just figured the answer was rather obvious and you'd be able to figure it out on your own."

"I get that it has something to do with being a Kriger."

Bending, I plucked a rock small enough to fit in the palm of my hand.

Anders spun around and grabbed my arm. "If you throw that at me, I'll gut you."

I yanked away. "I just wanted something to hold on to."

"Oh." He turned and started walking again. "Well, don't assault anymore trees either." I rolled my eyes. "And don't roll your eyes at me. It's rude."

"How did—"

"The pain you feel occurs when you're in danger," he said, cutting off my retort. "The power within you is seeking its weapon."

Again, at the mere mention of my weapon, my body hummed. "How do you know so much about all of this?" I rolled the rock between my fingers, easing my nerves.

Anders sighed. "Can we please travel in silence? All of your questions will be answered when we arrive."

"Why can't you just tell me what's going on?" I asked, squeezing the rock. It started to warm.

He halted and turned to face me. "Do you ever stop talking?" He pointed his finger at me. "You're impossible."

His dark eyes and the fury lines in his forehead should have frightened me. Yet, the rock somehow sapped the panic from my bones. "Why? Because I ask a few simple questions trying to understand what's happening to me? I'm not the impossible one. You are." I pushed around him and continued walking, hurling the rock as far as I could into the trees. I'd never met anyone who grated on my nerves as much as Anders did. It was infuriating, annoying, and exasperating.

"Kaia," Anders said from behind me. It was the first time he'd used my name.

"What?"

"You're going the wrong way."

Surveying the surrounding area, there weren't any trails. "Well, which direction are we headed?" I folded my arms against my chest.

"That way." He motioned to the left, the corners of his lips pulling up ever so slightly. "There's a cave thirty feet ahead. It's small, but it'll offer us some protection for the night. And seeing as how I haven't slept in two days, I'm rather tired."

I trudged off in the direction he pointed, navigating between several trees to a cluster of boulders covered with bright green moss. Anders went around the side to a narrow, dark crevice between two of the boulders. Turning sideways, he shoved his way into the darkness.

"That's a cave?" I asked, reminding myself that the assassin wouldn't kill or harm the last Kriger. After all, he needed me.

"Sort of," he called out. "Before you come in, grab some branches and pine needles so I can light a fire."

Within five minutes, I'd managed to pick up an armful of fallen branches. After shoving them through the opening, I crawled on the ground and collected two handfuls of pine needles and squeezed inside the cave.

"Here." I stuck out my hands, not able to see a single thing since my eyes hadn't adjusted. Anders's fingers touched my stomach, and I squealed with surprise.

"Sorry," he murmured. His fingers fumbled down my arms to my hands. He took the pine needles and quickly withdrew. "Can you move away from the opening so I can see?"

I scooted over and gingerly sat down. A few moments later, there was a spark, and the fire took. Anders knelt on the other side of the flames, avoiding me. He wasn't kidding when he said the cave was small. It was barely large enough for the two of us to sleep in. I removed my boots and rubbed my sore feet.

"Hungry?" he asked, his voice hoarse. I nodded. "I'll find us something to eat. Stay here."

After he hurried from the cave, I removed my knit cap and massaged my scalp. I wanted to arrive at our destination tomorrow so my questions could be answered. Who was Vidar, and how did he fit into all of this? How did Anders, an assassin, end up helping the Krigers? Why was I the only female Kriger, and how did I come into my powers early? And above all lingered the question I feared the answer to—did I have a nightmare about Morlet, or did he somehow communicate with me? The image of him standing before me in that eerie, black cloak was seared into my mind.

A short time later, Anders returned carrying a small jackrabbit. He'd already skinned and tied the animal to a stick. He sat across from me and began cooking it. The shadows from the flames flickered on his face, making him look foreboding and harsh— every bit the assassin he was.

"When I met you in the Town Square," I said, "what was the black jar I gave you?"

He kept his focus on the jackrabbit. "Does it matter?"

"No, not really." Was it poison? Medicine? Or something else?

"You didn't give me anything," he said. "You simply delivered something that was already mine."

Why couldn't he just answer a simple question? Why did everything have to be so complicated with him? Fine, if he didn't want to converse civilly, I would ignore him.

Once the meat was cooked, he handed me my portion, and I devoured it. After licking my fingers clean, I turned my back to

Anders and lay down. There wasn't enough room for him to do the same unless he put the fire out and removed the ashes. At this point, I didn't care. He could fend for himself. Why should I be polite to him when he was barely civil to me?

Anders sighed. "A sleeping potion."

"Excuse me?" I didn't bother to look at him. The wall of the cave was right in front of my face, making my voice echo in the small area.

"You asked what was in the black bottle, and the answer is a sleeping potion for my darts."

I remembered seeing darts embedded in the *soldats'* necks when Anders rescued me. "Deadly?"

He grunted as he kicked dirt onto the fire. The warm blaze on my back faded away. "It can be," he answered.

"Is the apothecary involved with the secret organization that aids the Krigers?"

"No," he replied. "He is simply my supplier. That is all."

I kept perfectly still as Anders situated himself next to me. "How come—"

There was a small prick on my back. "I'm sorry," the assassin whispered. "But I'm tired, and you enjoy talking far too much for my taste."

My eyelids felt like lead, and then blackness engulfed me.

*"Wake up," a soothing voice whispered in my ear.*

*I squeezed my eyes shut tighter, pretending to still be asleep, too exhausted to walk again all day.*

*"I can feel you're outside the capital's walls, but where? The Forest of a Thousand Lakes is large, and I don't want to spread my resources thin searching for you."*

*My eyes flew open, and I bolted upright, finding myself on a soft, feather mattress, wrapped in silk sheets. Heavy fabric was draped above the bed and tied to each of the four posts. Soft wallpaper covered the walls, and several paintings framed in gold hung on them. A roaring fire in the hearth heated the room.*

*The mirror next to the bed revealed dirt and grime covering the side of my face, and my hair stuck out in all directions. I still had on the same clothes. Standing behind me was a black-caped figure. Twisting around, I came face-to-face with Morlet holding a small tray laden with food. It seemed like such an odd thing for a king to do. Almost ... ordinary.*

*"I think we got off on the wrong foot," he pleasantly said. "Let's start over, shall we?" He sounded calm and cordial.*

*"Are you really communicating with me in a dream?" I demanded, wondering how his magic worked.*

*He chuckled. "I bring you food because you appear to be starving and instead of thanks, you question me. You are an interesting one." He sat on a plush, red velvet chair next to the bed and slid the tray of food toward me.*

*Unable to resist, I grabbed the spoon and devoured the stew. The meat melted in my mouth, and the vegetables tasted divine. After scarfing down every last morsel, I pushed the tray to the end of the bed and sat cross-legged, facing him.*

*"You have questions," he mused.*

*"I do." Even though it seemed impossible, I knew this dream was somehow real, that I was with the man I was supposed to defeat—a monster that set people on fire and murdered hundreds for his own pleasure. This was the reason I existed. And here we sat, facing one another in his bedchamber. If only he would remove his cloak so I could see the man underneath it.*

*"You'll need to refrain from asking anything tonight," he kindly said. "I brought you here, so I will ask the questions. If you cooperate, the next time we meet you may ask me anything you wish. Understand?"*

"No." There was no way I was going to play along with him. "I want to know—"

"I'm asking the questions, not you," he said, his voice instantly harsh. He tilted his head to the side, and light illuminated his chin and nose, revealing a fraction of the man beneath the cape. When he realized I was staring at him, he moved his head, once again concealing himself in the shadow of his hood. "Where are you?" he demanded.

"I don't know."

"Hmm," he said, drumming his slender fingers on the arms of the chair. "Do I need to torture a child in front of you in order for you to cooperate?"

It sounded as if he was discussing what to have for dinner, not threatening me. "I honestly don't know where we are."

"We?"

My breath caught as I realized my error. "You and me," I quickly answered, trying to play it off. "Is this the castle?"

He leaned back on his chair, observing me. Since I couldn't see his face, I had no idea if he bought my excuse.

"When you wake up, where will you be?" he calmly asked. "In the forest?"

"Yes." I was afraid if I didn't tell him something, he'd make good on his threat. Since he already suspected as much, this truth could do no harm. Besides, I'd never be able to watch a child be tortured.

"How did you get out of the capital?" he asked, leaning forward. "I sealed the gates."

I needed to tread carefully. "It was late at night, and soldats were after me. I ran until the wall was in sight."

"Go on," he encouraged.

"I'm not sure what happened," I lied. "One minute I was inside the capital, the next, I was standing on the other side of the wall." At *first, I considering telling him that a citizen had helped me escape, but there was no reason to doom an innocent person. And under no circumstances could he know that blocks in the wall came loose. There needed to be a way to get back inside.*

*"And then you ran into the forest?"*

*"Yes."*

*He crossed his legs. "There's something you're not telling me. I can feel it." His voice was soft and seductive, making my head swim.*

*Wanting to change the subject, I stood and examined the room. Twelve paintings hung on the walls, each depicting a weapon of some sort. One in particular felt as if it had a life all its own. Moving toward the long, wooden pole, the elegant but deadly looking weapon mesmerized me. It appeared to be about five or six feet tall with intricate carvings along the entire length of it.*

*"I always wondered why I never found all twelve Krigers. It never occurred to me that one of them could be female. It's clear you're a Kriger. Not only can I feel your power, but you're drawn to your weapon. That's a bo staff."*

*Forcing myself to look away from the painting, I felt the compulsion to touch it instantly vanish. Turning my attention to Morlet, my head suddenly felt like someone was squeezing it, and my eyes grew heavy. "I'm in a cave," I murmured against my will.*

*Morlet tilted his head back, revealing his callous smile. "I'd like to be friends," he purred. "What's your name?"*

*"Kaia," I responded, unable to stop my mouth from speaking. Forcing myself to look away from the king, my head immediately cleared. He chuckled. I moved to the bed and sat down, not sure where to look in order to keep my wits about me.*

*"You're stronger than the others," he mused. "I wonder why."*

*Clasping my hands together, I bit my tongue to try to wake myself up in order to break my connection with the king.*

*"Since you're being honest with me,"* Morlet said, interrupting my thoughts, *"I'm going to tell you something personal about me."* Curiosity overruled practicality, and I unclasped my hands, waiting for him to continue. The only information I knew about the king was whispered stories told by my father or the few people I'd come across who were willing to speak. Those stories were violent nightmares of terror, destruction, and death.

*"My name is Espen,"* he revealed.

The words dangled in the air, teasing me. *"I thought it was Morlet."*

*"That is the name most people know me as,"* he said, uncrossing his legs under his black cloak. *"Morlet Forseve—the dark force. My birth name is Espen, although no one has called me that in years."*

*"Then why did you tell me?"* Did it make a difference what his name was?

*"Because someone should know."* Scooting to the edge of his chair, he said, *"You're going to change everything. You will either be the death of me, or set me free."* He reached toward me. *"Why do I feel us losing our connection?"*

*"I don't know."* The air around us shimmered.

*"There has to be a reason I can only communicate with you at certain times. It's like there's something preventing me from linking to you."* There was desperation in his voice that I didn't understand. *"Find out what's blocking my ability to sense you,"* he pleaded as my body faded away.

I woke up. Anders hovered above me, one hand on my arm. "What's the matter?" he asked. "Another bad dream?"

"I don't know."

He released me and laid down, the medallion slipping out from under his shirt, dangling around his neck.

"The medallion blocks magic from being used on you?" I asked, pointing to it.

"It blocks whoever is wearing it from magic. Why?"

"We're far enough outside the capital that Morlet can't sense me, right?"

He nodded and yawned.

"Sorry I woke you up," I whispered.

"You didn't," he mumbled. "I went outside for a moment."

Both times Morlet managed to link with me, Anders had left me alone while I slept. "Can the medallion serve as a block for me even though I'm not wearing it?" Was being near it enough?

"If we were touching, it would. What are you getting at?"

Staring up at the ceiling, I was certain the first night Morlet contacted me, I hadn't been touching Anders. In fact, we'd been on opposite sides of the fire. Tonight, given our close proximity in the cave, we could have been inadvertently touching while we slept.

"When you were gone, I had another dream about Morlet." Anders stiffened but didn't say anything. "Only, I'm not sure it was a dream. I think he is somehow communicating with me."

"That's impossible," he said with an air of certainty. Perhaps in his quest to aid the Krigers, Anders had access to information about the king that the average person did not.

"Do you know anything about Morlet?"

"A little."

"What about his birth name?"

"What about it?" he asked, his voice unnaturally calm, making my skin prickle.

"Is it Espen?"

Anders rolled over and grabbed my upper arms. "What did you say?" he demanded, squeezing me so tightly it hurt.

"Let go!" I yelled, struggling to pull free.

His eyes widened, and he jerked back, releasing me. Instead

of apologizing, he asked, "How do you know his birth name is Espen?"

Rubbing my arms, I sat up and replied, "He told me, right before he said something was blocking our connection. Then I woke up, and you were here with the medallion."

"He's never communicated with any of the other Krigers." Running his hands through his hair, he looked uncertain. "This changes things," he mumbled as he sat up. "What else did he say to you?"

"He wanted to know where I was. He … he did something to me. He forced me to tell him I was in a cave in the forest, but I didn't reveal anything about you."

Anders slammed his hand on the ground and yelled, "Why don't you just wave a flag, announcing our location?"

"Seems like you're already doing that with your outburst. Keep your voice down." Anders huffed. "Besides," I continued, "Morlet used his powers on me. I couldn't stop myself from answering him."

"I guess it's a good thing I got here in time to save you. Again."

Rage filled me, and I clambered to my knees, ready to wrap my hands around his neck when I remembered the prick on my back. "You used your sleeping potion on me." He could have killed me.

"Hardly any," Anders said, lying down again, not perceiving me as a threat. "Just a little so you'd stop talking long enough for me to fall asleep."

"You're despicable."

"And you're a chatty, naive girl."

Some of my anger evaporated with the truth of his words. As much as my father had taught me about fighting and the politics of Nelebek, I was relatively sheltered. Needing to salvage what little dignity I had left, I said, "If you ever use your poison on me again, I'll kill you."

"I'd like to see you try."

"Don't tempt me."

\*\*\*

Anders handed me some berries.

"No thank you," I said, ducking under a low branch. "I'm not hungry."

"You should be starving since you didn't eat anything for breakfast either."

I shrugged, surprised he'd even noticed. After eating the stew in my dream, I was full. But I didn't care to share that information with him.

"There's a pond up ahead where we can wash." He smiled. I'd never seen him smile. "Come on." He started to jog.

I glanced around wondering where the moody, insufferable Anders had gone.

"Hurry up!" he yelled.

I ran after him as he sprinted between the dense trees. He stopped before a good-sized pond that had steam billowing off it.

"What's that smell?" I asked, scrunching my nose.

"The water is heated from the earth." Anders peeled off his sweater and started untying his pants.

"Um," I mumbled, "would you like me to keep watch while you clean up?"

"No," he answered. "I want you where I can see you. Just face the other way."

With my back to him, I heard him undress and enter the water.

"Now it's your turn," he said.

"Aren't you still in there?"

"Yes, but you can't see anything. Get in. I won't look."

Glancing over my shoulder, I saw Anders neck-deep in greenish water, steam rising around his head. Everything below the surface was murky. Not that I was trying to see him, but I needed to be certain he wouldn't be able to see me. After telling him to face the other way, I removed all my clothing and quickly slid into the water, making sure it went up to my chin. The warm water felt better than I imagined it would.

"See," Anders said, facing me again. "Sometimes you just have to trust me."

I'd had a hot bath only a couple of times. Usually I was forced to clean myself in a tub of frigid water that had already been used by several other people. Even though this pool had an odd smell to it, I didn't care. I wanted to relax and fall asleep right there in the middle of it.

Just thinking about going to sleep made me tense. When I closed my eyes tonight, would Morlet visit me again? Why was he communicating with me? Was it simply so he could capture me or was there more to it?

Water hit me in the face. Startled, I glanced at Anders. "What was that for?"

"You looked scared," he said, a wicked grin spreading across his face.

"So?" I challenged. Right when he shook his head, I swiped my arm over the surface of the water, splashing him. A gush of water came whooshing back at me, and I ducked under to avoid it. I suddenly felt light-headed and resurfaced. Maybe the heat was getting to me.

"Are you okay?" he asked.

My palms tingled. "No," I said, holding up my hands. "They hurt." Glancing around the lake and shoreline, I didn't see anything out of the ordinary.

Anders swam closer to me. "I need you to focus," he said, instantly serious. "Shut your eyes." Without hesitating, I did as he instructed. "Put your hands in the air and feel your surroundings."

A pull came from behind me. Facing that direction, I opened my eyes and searched the area.

"Trust your instinct," he said, his deep voice close to my ear. "Keep your hands out in front of you. Direct your power to the source of the pull."

I took the odd sensation inside of me and pushed it out. Nothing happened.

"Are your hands still painful?" Anders whispered, close behind me.

"No," I said, realizing the feeling had gone away. "What happened?"

"I don't know," he replied. "But when you force your power out, it serves as a warning to those wishing to harm you. A predator could have been stalking us."

Facing Anders, the top of his chest and shoulders were exposed as he stood a mere foot away from me. Biting my bottom lip, I unexpectedly became nervous from being so close to him.

"We should leave," he said, his voice gruff, "in case whatever's out there returns." Moving to the edge of the pool, he hesitated. "Would you mind turning around while I climb out and put my clothes on?"

Horrified he'd caught me staring at him, I immediately spun away, my face flushed. I ducked under the water, for once wishing it were cold instead of hot.

# Chapter Five

As I left the water, freezing air engulfed my body; I swiftly pulled on my dry clothes. Shivering, I ran my fingers through my dripping wet hair.

"It's not far from here," Anders said, sheathing the small dagger he'd been playing with. "Vidar can light a fire for you to warm up."

After five minutes of walking, we reached a stream and followed it northward. The trees thinned, and the ground became rockier. Gradually, the clouds parted until the sun shone bright overhead. I stopped, dropping my head back and allowing the rays to warm me. "What?" I asked, noticing Anders staring at me.

"You don't smile very often."

Neither did he. Instead of arguing, I said, "I haven't seen the sun all season. It feels wonderful."

"Let's keep moving." Anders effortlessly jumped to the other side of the stream.

The water steadily swelled until the stream turned into a rushing river. We climbed over rocks, sticking close to the bank. Eventually, it opened onto a small lake. Sunlight glistened off the water, fed by an enormous waterfall easily as tall as a four-story apartment building and ten feet or so in diameter.

"There are even more waterfalls farther up the mountain," Anders said. "We found that this location suits our needs. Not only do we have fresh water, a bathing pool, and a great fishing area, but it's close to several villages and only a two-day journey to the capital."

There weren't any structures visible. "You live here?"

Anders shrugged. "In this general area. Our place is over there." He nodded toward the trees. "Come on."

A voice hollered, echoing with the wind. It sounded as if someone had yelled in excitement. Movement caught my attention, and I observed the top of the waterfall where a man stood, arms spread wide, his head thrown back.

"There's someone up there." I pointed, unable to take my eyes away from the man. He bent his knees and then jumped, his body arching through the air as he went headfirst alongside the waterfall. I grabbed Anders's arm, squeezing hard, my heart about to leap into my throat.

Anders chuckled. "He's fine. He does this all the time."

I watched the man's body cut through the water, disappearing below. He surfaced and swam toward us, climbing out of the water wearing only a pair of pants cut short above his knees. Before today, I'd never seen a man shirtless. Within the past hour, I'd seen Anders and now this man's torso.

"Glad you're back," the man said to Anders before turning his attention to me, his blond hair shining in the sun. Half a smile spread across his handsome face.

"I brought someone with me," Anders said.

"I see that." He stuck out his hand.

I awkwardly grabbed it, and we shook in greeting. "Kaia."

"Vidar," he responded with a cocky grin. His blue eyes—like two pools of water—were mesmerizing. He reached out and gently tugged a strand of my wet hair. "Looks like you've been swimming, too."

"Down below in the hot spring," Anders said.

"Where are you from, Kaia?"

Before I could respond, Anders replied, "She's from the capital."

Vidar rubbed his chin, his eyes darting between Anders and me. "I've never known you to be interested in someone long enough to bring her home with you."

My body prickled with heat from his mistaken read of the situation.

"We're not together," Anders hastily replied. "And I'm not interested in her that way."

Vidar raised his eyebrows, awaiting an explanation.

"She's a Kriger. I brought her here for you."

"A Kriger?" Vidar laughed. "I'm not sure what's more amusing—you claiming to have found a female Kriger, or that you're not interested in her." He draped his arm around Anders's shoulders. "Kaia, please give us a moment alone."

They went just out of earshot. Vidar bent over and grabbed his shirt, putting it on while Anders spoke to him. After a few minutes, they both turned to stare at me.

"What?" I demanded, walking over to them. "This better not have anything to do with me being a girl. I've left my sick father behind, been traveling for two days, and am cold. I'd like to go inside and rest for at least one night without worrying if a *brunbjorn* is going to eat me." There still weren't any structures visible. "Please tell me there is actually a roof with walls and that you don't live in a cave?"

Vidar burst out laughing while Anders shook his head, fighting a smile.

"My friend briefly filled me in on the events of the past two days," Vidar said. "He told me he promised to check on your father." He paused, awaiting confirmation.

"Yes," I replied, surprised Anders intended to keep his promise.

"I'll be back as soon as possible," Anders said.

"Don't you want to rest?" I asked. "Or eat something before you go?" It wasn't as if we were friends, but I'd been with him for two days, and he'd saved my life. The prospect of being alone with Vidar made me edgy.

"I'll bring proof, like I promised." Anders patted me on my shoulder, the gesture awkward.

"Please tell my father that I love him."

"Of course." He went to take off the medallion, but Vidar stopped him. "Keep it on," he said. "We can't afford to have anything happen to you."

"But Kaia—"

"Will be safe with me." Vidar spoke with authority, as if used to getting his way.

Anders nodded and left without saying goodbye. I watched him navigate between the trees until he disappeared.

"We have a lot to discuss." Vidar placed his hand on my lower back and guided me up the bank and into the forest, away from the lake. We stopped before a tree that had a tall opening in its trunk. "Follow me." He grinned as he stepped inside and vanished from sight.

"Vidar?" He didn't respond. Not keen on being left alone in the forest, I ducked my head and went in after him, unable to see anything inside the dark tree trunk. Something grabbed my waist, and I screamed.

Vidar laughed. "Jumpy little thing, aren't you?"

I whacked him. "You scared me."

"You're a Kriger. You have nothing to be afraid of."

"Speaking of which, I have questions."

"I'm sure you do," he said. "For now, up."

He took my hands and guided them to a rope ladder. I clutched onto a rung and started climbing, thankful beyond belief I had pants on. The ladder finally ended at a wooden platform, and I hoisted myself on top of it.

The sight astounded me. Three separate bridges were attached to the platform. Each led to a different tree. Those trees had additional bridges connecting to more trees. Built around each trunk were small, wooden structures complete with windows and chimneys.

Vidar joined me. "Welcome," he said. "I'll show you to the main house where you can rest and have something to eat."

I followed him along one of the bridges as it swayed from our weight. Clutching onto the rope railing, I judiciously made my way across. A bird flew below me—we had to be at least five stories in the air. "This is amazing," I said, the wind caressing my face. "How long have you lived here?"

"A while. It took years to acquire all the necessary supplies and build these structures."

Vidar appeared to be about twenty years old. Since it took years to build, perhaps his father was the one who built this place. "Who else lives here?"

"Just Anders and me."

We reached the end of the bridge and stepped onto another platform. Vidar opened the door to the house and ushered me inside. It was a cozy sitting room complete with couches, tables, and books. Off to the side, a door led into another room. Through there I spotted an oven, cabinets, and a table. This was nicer than any apartment I'd ever seen.

"Who built this?" I asked, fascinated by the luxury of this house hidden among the treetops.

"I did. Please make yourself comfortable. Once your belly is full, we'll talk."

Plopping on the couch, my body practically melted against the supple cushions. Vidar went into the kitchen whistling a tune I'd never heard before. He returned a few minutes later, handing me a plate piled high with bread and cheese.

He sat on the floor before the fire, resting his elbows on his legs.

I finished eating and said, "Why am I the only female Kriger?"

Vidar chuckled. "You are rather direct, aren't you?" He stood, then sat next to me on the couch. "In all my years, I've never met a female Kriger." He tapped his hand on his leg. "Of course, I've never known all twelve Krigers at once either. As soon as we got close to finding them all, one died and another was born. Then we had to wait eighteen years to discover the new Kriger."

"How do you know so much about us?"

He smiled, his piercing blue eyes drawing me in. "Well … that's a complicated question and it's getting rather late." He went over to the shelves, pulling down a black, leather-bound book. "This has a complete history of the Krigers. Can you read?" Vidar handed me the heavy book.

I nodded. My father had taught me years ago. We used to stay up late at night reading books and discussing politics. One of my favorite stories was about a far-off land where a young peasant girl discovered she was the true heir to a kingdom and fell in love with the evil king's son.

"Come," Vidar said, interrupting my thoughts. "I'll show you to an extra bedchamber. You can read the book in there."

Following him out of the house, he led me across another swaying bridge to a small wooden structure attached to a different tree trunk. Sturdy branches surrounded the house. He opened the door and ushered me inside. There was a bed, dresser, and a chair situated between two large windows.

"Is this for me?" I'd never had a room of my own before.

"Yes." His eyes roamed over my body, making me flush. "Do you have any other clothes?"

"No." I carefully laid the book on the bed and removed my jacket, placing it on the chair.

"Some of my old shirts are in the dresser. You can wear one of them for tonight. Tomorrow we'll go to the nearby village. I'll purchase some appropriate clothing for you."

"You don't have to do that." I fidgeted with the end of my shirtsleeve.

"I know, but you've been through a lot. It's the least I can do." He turned to leave. "Oh, and if you need anything, my room is the next house over." He pointed to the right. "I have a few things to tend to before I retire for the night. I advise you to stay inside where it's safe from *brunbjorns*." He smiled sardonically and left.

Shaking my head to clear it, I went over to the bed and sat down, eager to read the book. Engraved on the front was the title: *The Order of the Krigers*. Peeling open the cover, the front page contained sketches of twelve weapons. My fingers trailed over each of them. When I came to the bo staff, a pulsing sensation bloomed in my chest, expanding to my hands and feet. I quickly turned the page. At the top was the title: *Known Krigers*, followed by a list of names. Reading through them, I felt my eyelids grow heavy.

*Blackness surrounded me. Air started to whirl, whipping my hair every which direction.*

*"Help me, Kaia!" a man yelled.*

*Hands tried to grab hold of my legs, but they kept losing their grip. I squatted down and reached out, wanting to help the person. Warm, solid fingers found mine. The wind immediately died, and the darkness receded. I found myself sitting on the forest floor, Morlet in front of me, our hands clasped together.*

*"You did it," he said, a hint of awe in his voice. "I knew you could."*

*"Did what?" I asked, trying to pull my hands away. He squeezed them tighter, keeping me in place.*

*"You sensed me searching for you. Your own power reached out to help forge our connection."*

*There was no way my power did this. "You're the one communicating with me," I insisted. I didn't even know how to use my power. The only time I'd tried was in the pool with Anders, and even then I wasn't certain what I'd done.*

*"You mean to tell me you aren't even aware of what you're doing?"*

*"Please let me go," I begged, trying to pull away from him.*

*He released me. "You must be a good distance from the capital. In order to find you, I had to use a tremendous amount of energy. Luckily, the block I felt earlier is gone. Did you figure out what it is?"*

*"I'm not certain."*

*"But you have some ideas as to what it could be?" he asked.*

*We were sitting crossed-legged facing each other. Me, a peasant girl Kriger, and him, the evil king of Nelebek.*

*Certainty filled me—Morlet couldn't find out about the*

medallion. "You told me I could ask the questions the next time we met."

"Ah," he mused, "I did. But I wasn't finished with you when you so rudely disappeared."

No animals lurked in the surrounding forest. "Where are we?" The air was unnaturally still.

"Somewhere between your location and mine," he answered. "Would you like to go somewhere else? I can take you back to my castle now that we've established a connection."

"Here is fine, thank you."

"Are you alone?" he asked, his voice etched with curiosity and something else I couldn't quite pinpoint.

Like before, my gut told me to keep Anders and Vidar a secret. "No, I'm here with you."

He reached out, as if to touch my face. I leaned back, and he dropped his hand onto his lap.

"Why do you wear that black cape? Is there something wrong with your face?"

"I never let anyone see me," he answered.

"Why?"

Morlet laughed. "No more questions from you. Not until I'm done asking mine." He leaned forward. "My dear Kaia," he murmured, his face only a few inches from mine. Blue eyes glowed beneath the hood, and I sat mesmerized by the two pools of light. "I want you to come to me."

A pull emanated from his body, and I leaned toward him.

"That's right," he purred. "Come to the capital. I need you, and I have something you need, too." He placed his finger on my cheek, and desire flooded into me. "I'm waiting for you."

I wanted nothing more than to do as he said. "Yes," I replied. "I'm coming."

Something shook my body, waking me. I was lying with my cheek on the book.

"Kaia," Vidar said, kneeling next to the bed. "What's the matter?" His face was creased with worry.

Sitting up, I felt horrible; my hands shook and my head pounded. "Morlet," I croaked. "He wants me to go to him." I half expected to see him lurking in the corner of my room.

Vidar sat on the bed next to me, his face turning as white as his shirt. "Morlet?"

"He's communicating with me when I sleep."

"First a female Kriger and now this," he said, gently patting my back. "You're changing everything."

I rested my head on his shoulder, welcoming the warmth and steadiness of his body. "The only time Morlet contacts me is when I'm asleep, and the medallion isn't nearby."

"Have you worn the medallion?"

"No."

"So just being near it is enough?" I nodded. "Unfortunately, Anders left with it. He won't be gone long though. Until then, we need to be careful. I have no idea what power Morlet has over you when you're in a dream state."

Remembering my lack of control in the dream, I shivered. "If you hadn't woken me up, I probably would have left and gone back to the capital."

Vidar rubbed his face. "This complicates matters. Morlet can't get his hands on you. If he does, it's over."

"I'll just try and stay awake until Anders returns." I yawned.

He smiled, his eyes kind and gentle. "He could be gone a few days. You look exhausted." Vidar placed his hands on my shoulders. "Why don't you sleep in my bed?"

I shook my head.

"I'll sit at my desk, working, and watch over you. If you become restless, I'll wake you."

"What about when you need to sleep?" He'd already given me an entire room to stay in; sleeping in his bed would be far too much of an imposition. Not to mention skirting the line of impropriety.

"I'll stay up all night," he insisted. Before I could object, he stood and scooped me up in his arms.

"I am perfectly capable of walking." I wasn't a child who had to be coddled.

"Oh, I know," he chuckled while shouldering past the door.

"Put me down." My face turned red.

He carried me as if I weighed nothing. "Sorry," Vidar said, suddenly serious. "Anders told me you fell and hit your head. I can't have you walking around an unfamiliar place late at night when it's difficult to see and we're high up in the treetops."

I rolled my eyes. Anders managed to irritate me without even being here.

Vidar pushed the door open and stepped inside his room. It was large, perhaps five times the size of my room, and packed with items. Shelves filled with hundreds of books, statues, and rocks covered one of the walls. Another wall had several swords, daggers, and bows hanging on it. Area rugs littered the floor while a massive desk piled high with papers took up an entire corner of the room. Maps and diagrams were strewn all over his bed. A small fireplace was situated near the bed, although it wasn't lit. A few candles burned, illuminating the room.

Vidar set me on my feet. He went to his bed, rolling up the papers and placing them on his desk. "As I said before, I have some work to do." Pointing to his bed, now cleared off, he said, "Make yourself comfortable."

I crawled onto the enormous feather mattress and slid under the silky sheets that smelled of pine. Vidar blew out all the candles except for the ones on his desk before sitting down and reading through some papers.

I decided to close my eyes and rest—not that I'd be able to fall asleep in his room with him watching me, no matter how comfortable the bed was.

*"Kaia, come to me." My body felt as if it were tied to a rope, being tugged toward the voice. "That's right, come."*

*"No." I kicked the invisible force, but I wasn't strong enough to break free. Morlet's arms wrapped around me, and I stiffened. This felt wrong. I needed to sever the connection.*

*He stroked my hair. "My Kaia."*

"Wake up."

My eyes flew open.

Vidar rested his hand on my forehead. "You were mumbling that you needed help to break free."

"Morlet used his magic on me." Sitting up, I rubbed my eyes. "When he communicates with me, each time it's becoming difficult to remember who and where I am." What was I going to do?

Vidar kicked off his boots and climbed under the covers.

"What are you doing?" I swiftly scooted to the other side of the bed.

"I'm going to sleep next to you. Perhaps you'll dream of me instead of Morlet." He wiggled his eyebrows.

Even though Anders and I had slept side by side in caves, there hadn't been any romantic inclinations between us. However, being in the same bed as Vidar felt forbidden. I crawled on top of the blankets, wanting to put space between us.

The corners of his mouth pulled up into a devious smile.

"You know, usually when I tell a woman I'll sleep with her, she's thrilled." He chuckled. "I've never had your reaction before."

I bolted out of bed. My father would be furious if he found out I was alone in a room with a man, let alone in his bed.

"I'm just teasing you," Vidar said. "Sorry, couldn't help myself. You're adorable when you're embarrassed."

Folding my arms, I wanted nothing more than to go back to my own room, away from this man with beautiful blue eyes that were constantly looking at me as if I were interesting.

"Come on." He patted the bed. "I won't bite. Much."

"I'll take my chances in the other room," I whispered, refusing to banter with him. He made me uncomfortable, made me feel things and think about things I'd never experienced before.

"Fine." He stood and walked to the door. "At least allow me to escort you to your room."

Remembering how he'd carried me here, my face flushed, not wanting him to hold me so intimately again. "Very well," I said. "But I'm walking on my own this time."

"Suit yourself."

Crossing the bridge, I saw thousands of stars dotted the sky. An owl hooted, and a soft breeze rustled the leaves.

"Just so you know, I'm sitting in a chair and watching over you, whether you like it or not."

I didn't care for the idea of him looking at me all night. However, if Morlet returned, I needed someone to wake me. "Thank you," I said, trying to sound sincere.

"The pleasure is all mine."

I preferred the assassin's aloof demeanor to Vidar's blatant flirting. It was going to be a long couple of days until Anders returned.

# Chapter Six

When I peeled my eyelids open, the sun shone bright outside. I sat up and observed the disarray before me. The lower portions of my legs were tied with rope to Vidar's hands and arms.

Lying on the bottom half of my bed, he looked up at me. "Morning," he said, his voice gravelly.

"What happened?" I asked, not sure I really wanted to know.

He smiled. "After you fell asleep, you tried to leave. Several times, as a matter of fact. When I started to doze off, I tied myself to you to make sure you didn't go anywhere."

"What if I untied myself once you fell asleep?"

"I didn't think of that." Vidar chuckled. "Care to untie me now? Unless you prefer to stay this way?"

Heat coursed through my entire body. Taking a deep breath, I blew a stray hair off my cheek, trying to act nonchalant. "You mean to tell me you can't undo a few knots?"

"I can." He shrugged. "It's just easier for you since your hands are free."

I reached down and worked on the complicated knots. His face was only inches from mine as he sat there staring at me. "Stop watching me."

"Why?"

"You're making me nervous," I admitted, pulling a knot free.

"Better?" he asked, facing the ceiling.

"Much. Do you know if there's a way I can use my own power to block Morlet?" That way we wouldn't have to resort to drastic measures—like being tied together—just to sleep.

"Not that I'm aware of," Vidar answered. "It's your power that allows him to connect to you in the first place."

The last knot on my right leg came free. I moved to the left one, working as fast as possible. "So you're saying the only way to stop him is with the medallion?"

"Correct."

"How am I supposed to defeat someone so powerful?"

"You're not," he said, looking back at me. "That's why there are twelve Krigers. It takes each Kriger with his own weapon, his own power, working together. Then, and only then, can Morlet be destroyed."

I undid the remaining knot and moved away from Vidar, rubbing my ankles. "The other eleven Krigers are all imprisoned?" He nodded. "What about their weapons?"

"I suspect Morlet has stashed them somewhere in the castle."

"And mine?" I stood and stretched.

"We'll talk about it later." He got up and grabbed his boots off the floor. "I don't know about you, but I'm famished." He left the room, whistling as he strolled away.

\*\*\*

I bent over, resting my hands on my thighs, gasping for air.

Vidar patted my back. "You're not out of shape, exactly, but there's definitely room for improvement." He stepped around me, not even winded, and walked along the dirt road that led to the center of the remote town. I hurried after him, still unable to believe he'd forced me to sprint the entire three miles here.

The village was nothing like the capital. All the buildings were single story structures of varying shades of brown, blending in with the surrounding land. The entire town was only a few blocks wide with a large, prominent farm on the west end. About a dozen people were in the field tending to the vegetables. Not a single *soldat* was anywhere to be seen.

Vidar took me to the only tailor shop in town. Inside the tiny store, a woman in her thirties sat sewing. Her blond hair was pulled back into a messy bun, and her blue eyes darted between Vidar and me. "Good to see you again, milord."

He smiled kindly at her. "It's good to see you, too, Aina." He waved me forward. "My sister needs some help."

She put her sewing down and stood to examine me. "What would you like?"

"Sturdy pants and tunics for working and moving freely about in," he answered.

"No dresses?" the woman asked.

"She has no need for them."

Aina picked up a long string with marks evenly spaced on it. "Let's take some measurements."

"That's my cue to go," Vidar said. "I'll be back later. Take good care of … my sister." He winked at me and ran from the store.

I bit my lip, furious he'd left me there. After being poked, prodded, and thoroughly measured, Aina ordered me to sit on a small wooden stool in the corner of the shop while she cut and sewed two pairs of trousers and three shirts.

An hour went by. I started to nod off. Needing to stay awake, I begged the seamstress to allow me to help. She reluctantly put me to work sewing the seams of my shirts, which apparently I didn't do very well, but good enough.

Vidar finally returned, carrying several bulging burlap sacks. He paid Aina for my clothing, and I took the completed items. As we left the store, I inquired about the contents of the bags.

"Just some necessities, like food. Oh, and rope." His eyes sliced over to mine, and he grinned.

I whacked his arm, still embarrassed that he'd tied himself to my legs just to make sure Morlet didn't lure me away. Wanting to change the subject, I asked, "Are you going to make me run home?"

"No." He nodded to the large bags swung over his shoulder. "We're going to go and visit someone before we *walk* home."

We went to the outskirts of the village where a small hut stood at the edge of the woods, separated from the rest of the town by a large clearing. Smoke rose from the chimney. Vidar dropped the sacks to the ground and knocked on the door. I put my new clothes on top of the bags. The door creaked open, and a hunched-over woman with white hair sticking up in all directions answered.

"Ah, I was wondering when you'd show up," she said, ushering us inside.

The only light came from the orange glow of the fireplace illuminating a bed situated in one area, a small chair before the fire, and an old table placed in the center of the hut.

"Grei Heks, I'd like for you to meet Kaia." Vidar put his hand on my lower back and pushed me toward her.

She was a witch endowed with immense powers? I'd never seen a *Heks* before. Grei Heks were ancient beings who used their magic for good. The kingdom of Nelebek was rumored to have only one. My father spoke of her with great reverence since she created the Order of the Krigers and bestowed on us the power to destroy Morlet.

The old woman smiled, revealing several missing teeth. "I've been waiting for you," she said by way of greeting, taking a seat on the chair near the fireplace. Vidar and I each sat at the table. The small room smelled of lavender and rosemary. "I felt your presence and knew your power came early." She glanced at Vidar. "What have you told Kaia?"

"Nothing. She only arrived yesterday."

"Ah, child," she mumbled, facing me. "You come from a line of very strong Krigers."

"It has never had anything to do with family lines," Vidar said. "It has always been random. When one Kriger dies, another is born. Power is dormant until the age of eighteen."

Grei Heks leaned back against her chair. "True," she nodded, "for the other eleven Krigers. The twelfth is different—that's why you've never found her. It has always been a female from Kaia's family."

Confusion overwhelmed me. My father never mentioned anything about the women in our family being Krigers. No one else in my family was even alive. If my own mother had been a Kriger, certainly Papa would have known and told me. Our last conversation replayed in my mind. He'd wanted to tell me something important. My heart sped up as the pieces started fitting together. Is that why he'd spent so much time training me to fight?

"Did your mother die in childbirth?" Grei Heks asked, reclaiming my attention.

"Yes," I replied. "But Papa never told me anything about her."

"She was a Kriger," the old woman said.

The word Kriger echoed in my head, like a bird singing, and I felt the truth of her words deep inside my bones.

"When she died, her power shifted to you."

Vidar leaned forward, placing his arms on his legs. "Why is the twelfth Kriger a woman from Kaia's family?" He spoke to Grei Heks with a warm familiarity, hinting that they were well acquainted.

She smiled kindly at him. "I'm surprised you don't know, Vidar." What was their connection to one another?

"I have a few theories," he mumbled. "Nothing definitive."

Grei Heks twitched. "We don't have much time," she said, jumping to her feet. "Morlet is searching for her—I can feel it. As her power grows, so will his. Keep her hidden until the time is right. Once you've managed to free the other Krigers, we can meet again. Until then, it's too dangerous."

Vidar stood. "I understand. Thank you for speaking with us." He went over to the old woman and kissed her cheek. He whispered something in her ear, and she smiled, patting Vidar's shoulder.

"Come, Kaia," he said. "We must be going." He took hold of my hand and pulled me from the hut.

I picked up my clothes, and Vidar heaved the sacks over his shoulder. "Do you know the word Kriger means warrior?"

"No." My father had often spoken of the Krigers and their fighting abilities, but he'd never mentioned what the word meant. In hindsight, my father knew more about Krigers than the average citizen did. All the training, all the fighting; I thought he wanted to empower me against the *soldats*—not prepare me to fight the king. It all seemed so obvious now.

"It's going to take twelve warriors to destroy one man."

"Are you certain Morlet isn't a *Heks*?" No one but *Heks* could wield magic.

"He is a man tarnished and changed by dark magic." We walked in silence for several moments. Just when I thought he wouldn't elaborate, he said, "Years ago, Morlet sought out Skog Heks. They made a bargain that resulted in him being able to use her magic. That's how he managed to kill the king and queen." The corners of Vidar's lips pulled down.

I had so many questions but decided to keep my mouth shut. We walked in silence, my mind reeling over everything that had just been revealed.

\*\*\*

Sitting on the chair before the hearth in the main room, I peeled open *The Order of the Krigers* and started reading the section on how to defeat Morlet. It explained that the twelve warriors had to link their powers together using their weapons, which contained magical properties bestowed by Grei Heks.

My eyelids eventually grew heavy, and I drifted off to sleep.

*A gentle hand caressed the side of my face. "Since you won't come to me, I've come to you."*

*I was still on the chair with the book resting on my lap. The only difference—Morlet knelt next to me. Was this a dream or reality? I furtively glanced about the room to make sure Vidar wasn't present. Morlet plucked the book from my lap, placing in on the ground. "It's time we get to know one another better." His voice was smooth and seductive.*

*Afraid he'd use his magic on me, I stood and walked to the window, staring outside into the starless night. Dealing with him required the utmost caution. There was a reason it took twelve Krigers to defeat him—he was powerful, perhaps more powerful than even a Heks.*

*"Kaia," he purred.*

*I closed my eyes and focused on my surroundings, allowing instinct to take over. Morlet's magic felt weakened. It had to be taking an enormous amount of energy for him to be here with me. Somehow, I knew he couldn't control me as he'd done before. Relief filled me, and I turned to meet his gaze from across the room. The only light came from the dying fire in the hearth.*

*Morlet stood and reached up, pushing back his hood to reveal his striking face. The gesture seemed intimate, forbidden. I couldn't help but stare. He had a handsome square face, coal black hair, and crystal blue eyes.*

*He sauntered toward me with a wicked smile and seized my hands, holding them tightly. "I want us to be friends. You're unlike anyone I've ever known." Something flashed through his conflicting, dangerous eyes, hinting at a deep pain. "I don't have anyone who knows or understands me."*

*I believed he was telling the truth and found myself wanting to help him.*

*His head jerked toward the door. "Who's there?" he demanded. "Are you with someone?" His face contorted with fury and rage.*

*Was it possible for Vidar to enter my dream? In case he could, I wanted to placate Morlet and keep his focus on me. "I'm alone. It's just the two of us."*

*"I feel I'm losing you." His eyes sought mine, revealing betrayal. "Please help me. I don't want to live like this any longer." He placed his hands on each side of my face, cradling it as if I were precious. "I need you."*

I woke up, once again sitting on the chair, Vidar now kneeling next to me. Both of his hands were on my cheeks, in the exact placement Morlet's had been a moment before.

"Are you okay?" he asked, his forehead pinched with worry.

Closing the book, I leaned forward, and Vidar released me. "I'm fine," I said, placing the book on the ground.

"You're shaking. Did Morlet contact you?"

"Yes. This time was different, though." Not only did Morlet come to me, he had shown me his face. Something about the intensity in his eyes hinted that there was more to him than simply the evil man everyone claimed him to be. There was definitely darkness and cruelty in him, but that innate feeling that told me to trust Anders now told me there was great sadness in Morlet. Against all common sense, a desire to understand him took root.

"What happened?" Vidar asked.

Not wanting to tell him about seeing Morlet's face or about being drawn to him, I said, "He was here, in this room."

Vidar let out a deep breath. "Grei Heks told us his magic would grow stronger." He rubbed his face. "I didn't expect it to be at this rate."

My hands started to pulse with a dull pain. I frantically searched for the source of the danger lurking in the shadows.

"What's the matter?" he asked, pulling me to my feet.

I rushed over to the window. "Could Morlet be outside?" The dark forest appeared normal.

"I don't think so," Vidar whispered behind me. "Why?"

My spine tingled as if spiders were crawling up it. "My hands hurt. It's only a mild throbbing and not the awful feeling I usually get before something bad happens."

"If they were painful, I'd say you're in danger. However, since it's a dulled sensation, it's probably just from your dream. A delayed reaction, if you will."

My hands never hurt with our previous communications. Gazing through the open window at the forest, the chilly night air engulfed me with its heady pine scent.

Vidar placed his hands on my shoulders, rubbing them. "I'm sorry," he said. "It'll be better once Anders returns with my medallion."

"Did Grei Heks give it to you?"

"Yes. It was a gift to protect me from Morlet. It's imperative that he doesn't know I'm alive."

My suspicions were confirmed. "How are you and Anders tied to all of this?"

His hands slid down my arms, instantly calming me. "I'll show you." He led me out of the main room, across the bridge, and to his bedchamber. He built up the fire and then searched his bookshelves. "Here it is," he said, pulling out a small wooden box that had been hidden behind several books. Sitting on his bed, he patted the spot next to him.

Something shifted between us, and I no longer felt nervous around him. Instead, his friendship soothed me. I sat down and he opened the lid. Inside, a sapphire roughly carved into the shape of a ball rested on a white handkerchief. He lifted the stone, placing it on the palm of my hand.

The light sparkled on the polished sapphire, reminding me of Morlet's eyes. "It's beautiful, but what is it?"

Vidar lay back on the bed, staring up at the ceiling. "Everything," he responded, flinging his arm over his eyes. "It means everything."

The stone felt warm, as if it had a life of its own. It began pulsing slow and steady, a soft glow emanating from the middle, growing until the entire sapphire shone brightly. "It recognizes I'm a Kriger, doesn't it?" I asked, captivated by the blue light that somehow felt familiar.

"Yes."

I carefully placed the stone back in the box and closed the lid. I lay on my stomach next to Vidar, waiting for him to explain.

"Grei Heks gave it to me," he said. "It's a sapphire infused with a sliver of magic. It allows me to properly identify a Kriger. Although, I've been doing this for so long, I can feel a Kriger's power. The stone also allows me to communicate with Grei Heks—similar to the way you do with Morlet."

"But you yourself have no power?"

"No, none at all." He sighed and moved his arm down so he could look at me. "Today, in the kingdom of Nelebek, only two witches exist. Grei Heks and Skog Heks. They always have to be balanced with one another. When they're not, something happens to right the wrong and create balance again."

Thunder boomed. I hoped it didn't start raining until after Anders returned. He shouldn't have to travel through treacherous conditions on my account.

"You look tired," Vidar commented.

Laughing, I said, "Haven't been sleeping well." I rested my head on my arms. "How are you involved with the Krigers?"

His penetrating blue eyes stared at me. "Like you, I'm faced with a destiny whether I want it or not."

"What about Anders?"

His eyebrows drew together. "What about him?"

"He's an assassin who considers you his best friend, as close as a brother. How does he fit into all of this?"

"He's cursed like you and me. He won't be free until the twelve Krigers defeat Morlet."

"Who cursed him?"

Vidar chuckled. "Hard to say."

"What was he doing in the capital the day I met him?"

"Why are you asking me? Why don't you ask Anders?"

I wanted to scream that Anders never spoke to me and refused to answer any of my questions. "Was he there on a mission? Or for some other reason?"

"He was checking on the Krigers," Vidar admitted.

"Aren't they locked in the dungeon?" He nodded. "Was he going to rescue them?"

"He can't." Vidar rolled onto his side, propping his head up on his hand, facing me. "The Krigers are in cells that have a magical ward on them. Only a *Heks* or someone with power"— he looked pointedly at me—"can break the ward."

My stomach dropped. "Why don't they free each other?"

"The ward prohibits them from accessing their powers while in the cells. You can free them so long as you're not in there with them."

"And you're going to ask me to break into the fortified castle and rescue the Krigers, aren't you?"

"No, I'm not going to ask you. I'm going to train you. And when you're ready, I expect you to save your fellow Krigers. Because then, and only then, can the group of you link your powers together to defeat Morlet. Once he's gone, we'll all be free from his tyranny."

"Why doesn't Grei Heks save them?"

"When she created the twelve Krigers to defeat Morlet, she greatly diminished her own magic. She rarely leaves her home." My eyelids were getting heavy. "How do you propose I make it through the night? Are you going to tie us together again?"

"Speaking of which, you never told me about Morlet's visit. You simply said he came here to see you. Was that the only reason you were so afraid?"

I didn't want to reveal anything about the strangely intimate encounter.

His eyes narrowed. "You can tell me. I'll help however I can."

"He still wants me to go to his castle."

"What did he do to entice you this time?"

How did he know Morlet had done something different? I shook my head and yawned, wanting to end this conversation.

Vidar got up and took the box over to the bookshelf, putting it away. "Just know that Morlet has been around for a century. He's very good at manipulating people to get what he wants. Always remember that, and whatever you do, don't trust him." He turned and faced me, rubbing the back of his neck. "When he visits you, how does he appear?"

I fidgeted with the edge of my sleeve. For some reason, revealing that Morlet had shown me his face felt like acknowledging I'd done something wrong. "He's always wearing a black cape." Which was true.

"Well," he said, coming to stand before me. "His magic is probably depleted after reaching all the way out here to visit you in your dream. It takes much less effort on his part to bring you to him." He rubbed his face. "I'd like to try and catch a few hours of sleep. Would you mind staying in here tonight?"

I didn't want to sleep in his room; however, I understood why he wanted me to. Considering all he'd done for me, it was the least I could do.

\*\*\*

The sound of people talking roused me. Opening my eyes, I found myself in Vidar's bed, wrapped in his arms, my head on his chest. Thunder boomed in the distance. "We'll discuss it later," he whispered. "Go before you wake her."

Realizing Vidar wasn't talking to me, I flew to a sitting position and twisted around. Anders stood in the doorway, dripping wet from the light rain. "How's my father?" I asked. Anders turned and trudged away without acknowledging me. Wanting to speak to him, I went to climb out of bed.

Vidar's arm tightened around me, and he tapped the end of my nose with his finger, capturing my attention. "You're adorable in the morning." His lips curled into a slow smile. "I slept like a baby. How about you?"

Both of us were fully dressed and lying on top of the blankets. Obviously, nothing had happened, but I didn't want Anders to get the wrong idea. I shoved away from Vidar and scrambled out of bed. "I slept just fine, thank you."

"Morlet will try to communicate with you again as soon as he's strong enough. I'd recommend not napping." He sat up and stretched.

"I'll make sure I'm near Anders and the medallion."

"That won't work." Vidar ran his hands through his rumpled

hair. "The medallion is mine, and I'm supposed to wear it at all times." He pointed to the door handle where the necklace hung. "See, Anders already gave it back to me." Vidar got up and took the medallion, placing it around his neck so it rested against his chest. He glanced at me and chuckled. "Guess you'll just have to sleep with me from now on."

I rolled my eyes. "You should be so lucky." I hurried from the room, eager to talk to Anders about my father.

# Chapter Seven

The light rain picked up, turning into a heavy downpour. I ran to my room and changed into a clean pair of trousers and a thick shirt. When I entered the main room, Vidar was kneeling at the hearth, nursing the flames back to life. Banging came from the kitchen, so I headed in there. Anders had his back to me while he stirred something in a pot hanging over a small fire.

"I'm glad you made it back safely," I said. "Were you able to find my father? Is he well?" Hopefully, Papa had not gotten worse. I held my breath, waiting for Anders to answer.

"I just returned," he mumbled, not bothering to look at me while he spoke. "Can I at least eat before you bombard me with a thousand questions?" He shook his head. "I forgot how much you love to talk."

Sitting down at the table, I drummed my fingers on the wooden surface. This was my father we were talking about. He was the only family I had. So no, I couldn't wait for Anders to do something so trivial as eat. I started tapping my foot.

After using a wooden ladle to scoop some white mush into a bowl, he sat across from me and ate, not once looking in my direction.

"Are you mad at me?" I asked. Another thought occurred— maybe my father had died and Anders was afraid to tell me the news. "Is my father … " I trailed off, unable to finish the sentence.

He glanced up with fierce brown eyes and said, "Your father is fine." Then he went back to eating, studiously ignoring me.

"Now that we're all here," Vidar said as he came into the kitchen, "we need to talk." He went over to the pot and scooped some white mush into two bowls. After handing one to me, he sat down. "Anders isn't the best cook," he loudly whispered, "but at least it's warm." Taking a spoonful, he elegantly ate the food.

I stirred mine, not really hungry.

"While you were gone," Vidar continued, "Morlet visited Kaia in her dreams. He has to know someone is helping her. It's only a matter of time until he discovers we're still alive."

Anders put down his spoon and observed his friend. "How is this possible?"

"I spoke with Grei Heks. She said he's feeding off Kaia's power."

Anders rubbed his face. "So now what?"

"We need to train Kaia. Then we'll rescue the Krigers."

"I'm not sure she's ready," Anders said. "She's only sixteen."

Vidar smiled. "True, but she's not like other girls. She's special."

Both of them spoke as if I weren't in the room. I pushed away from the table, not caring to hear any more of their conversation, and walked out of the kitchen. The walls felt confining, suffocating. I needed some time alone to sort through my thoughts. I left the house, crossed the bridge, and climbed down the tree. I stepped out of the trunk, the rain pounding on the ground. I closed my eyes and tilted my head back, letting the cold water wash over me. Papa was okay. Morlet hadn't captured him nor had my father's illness taken him.

My clothes were drenched, but being alone in the forest in the pouring rain was liberating. I could almost forget Anders's degrading words: *I'm not sure she's ready. She's only sixteen.* Neither Anders nor Vidar looked much older than I was. Granted, I wasn't an assassin skilled in the art of killing. However, I was more than capable of taking on a larger opponent and winning. After all, I'd been training my entire life for this—I just hadn't known it.

The sound of raindrops hitting the leaves and branches soothed me. On a whim, I decided to try to find the lake with the large waterfall. Heading east, I had difficulty seeing more than a few feet in front of me. Thunder boomed and lightning sliced across the sky. After five minutes of walking, my hands pulsed with acute pain, almost knocking me over. It was stupid to have come out here all alone during a storm when I was so unfamiliar with the area.

Closing my eyes, I thought back to what Anders said at the pond. I raised my hands out before me and slowly turned around, searching for some sort of pull. The only thing I felt was the rain pounding on my body and the throbbing in my hands. Squinting, I searched for an animal or someone lurking nearby. Nothing.

The ache intensified, and I fell to my knees, crying out. My arms shook, and I glanced at my palms, expecting to see them on fire. They appeared normal, but the cool rain did nothing to soothe them. The ground beneath me suddenly gave out, and I dropped into the earth, screaming as I fell through darkness.

I slammed against a hard surface; a sharp shooting pain pierced my right leg. Luckily, my head didn't hit anything. The only light came from the opening through which I had fallen, a good ten feet above me. My clothes were soaking wet, and cold seeped into my bones. Taking a deep breath, I moved my foot in slow circles. My ankle was sore, but not broken. Relieved, I bent my knee and discovered it too was just bruised.

My father told me there were hundreds of underground caverns throughout Nelebek. Some of them opened up to the middle of the world, causing people to disappear forever. I would have to use the upmost caution searching for a way out.

Standing, I yelled in case someone above could hear me. No one came. The rocky floor sloped to my right, so I headed in the opposite direction, hoping there was an exit. Sliding one foot forward to ensure the ground didn't suddenly open up, I shifted my weight, and then slid my other foot forward. It was slow going, especially since my leg was sore. The farther I moved from the small opening in the cavern's ceiling, the darker it became until complete and utter darkness took over.

It smelled of damp sulfur like the pool Anders and I had bathed in. I shook my head, not wanting to think about the assassin right now. It was eerily quiet—the only sound coming from my feet. The darkness started playing tricks on me. I kept imagining someone grabbing me from behind. Balling my hands into fists, I continued on.

If I reached a dead end, retracing my steps would be difficult, if not downright impossible. This reminded me of being stuck in the closet when I was younger. Since my mother died in childbirth, there was no one to care for me when my father went to work. At first, he left me with a neighbor who had six children of her own. Papa never talked about it, but I got the impression she didn't take very good care of me. He started leaving me home alone to fend for myself when I was only four years old. When *soldats* came to search the apartment building, I would hide in the secret closet my father built, staying in the dark, cramped space until he returned in the evening. Often times, I'd go all day without food and water.

A noise came from up ahead. I started shuffling my feet faster, hoping there was an opening and that sound was rain. Gradually, the floor and rocky walls became defined, a soft gray light filtering in from somewhere. I went around a bend and entered a large circular area in the cavern approximately fifty feet wide and thirty feet tall. An opening directly above illuminated the pool before me. A waterfall cascaded down from a cave twenty feet above the pool. Sun sparkled on the beautiful greenish-blue water. Kneeling, I stuck my hand in. The water was hot. Shivering from my wet clothes, I stripped and climbed in, basking in the water's warmth.

After rinsing the dirt and grime from my body, I floated on my back with my eyes closed, trying to relax. Anders's angry face appeared before me, shaking his head as if I'd done something wrong. His face melted away and was replaced with Vidar's handsome one, smiling sardonically as if he knew a secret I didn't. His face dissolved and Morlet appeared in his bedchamber, standing in front of a tall mirror, lacing up his shirt.

*"Kaia?" Morlet asked, his voice hesitant.*

*Shock rolled through me—were we somehow linked together? How was that possible since I wasn't asleep?*

*"You're cape isn't on," I lamely said, noticing it draped over a nearby chair. The mirror reflected his beautiful face, tousled black*

*hair, and penetrating blue eyes. There was something dark and sinister yet alluring about this man.*

*"I can hear you," he softly replied. "But I can't see you. Where are you, my Kaia?" He turned away from the mirror, searching for me.*

Remembering that I was swimming naked, my concentration faltered and our connection severed. Did I just invade Morlet's thoughts? Swimming to the edge, I swiftly climbed out of the water and put my heavy, wet clothes back on, trying to mask my feeling of vulnerability.

Before I could think about my power, how to control it, and what just happened, I needed to find a way out of the cavern. Looking at the opening far above me, I searched for a way to climb up there. It didn't appear possible. Maybe if Vidar threw a rope down, but even that seemed sketchy.

My father taught me to be resourceful and to use the environment to help me. I focused on the details of the cavern. The waterfall came from somewhere, filtered into this pool, and then what? Was this where it ended? If so, why wasn't the water filling up more? There had to be an outlet. I observed the pool's movements. The waterfall came down, swirled around, and then headed toward the right. I went over to that area, looking for additional clues. The water flowed below the surface where I stood. There had to be a way out through there.

Keeping my clothes on, I took a huge breath, jumped into the water, and let the current carry me below. It was stronger than I anticipated, and my clothes weighed me down. Panic filled me, but Papa always said that panicking only made things worse. There was nothing I could do except allow the water to take me where it wanted. It carried me into a narrow tunnel. If my lungs didn't get air soon, I'd drown.

As I was jostled forward, I kept my legs together and my hands on my head, protecting myself from the rocky wall. Suddenly, I fell in a gush of water, gasping for air. My arms flailed about in the darkness. My body hit water again. This pool was much colder than the previous one. The current carried me along. When I felt it pulling me down, I took a big breath and went under. The water pressure was so strong, it shoved me right along.

The tunnel spit me out, and my body fell a short distance to a small pool bathed in sunlight. Gasping for air, squinting, I stared at the open sky with a huge sense of relief. I was out of the cavern and the rain had stopped. The water kept shoving me forward, too deep to gain my footing, as the edge of the pool neared. The sound of roaring water was the only indication of what lay ahead. There was nothing I could do to stop myself from going over the edge of a steep cliff.

My stomach gave out as I fell with an enormous surge of water.

# Chapter Eight

After falling a good thirty feet, I slammed into another pool of water. My body twisted every which way as water continued to crash on top of me. I tried swimming to the surface, but the force from the water was too strong. I sank lower and lower.

Desperately needing air, I let instinct take over and swam sideways, away from the waterfall. Kicking furiously, I finally broke the surface, gasping for air. My chest felt like it was being crushed. Heaving deep breaths, my arms and legs spent, I could barely keep my head above water. Angling straight toward the closest bank, I forced myself to swim until my feet touched bottom. I trudged out of the water, crawled onto one of the boulders that surrounded the lake, and collapsed.

*"Kaia,"* Morlet *frantically whispered. "Are you all right?"*

*I was lying on Morlet's bed, soaking wet. He sat next to me, his hand pulling wet strands of hair off my face. I must have fallen asleep* on the boulder. "I'm fine," I croaked, my throat sore. I nuzzled the silk blankets, the roaring fire warming me.

"Earlier, you found me." He drew his eyebrows together.

"I have no idea how that happened," I mumbled. His hand reached out, cradling my face. The intimate gesture shocked me. We stayed that way for several minutes, neither of us moving.

Morlet's face was rarely uncovered, so I used the opportunity to study him. His dark hair and thick eyebrows accentuated his bright blue eyes. "How old are you?" I asked. He looked nineteen years old, but he'd been ruling over Nelebek for at least a century.

Instead of answering, he asked, "What do you know about being a Kriger?" His hand dropped from my face.

I pushed myself into a sitting position. "Very little." Would Morlet be willing to share his knowledge about magic with me? Would he teach me how to use my power? However, this was the man the Krigers were supposed to defeat. He couldn't be trusted. "I don't understand my role as a Kriger. Frankly, it makes me feel very lonely."

"You don't have to be alone," he gently replied. "I'm here. You can come to me." He took my hand, tracing small circles on my palm.

"So you can kill me?" I asked. Or was there more to it than that?

Morlet abruptly stood and went to the fireplace, his back to me. "Yes," he finally admitted.

"Then you know I can't come to you."

"It's the only way to end the curse," he said. "I have to eliminate all the Krigers."

"Why?" Vidar's warning not to trust Morlet came back to me. However, right now, it seemed like he was being honest with me.

Morlet turned around, and his face hardened, making him look malicious. "I won't live another hundred years like this," he sneered, the gentleness and concern from earlier gone. "I hear you're close to *your father. If you don't come to me, I'll hunt him down and kill him."*

*My heart pounded, and terror filled me. I couldn't allow Papa to suffer because of me.*

*Morlet's head tilted to the side. "Who's with you?" he demanded. "I can feel something severing our connection." He grabbed my upper arms, squeezing hard. "I can't lose you!" he yelled, his face turning an angry shade of red.*

*A surge of magic coursed through me, hot like fire. I screamed in pain.*

"Kaia," Vidar cried. My eyes flew open. Vidar hovered over me on the rock, the medallion hanging around his neck. "What happened?"

My body ached from everything I'd been through, and I was shaking from the frigid air, my clothing and hair still dripping wet. Vidar patiently waited for me to answer, but I didn't even know where to begin. Tears filled my eyes. Morlet had threatened my father.

Vidar scooped me up. I didn't have the energy to argue with him to put me down. As he carried me in his arms, I drifted off to a peaceful sleep, my hand clutching the medallion.

\*\*\*

Rubbing my eyes, I sat up, still wearing the same clothes from earlier. Although now dry, they were stiff from the water. My boots and socks had been removed and were on the ground next to the bed.

A blazing fire roared in the small hearth, making my

bedchamber hot and stuffy. Something moved in the corner of the room, and I twisted around to see Anders sitting on a wooden chair, staring at me, the medallion dangling from his hands.

"What are you doing here?" I asked.

He watched me with hooded eyes. "I want to make sure you're okay," he said, his voice barely audible.

He only cared about me because I was a Kriger. My life was precious and valuable. He didn't actually care about *me*.

"And I want you near the medallion," he added, glancing away.

"I'm all right. You don't need to watch over me." Morlet's haunting words replayed in my mind. Was he honestly going to search for my father? If so, I had to find a way to protect Papa.

"I was hoping we could … talk." Anders fiddled with the medallion's chain, not looking at me.

I laughed. "Sorry, it sounded like you said you wanted to talk."

"You heard me correctly."

The one time I needed to be alone in order to sort through my encounter with Morlet, and Anders wanted to talk. I could scream. Sitting on the edge of the bed, I patiently waited for him to speak.

He slouched forward, resting his arms on his knees, his focus on the ground. "I'd like to apologize for my behavior." His words caught me off guard. "I'm still getting used to the idea of the final Kriger being a young, attractive girl." He peered into my eyes.

He thought I was attractive? No, most likely he needed something from me. "Why the sudden change?" I folded my arms across my chest, trying to appear aloof.

Anders came over and sat next to me on the bed, the medallion resting on the palm of his hand. "I spoke with your father," he softly said. "Working underground in the mines, even as a guard, can damage one's lungs."

Without Papa, I'd be all alone. Tears filled my eyes. I tried holding them back, not wanting to show any weakness in front of Anders. "He'll improve with medicine."

He placed the medallion around my neck. "I promised your father I'd look after you."

Papa must have taken to Anders to ask such a thing—he never would have done so unless he trusted him. I could see Papa liking him since they were both private, stubborn, and intelligent. My breath caught, and I focused on my hands, not wanting to look at Anders. Not able to look at him.

"He's a good man," Anders whispered.

I needed to change the subject. "I thought Vidar had to wear the medallion."

"He does. But for now, I want it around your neck."

This was the first time he'd ever opened up to me. Perhaps he would be willing to share more about his past. "How did you become involved with the Krigers?"

Anders sighed and rubbed the back of his neck. "It's a long story."

"I have time."

"I guess you could say I deserve this fate ... a fate worse than death."

His words froze my insides. "You don't want to help the Krigers?" Then why was he here?

"I'm an assassin," he said. "I took an assignment I shouldn't have. I was greedy and only concerned with making money, not the consequences of my actions. Now, I'm paying for it." He stood and went to the window, gazing outside at the forest.

Sensing his hesitation to continue, I asked, "How did you

become an assassin?"

"It was a long time ago, and I don't remember much."

It couldn't have been that long ago—he didn't look older than twenty. Although, neither did Morlet, and somehow he'd managed not to age for over a hundred years.

"How old are you?"

He glanced over his shoulder at me, smiling. "Eighteen." Looking back outside, Anders continued talking, "I was born into slavery in Hoverek—the kingdom to the north of us. At the age of ten, my owner sold me to a man who trained assassins. He taught me to fight and kill. At fifteen, I started going on assignments."

"How did you enter Nelebek?" Our borders had been closed by a magical barrier for over a hundred years. "And how did you become friends with Vidar?"

He sat next to me on the bed, searching my face for something. I flushed. His brown eyes revealed painful memories, danger, and a depth of emotions I couldn't even begin to comprehend.

"Vidar and I share a common goal."

"To defeat Morlet."

"Yes. In order to do that, we need you. I'd like to start your training."

If I was going to be here for a while and Morlet was hunting my father, I needed to figure something out to ensure his safety. "Can my father join us here?" I asked. "Morlet threatened him."

"You need to trust me when I say he's safe where he is. There's no way the king will be able to find him. I promise." The confidence with which he spoke made me believe him.

"Then let's get started."

"Are you feeling well enough?"

My leg was sore and my chest tight. Yet, I was eager to do

something physical to get my mind off Papa. "I'd like to get this over with."

Anders raised his eyebrows. "Am I that awful to be around?"

*Yes.* "That's not what I meant. The sooner we defeat Morlet, the sooner I can return to my father and my life."

His forehead creased. "Didn't you say you worked as a laundress?" I nodded. "You're eager to return to that?"

"I miss my home," I said, turning away as embarrassment consumed me. There was nothing for me to go back to except Papa; yet, it was all I knew and was familiar with. Perhaps once we defeated Morlet, things would change, and I'd have an opportunity to do something else—something better and more exciting with my life than wash people's clothes.

\*\*\*

Standing on the forest floor beneath the towering pines, I could hear birds singing all around me. In the capital, I never heard birds chirping or wind tossing the leaves of trees. Instead, the sound of *soldats* beating citizens, children screaming, and people crying in pain echoed everywhere.

Anders and Vidar stood off to the side, speaking in hushed whispers. While I waited for them to finish, warring thoughts about the king entered my mind. Growing up, I'd always been told Morlet ruled the kingdom with his vicious army. He tortured citizens and kept us all in poverty. Now that I'd met him, there was more to it than that. Yes, he was evil, but there was also good in him—I was certain of it.

Vidar laughed, recapturing my attention. He wrapped an

arm around Anders's shoulders, and they walked over to me. I removed the medallion and handed it to him.

"Anders is going to teach you some basic fighting techniques, and I'll show you how to wield your power while using your weapon." He put the necklace on. A buzzing sensation radiated through my body. "My bo staff?" I eagerly asked.

They exchanged confused looks.

"How do you know that's your weapon?" Anders questioned me.

"When I saw a picture of one in Morlet's bedchamber, it called to me." Even now, my hands tingled, wanting to hold it.

"You were in his bedchamber?" Anders's face remained expressionless, but his voice was laced with a lethal fury that made my skin prickle.

"Yes," I answered.

His foot kicked a rock, sending it flying. "I can't believe he had you in such an intimate place. Why not his sitting room? Why his bedchamber?"

Vidar let out an odd noise—something between a laugh and a sound of disgust. "You don't know him like I do," he said, shaking his head. "Morlet always gets what he wants. And if he's trying to lure Kaia to him, he'll use whatever means necessary to do so."

"You know you can't trust him, don't you?" Anders asked me, his hands on his hips.

I looked between them. "Honestly? I don't know what to believe. Neither of you has told me about yourself nor how you're involved in all of this. You've both been vague when I ask you questions. Right now, Morlet is at least talking to me."

Vidar's face turned red. "He lies to get what he wants,"

he fumed. "And he wants you." His hands shook as anger overwhelmed him. "When I get my hands on him, I'll kill him." Vidar stormed away.

I watched him leave, wondering why he was so mad. He knew the king had been visiting me and that he'd tried more than once to lure me to the castle.

"So," Anders mused, "you have questions. I'll make you a deal. How about you train with me for a few hours, then I'll answer anything you want."

"Why can't we talk now?"

"Because we have a lot of work to do." Swinging his arms, loosening them up, he continued, "Most Krigers don't come into their power until they're eighteen. Since you're different, Vidar is worried you won't pass your trials. Now that Morlet knows who you are, he'll be hunting you. We don't have a lot of time."

"Trials?" No one had mentioned anything about any sort of trials.

"In order to enter the cavern where your bo staff is, you must pass a series of challenges." He slid a dagger out from his sleeve, laying it on top of a nearby boulder.

"Who gives them? And what sort of trials are they?"

Anders reached down and removed two knives from beneath his trousers, laying them on the boulder next to the dagger. "Grei Heks put a spell on the cavern to make sure only those who truly are Krigers, and worthy of the title, enter to retrieve their weapons. Neither Vidar nor I will be able to assist you. I don't know how you'll be challenged because everyone faces something different." Reaching behind him, he removed a short sword from under his shirt and placed it on the boulder next to the other weapons.

"Have the others passed?"

"Over the years, a few have failed. They were forced to return years later to try again. No one has failed a second time, though."

"How do you know this?"

"I'm always there, waiting in the cave outside the cavern whenever a Kriger faces the trials." Anders removed several pocketknives hidden within the folds of his clothing, tossing them onto the boulder alongside the others.

"How is that possible? You're only eighteen."

He bitterly laughed, shaking his head. "You keep asking how I'm tied to all of this. Well, I'm frozen in the body of an eighteen-year-old," he revealed. "I'm cursed. I assumed you knew. Otherwise I wouldn't be able to touch the medallion."

I couldn't believe what he just revealed. The forest went still, all life hidden within vanished, and all that existed were Anders and I, standing there, facing one another.

"When Morlet is defeated," he said, "I'll finally be free. I'll be able to age and live my life, no longer bound to Vidar."

"Bound how?" I whispered, taking a step closer to him.

His brown eyes seemed far away, lost in thought. I gently touched his arm, and he blinked several times. "Enough talking," he said. "We have work to do. Once you have your weapon, you'll be able to control the power within you. After you do that, you can save the Krigers." He took a step away from me, and my hand dropped to my side.

Was Vidar cursed as well? Was he stuck in a body that never aged? All this time, I thought Anders wanted to save the people in Nelebek, but he really just wanted to save himself.

The wind rustled the leaves above me, and I remembered what I was here for. "Let's get started."

Anders swung his arm, and I ducked. "Excellent reflexes," he said, surprised. Staying light on his feet, he bounced around, taunting me. "The first thing you must learn is basic combat techniques."

"Oh?" I raised my arms, prepared to block or strike as needed.

His eyes sparkled with amusement. "When we go into the dungeon to rescue the Krigers, we'll be in a small, confined space. We'll need to incapacitate the *soldats* quickly, before the alarm is raised."

"What do you mean, *we*?" I kept a close eye on him as he circled me.

"You and me." He kicked his leg and knocked me to the ground.

I jumped up, mad I didn't see that one coming. "I'm not going in alone?" He kicked again, and this time I swung my arm, hitting his leg before it could strike me.

"No," he said as he came closer. "I'm going with you. You don't know your way around the castle, and you don't have enough experience."

"What about Vidar?"

He swung his fist toward my face. I ducked and then countered by kicking his leg.

"He has other duties to attend to." Anders sidestepped to avoid being hit. He spun around and came up behind me, wrapping his arms around me. Instinct and years of my father's training kicked in. I stomped on his right foot. When he hunched slightly forward, I rolled my body to the side and swung my right arm, hitting him in the groin. His grip loosened, and I threw my elbow up, knocking his chin. He fell to the ground.

"Just as I suspected," he said. "You have some basic training. That will save me a lot of time. We just need to practice and make sure your stamina is up. Ready for another round?"

I nodded, excited to be able to spar so easily with him.

# Chapter Nine

My stomach growled from having spent several hours working with Anders and not once stopping to eat. We entered the sitting room and found Vidar sprawled on the couch, reading a book.

"About time," he said, not bothering to look up.

Heading into the kitchen, we saw two plates piled high with bread, cheese, and some sort of meat.

"Duck," Anders said, answering my unvoiced question. He picked up his plate and took a bite of the bread. "I'm going to get cleaned up."

"You promised you'd answer my questions."

"Ask Vidar. He enjoys talking nearly as much as you do." At the doorway, he glanced back. "Make sure you're near the medallion at all times so Morlet can't contact you." He left, taking his plate with him.

Not wanting to eat alone, I went back into the sitting room

and plopped down next to Vidar. "What are you reading?"

"A book about the history of Nelebek," he answered, swinging his legs off the couch and propping himself up.

"So just some light reading for fun," I teased.

He smiled and closed the book. "I have it memorized from beginning to end. But I read it once in a while to remind myself what we're fighting for." He put the book down, giving me his full attention.

"What are you fighting for?" I asked. "The kingdom? To end the curse?" What motivated him to keep going, even after all the years of failure?

"As much as I'd love to end the curse, I fight for the people of Nelebek. We must kill Morlet so people can once again be free and live in peace."

"Was it peaceful before Morlet took over?"

He nodded, his eyes revealing a great sadness.

I longed for a kingdom where *soldats* didn't watch our every move, where people weren't executed for helping one another, and the ruler actually cared about his subjects. I finished my food and put my plate on the nearby table.

"Kaia," Vidar said, fidgeting with his hands. "Grei Heks ... well ... she told me something you should know." His eyes darted to my face and then quickly away.

"What is it?"

"That you and I ... well ..." He ran his hands through his hair, nervous about whatever it was he had to say. "We ... uh, just that we need to retrieve your weapon as soon as possible. I'd like to leave in two days."

Vidar was hiding something from me. Before I could ask him what it was, he said, "Anders told me you have questions about being a Kriger, and I should answer whatever you ask. So now is your chance. What do you want to know?"

One question had been nagging me since I first discovered I was a Kriger. "When the twelve of us link our powers together and go up against Morlet, will we all survive?"

After staring at me for several uncomfortable minutes, he finally answered, "No. Most of you will not."

My fear was confirmed. I was going to fight to save a kingdom I most likely would never see liberated.

"Don't look so sad," he pleaded. "There's a chance you'll live."

"You and I both know I probably won't make it out of this alive."

He reached out and gingerly touched my cheek. "I think that's why Anders is so upset that the last Kriger is a girl."

"It doesn't matter whether I'm a girl or a boy," I said. "I'm a person. And the death of any person is a tragedy." I stood to go. "If you'll excuse me, I'd like to go to bed."

"Uh," Vidar stammered. "I need to sleep close by so the medallion can protect you."

I'd forgotten about that.

"We don't have to sleep in the same bed," he continued. "The same room should suffice."

"Fine, but I'm sleeping on the bed. You can sleep anywhere you like on the floor." I turned and left, not waiting to see if he followed.

\*\*\*

After tossing and turning for several hours, I finally gave up trying to sleep. Vidar lay lightly snoring on the ground next to my bed, a pillow under his head, and a blanket strewn between his legs. I slipped off the mattress, careful not to wake him. My head tingled. Morlet must be trying to find me. Thankfully, the medallion blocked his ability to do so. I lit a candle, placed it on the bedside table, and picked up *The Order of the Krigers*. Sitting cross-legged on the bed, I started reading, hoping to understand more about being a Kriger.

One chapter went into detail about each of the twelve weapons, so I skimmed over it, wanting to read about the Order itself or the life of previous Krigers. The following chapter was entitled "Journals," and there were several loose sheets of paper wedged in the book. I started reading them:

*I am writing this account to serve as a warning to other Krigers. It's easier now, looking back over my life, to see all the mistakes I made. When I first learned I was a Kriger, I felt empowered. I thought I could save Nelebek by destroying Morlet. I was naive and had no idea what I was up against. The king is more powerful and far more sinister than I ever expected.*

*Morlet claimed he was searching for the* Heks *power source and needed more diggers in the mines. In an attempt to gain a larger workforce, he killed the eldest child in each family if they refused to send one able-bodied worker. All I could think about was retribution for the innocent lives taken. P. Vidar ordered us not to attack, but we didn't listen. That was our first mistake. We should have done as he said, but we didn't know or truly understand.*

*There were only four Krigers at the time. Together, we went to the capital. We had our weapons and knew how to fight using our powers. We easily fought off the* soldats *stationed throughout the castle.*

*When we arrived at the Throne Room, Morlet sat alone waiting for us. He removed his cape, and I saw he had not aged a single day in the twenty-two years I'd been a Kriger. I raised my sword and attacked. With a flick of his wrist, he threw me against the wall and I was rendered unconscious. It was over that quickly. Some warrior I turned out to be. When I came to, I was locked in the dungeon. While in that treacherous place, I was tortured daily. Years later, there was a fire in the castle, and Anders managed to sneak in and rescue me. I've lived with P. Vidar and him ever since. My fellow Krigers were not so lucky—they each died while being tortured.*

*To all future Krigers, wait until all twelve of you have come together. Learn how to work with one another and link powers. Then, and only then, will you be able to defeat Morlet.*

I flipped through a few more pages, looking for anything about why Morlet sought dark magic in the first place. Was it because he wanted to rule? Or was there more to it than that? In order to use dark magic, he had to be working with Skog Heks. How did the two of them come to work together? I turned the pages, searching for answers, and came to a passage that was barely legible. The writing was faded from time, the paper worn thin. I held the candle close, squinting as I read:

*A thousand years ago, this land was ruled by Heks, beings able to pull magic from the center of the world. Humans came from warring countries seeking peace. But they didn't ask permission to settle here. They took what they wanted thinking the Heks didn't matter.*

*Great battles between the two groups ensued. Even though Heks had immense magic, they were not immune to the humans' diseases, and many died. As the* Heks' *numbers decreased, so did their control over the land.*

*After years of fighting, the two sides finally came to a truce. The leaders of the* Heks *and the humans signed a peace treaty. The humans set up a monarchy in each of the twelve kingdoms and* Heks *were assigned to each region to work in conjunction with the king and queen. They held power equally and had to agree on all major decisions. Over the years, the* Heks *continued to die from the humans' diseases, and no new* Heks *were born. They became increasingly valuable for their powers. The balance of power slowly shifted.*

The rest of the page was faded, and I couldn't make out any more words. I didn't know *Heks* were here first and that humans took the land away from them. In Nelebek, we had only two *Heks*. But then again, our kingdom had been shut off from the rest of the continent for the past hundred years.

I rubbed my temples; the stuffy room felt confining. I carefully stepped around Vidar and went outside on the platform. Leaning against the railing, I was still close enough to the medallion for protection. Breathing in the fresh, crisp air, I gazed at the clear sky and the brightly lit stars above. The leaves gently rustled in the soft wind.

"You're up late," Anders said as he walked across the bridge toward me, hidden among the shadows of the trees.

I jumped, not expecting to see him at this hour. "I was reading."

"Anything interesting?" he asked, joining me on the platform. He wore all black and dirt was smeared over his face.

"No," I said, shaking my head and staring up at the stars. For some reason, being out here alone with the assassin unnerved me.

I didn't feel like talking about the book or *Heks* right now.

"You should go to bed," he said, leaning against the railing a few feet away from me. "We only have one more day of training before we leave to get your weapon. You'll want to be well rested to meet whatever challenge awaits."

"What are you doing up?" Given his attire, he'd obviously been out somewhere. Did Vidar send him on a mission? Did he just kill someone?

"I'd rather not say," he mumbled, rubbing his face. He sounded tired.

I moved closer to him. "Do you think so little of me that you can't tell me what you did tonight?" Or was he too ashamed to tell me he'd killed?

He went very still. "Is that what you think?"

"It's the only reason that makes sense." I must have been more tired than I realized because I felt like crying.

"Kaia," Anders said, letting out a deep breath. "You have to understand that I've been around for a very long time. Do you know how hard it is to lose a dear friend or someone you love?"

My father's illness was difficult to deal with. I couldn't imagine being stuck this age while everyone I knew grew old and died. It would be torturous. "So you don't even want to be friends with me because I'm eventually going to die?"

"Some deaths are harder to deal with than others. The last time I ... lost someone close to me, I decided to never go through that again."

Not only was he not aging, he wasn't even living.

"I'm sorry," he said.

"So am I. If you ever change your mind, I'm here." We stood in silence for several minutes.

He glanced sideways at me. "Vidar sent me on an assignment."

I closed my eyes. Anders had promised me no unnecessary killing.

"You have to know," he said, "part of my curse is that I am bound to Vidar. If he orders me to do something, I have to do it."

"I don't understand." Couldn't he make his own choices?

He gazed at the stars and sighed. "Vidar is a good man. Even if I weren't bound to him, I'd still pledge my life to serve him. He's never asked something of me that wasn't necessary or for the betterment of the kingdom." Anders curled his hands around the railing, his knuckles turning white.

I didn't have anything to say. After all, I was planning to kill Morlet for that very reason.

"What? No retort? No lecture?"

I laughed. "No. Right now, I want to enjoy the fresh air. It's beautiful out here."

He shook his head. "I've been around for so long that I forget what it's like to care for someone." He turned to face me, a small smile spreading across his face, softening the lines around his eyes and forehead. "You remind me of that." He reached out and squeezed my hand.

My breath caught, and my heart hammered in my chest. "I hope you consider that a good thing," I said, trying to ignore the sudden awkwardness I felt.

He chuckled. "Depends on my mood." He reached up and pushed a strand of hair off my forehead. "I'm exhausted. We should both get some sleep."

Suddenly eager to put space between us, I whispered, "Goodnight," and hurried back inside. Vidar was still in the same position, sprawled on the ground. Stepping around him, I crawled into bed, my hand tingling where Anders had touched it.

\*\*\*

"Faster!" Anders ordered. I spun and kicked my right leg, hitting his chest. "Excellent." He grabbed my wrist. "Now break away." Doing what my father had taught me, I leaned slightly forward, toward my opponent, and then pulled my arm up, breaking the hold. I immediately punched his stomach and when he doubled over, grabbed his shoulders, ramming my knee into his face.

He righted himself, breathing hard. "Good job," he said, his voice a little higher pitched than usual. "Just remember we're practicing. You don't need to hit so forcefully."

"Trust me," I said, smiling. "That was gentle. If I wanted to hurt you, I would have."

The corner of Anders's mouth pulled up. "With that attitude, you'll make it through your trials and receive your weapon without a problem."

After working together all morning, we finally stopped to rest. I sat on the ground, stretching my legs out before me. Somehow sparring with Anders was easier than talking to him. I learned to fight at such an early age that it was second nature to me.

"Here." Anders handed me a leather pouch with water inside. I took a sip and gave it back to him. "Your father trained you?" I nodded. "Where did you practice?" He plopped down next to me.

"In our apartment, even though there's hardly any space. There are only two rooms, and it's cluttered. But Papa doesn't care. He says it's more realistic since I have to move around objects. I've learned to use my environment to my advantage. My father is always rearranging furniture to keep it interesting."

Anders took a sip of water from the pouch. "My training was very similar to yours. Only, instead of a loving father, a master assassin taught me."

"Was he at least kind to you?" Probably not, since he'd bought Anders and only intended to use him to kill.

Anders leaned back against a tree trunk and closed his eyes. "Working for him was better than being a slave. But I was never ... happy."

"What about your family?"

Anders shrugged, keeping his eyes closed. His cheek twitched, haunted by some memory.

"Did you live with the assassin?"

"Yes," he said. "His house was high in the mountains. There was no one around for miles."

"This is the first time I've been outside the capital."

"I'm surprised your father kept you so close to the king's castle. Wasn't he afraid someone would discover you're a Kriger?"

"No, because I hadn't come into my power yet." Although, now that I thought about it, he rarely allowed me to leave our apartment.

"Still, I'm surprised your father risked being in the capital."

"Have you ever come face-to-face with Morlet?" I asked.

His eyes darkened, and he glanced away. "Our paths have crossed several times. When Morlet first took the throne, he personally hunted down the Krigers. He'd kill them, drag their bodies back to the castle, and put their heads on spikes at the front gates. That was before he realized that when one Kriger died, a new one was born in his place. Once Morlet understood the only way to defeat the Krigers is to kill them when their powers are linked together, he's been putting them in prison."

A thought occurred to me. "Can Morlet kill us if I don't have my bo staff?"

"No, because your power can't link with the others without your weapon. But once you have it, and all twelve of you link together, he can kill the Krigers. No more will ever be born."

"I thought you two were training!" Vidar called out as he approached, his eyes darting between the two of us.

I jumped to my feet. "We were just taking a break," I said, brushing the pine needles and dirt from my pants.

"Well the break is over," he said with a roguish smile. "You both need to go and pack. We depart tomorrow at daybreak." Vidar started to leave.

"Why are the two of you cursed?" I asked, crossing my arms and waiting for him to answer.

Vidar raised an eyebrow. "I think we'd all like to know *why*. Now hurry up. There's a lot to be done before we leave." He turned and strolled away.

***

We set out early the next morning, each of us carrying a sack with food, water, and blankets. Anders led the way, followed by me, and then Vidar. I pulled my knit cap over my ears, trying to stay warm in the crisp, cool air. Walking in silence, we made our way through the forest.

After a few hours, we reached a narrow path that skirted alongside a steep hill. I needed a moment to myself. Stepping off the path, I allowed Vidar to pass by. "I'll catch up with you in a minute."

"We stay together," Anders insisted, stopping to wait for me.

There was no way we were doing *this* together. "Then wait here," I said. "And face the hill." Suddenly realizing what I was about to do, Anders's face reddened, and both men quickly turned their backs, giving me privacy.

I went down the slope, wanting to go far enough so they couldn't see me relieve myself. I stopped, about to loosen my pants, when something jumped off a nearby tree, startling me. My feet slipped on the steep incline littered with pine needles. The stupid squirrel darted away as I tumbled down the hill, unable to stop myself. Up ahead, the ground suddenly dropped off revealing treetops below. This wasn't good.

I flew off the edge and into the air, squeezing my eyes shut, afraid I'd be impaled by a tree. My body violently jerked, and I screamed, dangling midair. My sack had gotten stuck on a branch, and it was the only thing keeping me from plunging to the ground. I wondered if I should yell out to Anders and Vidar for help, but decided against it. If they saw me like this, they'd never let me go on my own again. I had a couple of minutes before they came looking for me. My only option was to disengage myself from the sack and drop down. It appeared to be about fifteen feet. Taking a deep breath, I squirmed free and fell, rolling when I landed to avoid injury.

There weren't any low branches on the tree, so there was no way I could climb back up to retrieve my sack. Luckily, there were several large rocks and bushes along the cliff, which allowed me to easily scale it to where I'd fallen from. Then I retraced my steps back to the path where Anders and Vidar stood waiting for me.

When I reemerged, Vidar burst out laughing. "What happened to you?" he asked. "You're covered with leaves and twigs."

I plopped on the ground, trying to catch my breath. "Nothing," I said, realizing I still had to relieve myself.

# Chapter Ten

"Let's go," Anders said. "We need to reach our next location before nightfall."

"Don't worry," Vidar said, noticing my missing sack. "I have plenty of food."

We hiked the rest of the day and into the evening among the gigantic, towering trees. When the sun set, the temperature rapidly decreased. The scenery also changed as the trees thinned and massive boulders rose out of the ground.

"Are we nearing the edge of the forest?" I asked.

"Yes," Anders replied. "The mountain range straight ahead is where your weapon is located."

"For now," Vidar cut in, "we're going to that cave." He jerked his chin toward a boulder.

Heading that way, I searched for the entrance in the fading light, not finding it. Smiling, Vidar pointed to the ground. At the base of the boulder, there was a three-foot-wide hole. Anders squatted and grabbed a branch, wrapping dry leaves around the top of it, and lighting it on fire. "Wait here," he instructed, sliding his legs into the opening and dropping down.

I peered into the hole. Light from the makeshift torch bounced off the rocky walls. "All clear!" Anders hollered.

I mimicked what he did and dropped about six feet into the cave, landing on my feet. Vidar threw a pile of wood down after me and then gracefully jumped in. Anders arranged the logs and lit them on fire, the smoke exiting through the opening. There were notches on the wall so we'd be able to climb out.

I eagerly sat and removed my boots, stretching my legs out before me, exhausted from being on my feet all day.

Vidar pulled out two chunks of cheese, handing one to me. I took a bite, noticing him staring. "What?" I asked.

He smiled, shaking his head. "You have pine needles stuck to your knit cap." He reached out, plucking them off for me.

Anders made a sound of disgust as he unrolled his blanket. "Do you have to flirt with every girl? Kaia is a Kriger, not some barmaid."

"You can't tell me you don't think Kaia is pretty," Vidar said, folding his arms and pointedly staring at Anders.

My entire body prickled with heat. "Don't talk about me like that. Especially when I'm sitting right here. It's insulting." And extremely embarrassing.

The corners of Vidar's mouth turned up. "Here," he said, handing me a loaf of bread. "For the record, *I* think you're beautiful. A little short, but pretty nonetheless."

My fingers curled into a fist. A thought suddenly occurred to me that might be more effective than punching him. "Why thank you," I cooed. "I think you're mighty pretty, too. A little tall, lanky, arrogant, and conceited, but handsome nonetheless."

Anders laughed, the sound echoing in the small cave. "I think you've met your match Vidar. She's not going to let you get away with anything."

Vidar smiled and scooted against the wall, leaning his head back. "Speaking of getting away with things ... do you know how Morlet came into power?"

My interest rose. "He killed the king and queen and seized the throne," I replied. "However, I'm not sure why he did it." The book Vidar had given me didn't contain any clues as to a motive. It never occurred to me that Vidar might have firsthand knowledge of events. I ate my bread, waiting for him to shed some light on the past. Anders remained quiet, sharpening a dagger.

"At the age of nineteen, Morlet craved power," Vidar said, staring at the ceiling, lost in thought. "It wasn't enough for him to wield Skog Heks's magic; he had to usurp the royal family, too."

"How do you know he was the one who murdered the king and queen?" Maybe Skog Heks had killed them. I looked at Anders. His shoulders were hunched while he continued to sharpen his weapon. How did the assassin fit into all of this? My heart pounded, scared by the possibilities.

"*Heks* can't murder royalty," Vidar said. "A spell was cast five hundred years ago when the war between our kind and theirs finally ended." He shifted on the ground, bringing his legs up, his arms resting on them. "Thankfully, Grei Heks was in Nelebek when Morlet sealed the borders. Since the powers were out of balance, she was able to cast a spell to counter what Morlet had done with Skog Heks's evil magic. She created the Krigers."

"You told me Morlet made a bargain with Skog Heks and that was how he acquired dark magic which enabled him to kill the king and queen and take the throne. What did Skog Heks get out of the deal? Is she aligned with Morlet? Do they work together?" The story didn't make sense. Skog Heks wouldn't have given up so much without getting something in return.

Anders sheathed his dagger.

"Then the reign of terror began," Vidar continued as if he hadn't heard me. "When Morlet learned about the Order of the Krigers, he started torturing people in his quest to locate them. He killed the young and innocent alike. He is, and always will be, a monster." Vidar looked at me. His dull eyes came back to life, and he smiled. "Enough talking for one night. We have a long day ahead of us tomorrow. Get some sleep." He kicked dirt onto the fire, putting it out and sending the cave into utter darkness.

The word *monster* screamed in my head. Morlet was a monster, a murderer. He deserved to die for his crimes. Yet, something told me there was more to it than that.

A hand fumbled for my ankle, and I yelped. "Relax," Vidar said, his voice close by. "Here's a blanket." He found my hand and pulled it toward the wool fabric.

"Thank you." I took the rough material and situated myself on the blanket, wrapping it around my body.

\*\*\*

We set out early the next morning, traveling along the edge of the unusually quiet forest. Thick fog coated the land, concealing entire trees and boulders.

Anders suddenly froze, and I almost bumped into him. He slowly unsheathed his dagger and resumed walking at a snail's pace. I wanted to ask what spooked him, but knew not to speak if danger lurked.

After traveling another mile, the fog started to thin, allowing me to see about ten feet away. A twig snapped, and I jumped. Vidar chuckled from behind me. I glared at him, and he shook his head, amused. "If there was an issue," he said, not even attempting to be quiet, "your hands would give us sufficient warning."

I'd been so focused on my surroundings that I hadn't noticed the gentle throbbing in my palms. "They've been hurting since we left the cave," I admitted.

Anders spun around to face me. "Explain," he demanded, his voice low and deadly.

"I thought it was from being so cold," I whispered.

"We're being followed." His eyes darted all around us, searching for the threat.

"By what?" Vidar asked.

"I don't know, but something is out there." He rubbed the back of his neck. "Kaia, if the pain increases, let me know." I nodded. "For now, let's keep moving."

We continued, all of my senses on high alert. I mimicked everything Anders did as he slunk through the forest, trying to ensure each step was silent.

A deep growling reverberated through the air. Anders immediately took a step back toward me, Vidar doing the same so we were standing in a triangle, our backs touching while we searched for whatever animal prowled unseen in the fog.

Sharp shooting pains coursed through my hands, radiating up my arms and to my shoulders. I almost screamed but instead, bit my lip, drawing blood. The pain was so intense I fell to the ground. Grabbing moist dirt, I clutched the cool earth, trying in earnest to seek relief.

"Kaia," Anders whispered, "no jerky movements. Understand?"

His voice was soft, but there was a hint of panic to it.

I glanced up and saw his eyes focused on something in front of me. Following his line of sight, there were two bright blue eyes glowing in the fog, only fifteen feet away. The mist swirled, revealing a snow-white animal that looked like a large dog. It stalked forward, revealing a dozen more creatures behind it.

"*Ulvs*," Vidar hissed.

I remained crouched on the ground. Without my weapon, I didn't have access to my full power. Yet, there was still something in me. I slowly raised my hands, closed my eyes, and willed that force from my core down my arms and out through my fingers. A tingly sensation, as if a leg or an arm had fallen asleep, spread throughout my body.

Opening my eyes, the *ulvs* now stood ten feet away.

"My darts are loaded and ready," Anders quietly mumbled. "I can easily take down eight. That leaves five more."

"I have four throwing knives," Vidar said. "I can probably kill three *ulvs*. That leaves two to contend with."

"Kaia, stay behind us," Anders said. "On my count."

I slowly stood.

"What are you doing?" Anders demanded.

With my hands still out in front of me, I pulled on my power, once again forcing it down my arms and out through my fingers. Only, this time, I unleashed it. Fire rippled through my body, and I screamed. The *ulvs* turned and ran away as I collapsed on the ground, everything going black.

\*\*\*

It felt as if my body floated on water, rhythmically rocking up and down.

"Are you sure she's okay?" Anders's voice rumbled through my right ear. He must be carrying me. I wanted to jump from his arms but couldn't gather enough strength to even open my eyes.

"Kaia is fine," Vidar answered, his voice a few feet away. "She just needs to rest." He chuckled. "It was amazing to see her in action. The fact that she managed to use what little power she has without her weapon is astounding."

"I still can't believe the twelfth Kriger is a girl," Anders muttered.

"Does it matter?"

He sighed. "Not really so long as she can stomach killing Morlet, especially since he's communicating with her. You know how manipulating he can be. Will she be able to murder someone she knows?"

My cheek rubbed against his rough shirt.

"Of course she will," Vidar said.

"I sincerely hope you're right." It felt as if he climbed up something. He stopped and gently set me on the ground. "There's something different about her." Their voices trailed off, and warmth embraced me.

***

Peeling my heavy eyelids open, I found myself lying on a large boulder, the sun high above me. Vidar sat near my feet.

"Hungry?" he asked.

My stomach growled. "Yes." He handed me a water sack, and

I gulped down the liquid until there was nothing left. Vidar gave me a loaf of bread along with some cooked meat. I greedily ate both.

"We need to get moving," Anders said as he approached the boulder. "We've lost a lot of time." He grabbed his bag off the ground, shouldered it, and started walking. Vidar and I slid off the rock and hurried after him.

The fog had completely disappeared and scattered clouds shone in the sky. I moved between the tall pine and redwood trees, breathing in their heavy scents. A large falcon flew above me.

"Anders, if you're from a neighboring kingdom, and Nelebek's borders are closed, you must have entered before Morlet took over."

His back stiffened, but he kept walking as if he hadn't heard me. "Were you here on an assignment? Is that how you became cursed?"

He didn't answer. I was about to ask him something else when Vidar grabbed my arm, stopping me.

"Leave him be," he whispered.

"I have a right to know."

"When he's ready, he'll tell you." Anders had opened up a few times. I thought we were past this. "Besides," Vidar continued, "he gets moody when he's nervous."

"What's he nervous about?"

"He's worried about you facing the trials." Vidar headed in the direction Anders had gone.

Were the challenges a greater risk than either of them were letting on? "What happens if I don't pass?"

He stopped walking and turned to face me. "If the magic within the cave doesn't find you worthy, it will either tell you to come back later, or kill you."

# Chapter Eleven

*K*ill me? That didn't make any sense. Not ready was understandable, but not unworthy. Otherwise, the women in my family wouldn't have been chosen to be Krigers.

"This is why I tried not to tell you too much." Vidar pinched the bridge of his nose. "I thought it would be easier if I kept my distance, let you retrieve your weapon, and then told you everything."

"Easier?" I repeated, my fury building. "How many Krigers have died during the trials?"

"I don't know," he mumbled, diligently avoiding eye contact.

"One? Two? A dozen?" He had to have a general idea.

"Most have passed," he answered, attempting a smile to placate me. "But over the hundred or so years that I've been doing this, there have been half a dozen who were told to return when they were worthy and a handful who never exited the cave." He reached for my shoulders, squeezing them. "Anders is worried because you're young. He's afraid you'll be told to come back, and then we won't be able to free the Krigers."

"And end your curse," I muttered.

"That's not it," he insisted. "Those eleven men sitting in the dungeon being tortured are our friends." His eyes became glassy.

Shame filled me for doubting Anders. "I'll do my best to rescue them."

"That's all we ask."

"But ... what if I die trying to retrieve it? Since the twelfth Kriger is a female from my bloodline, how does it work if I'm the last one?"

"I'm not sure." He released me and started walking away.

He was hiding something. "Tell me what you know," I said, jogging after him. He didn't respond. I was sick and tired of him keeping things from me. Reaching for his wrist, I grabbed him. "Tell me."

Vidar tried pulling away. "I don't know."

I squeezed his arm tighter. "Tell me."

He chuckled. "Luckily, I'm wearing the medallion, or your anger would strike me down."

I released him but held my ground. "Please tell me."

"I asked that very question of Grei Heks," he said, rubbing his arm. "She laughed and said, 'She is not the end, but the beginning, of that I am certain.' Then she proceeded to tell me that you and I—"

A scream pierced the air. Vidar's eyes widened, and he took off running. I sprinted after him as he crashed through the forest searching for Anders.

At a small clearing, Vidar spun in a circle, frantically searching the area. "I don't see any trace of him," he said. "His trail just ends."

There weren't any signs of a scuffle, no animal footprints in the soft dirt, and no arrows lodged in the nearby trees. Anders couldn't have just disappeared. Then I remembered falling through a small hole in the ground and landing in the dark cavern below ground.

Kneeling, I started pushing the leaves aside, searching for a hole. Usually Anders was so careful and aware of his surroundings that it was hard to believe he could have fallen into a cavern. The possibility of him being hurt or dead was terrifying. Crawling, I retraced the footprints to a section where there were two sets of prints. Following the one that wasn't as pronounced, they veered off to the side by the rocks. My hands started to tingle.

"Vidar," I called. "Over here."

"What is it?" he asked, joining me.

"He fell through a hole in the ground right around here." We both shoved leaves and pine needles aside, searching the area. A small, black section hidden in the shadow of a tall redwood tree caught my attention. Lying flat on my stomach, I reached forward. As my hand slid into the shadow, the ground beneath disappeared.

"Anders?" I hesitantly called out. A moan sounded from below.

Vidar knelt next to me. "Are you okay?" he yelled down.

There was no response. "Do you have any rope?" I asked Vidar.

"No."

"Vidar? Kaia?" a voice called out.

"We're here!" I hollered down to Anders.

"My leg is stuck," he yelled. "But I'm okay."

Relief flooded through me. "How far down are you?"

"About twenty feet."

Searching the area, I found what I was looking for. "Give me your knife." Vidar slid his dagger from its sheath and handed it to me. I ran over to the base of a cliff where long vines hung all over it and started hacking them off, throwing them to the ground. Once there was enough, I tied the vines together, making a rope.

"Excellent idea," Vidar said, taking the vines from me. "I'll lower myself, free Anders, and climb back up."

I rolled my eyes. "And how do you propose I hold your weight?"

Vidar shrugged. "I'll tie it around that tree."

"It's not long enough to make it around the trunk, be tied to you, and then reach down twenty feet." I folded my arms. "Besides, I made it for me."

"It's not a good idea for you to go down there."

"Why?"

"Because you're ... well ... a girl."

My eyes narrowed. "Then go right ahead. With any luck, you won't fall and injure yourself."

Vidar went to a nearby tree, tying the vines around it. There was only about six feet left. He scratched his head and then untied the rope. "I'll hold it and lower you," he mumbled.

I stood and brushed myself off. "What a great idea!" I sarcastically replied. He was lucky the other eleven Krigers weren't girls. Otherwise, they would have killed him for his pigheadedness by now.

Vidar shook his head. "Be careful. We can't afford for you to get hurt." He wrapped one end around his hand several times and then threw the rest by my feet. "Tie the rope around your waist. Once you reach Anders and free his leg, I'll pull you out. Then I'll throw the rope down to him."

Taking a deep breath, I tied the vines around my waist, went to the hole, and slid onto my stomach.

"Okay," I said, lowering my legs.

Vidar sat on the ground, grabbed the rope so it was taut, and propped his feet against the nearby trunk. He released small portions of the rope, lowering me into darkness. I prayed the vines were strong enough to hold my weight. My body jerked downward until my feet finally touched solid ground.

"I'm at the bottom!" I hollered up, untying the vines from my waist.

Vidar's head poked over the edge. "I'll be right here," he called out. "Let me know if you need my help."

There was just enough light from the opening above to see a couple of feet in each direction. Anders lay on the ground, his foot wedged in a crevice. I knelt by his side. "Are you okay?"

"I am. Just wish you didn't have to see me like this."

"Oh please," I said, moving to the other side of him so my body didn't block the light. "Do you have feeling in your leg?" It was twisted at an awkward angle.

"Yes," he replied. "I tried wiggling my foot loose, but it won't budge."

"Maybe if we untie your boot, your foot will slip out?" I suggested.

He sighed. "I'm hot, and my feet are slightly swollen from walking. Perhaps once it's night, the cool air will allow me to yank it free."

"How's it going?" Vidar yelled down.

"He's okay! But his foot is stuck. We're going to wait until it cools and then try wiggling it free."

There was a pause before Vidar asked, "Do you need anything? Food? Water?"

Anders's face was hidden among the shadows. However, he

was breathing heavily and had to be thirsty. "Water please!" A few seconds later, a water sack landed a foot away.

"I have an idea," Vidar said. "I'll be back in a bit. Hold tight, it shouldn't take me more than an hour or two."

I handed Anders the water sack and he took it, drinking several gulps. "Does anything else hurt?" I asked, sitting near his head.

"I'm sore from the fall, but other than that, I'm perfectly fine." He handed the water sack back to me. "You didn't have to come down here. I'm capable of taking care of myself."

"I know. Regardless, I'm here if you need me." My eyes gradually adjusted to the dark cavern. After several quiet and uncomfortable minutes, I spoke again. "You didn't fall into the crevice, did you?"

His eyes sliced over to mine. "What are you saying?"

"You must have gotten yourself stuck after you fell."

He sighed. "Maybe."

"So you fell into the cavern and then what? Stumbled into this crevice?" I chuckled.

"It's not funny," Anders said, his jaw tight.

"I'm sorry," I said, trying not to laugh.

"If you must know, when I went to stand, my foot went into the crevice and got wedged in."

"You're lucky you didn't hit your head or break a leg." I took a sip from the water sack. We sat in silence for several minutes, neither one of us speaking.

"Do you like him?" Anders asked, his voice softly echoing in the cavern.

"Do I like who?"

"Vidar," Anders said, pushing himself to a sitting position.

I certainly enjoyed his company and felt an innate sense of

trust with him. "Of course I like Vidar. He's been nothing but kind to me." Unlike Anders, who seemed to irritate me every chance he got.

The corners of Andres's lips pulled up into a sly smile. "That's not what I meant."

I cocked my head. Was he asking if I had any sort of romantic feelings toward Vidar? "You can't be serious. You must have hit your head when you fell."

He held up his hands in surrender, laughing. "It's just that wherever Vidar goes, he seems to acquire several female admirers. He is very good at flattery. I thought perhaps you'd fallen for his antics."

Vidar certainly was appealing, and at first, I did think of him that way. But after I got to know him, all I felt for him was friendship. And I was certain, beyond a doubt, that was all he felt for me, too.

"Just because I'm young and haven't been courted, doesn't mean I'll fall for the first man who flirts with me."

"You've never been courted?" Anders raised his eyebrows. "I find that hard to believe."

I whacked his arm. "Don't tease me," I said, desperate to change the subject. "Now that you know something personal about me, why don't you tell me something about yourself?"

"There's nothing to tell." He looked away from me.

"In case you haven't noticed," I said, resting my arms on my knees, "we're stuck here. You're going to need my help to get your foot out of that crevice. I suggest you tell me something worthwhile for my trouble."

"I don't like talking about myself."

"You don't trust many people, do you?"

"No," he muttered.

Why did I care about this man? If he didn't want to talk or share his life with me, he didn't have to.

He tilted his head toward me and our eyes locked. My heartbeat sped up under his scrutiny. "My life before Vidar was a nightmare. Talking about it only makes me relive that time in my life. I was forced to become a monster and commit such atrocious crimes it makes me sick."

I glanced away, unable to take his piercing gaze. "I didn't realize."

"Of course not. You had a loving father raise you, not a sadistic man who only saw you as a piece of property—something he could make money from."

Mustering the courage to peer into his glassy eyes, I said, "If you ever want to talk, I'm here for you." I patted his shoulder and then scooted away so he'd know I didn't plan to push the matter any further.

"I'll make a deal with you," he said with a devious smile. "If you pass the trials and receive your weapon, I'll answer *one* question."

The awkward tension faded away. "Any question?"

He nodded.

"Then be prepared, because it's not *if* I pass, but *when*."

# Chapter Twelve

"Watch out!" Vidar yelled as he lowered something through the hole. I reached for the basket woven from leaves and twigs, releasing it from the vine rope. Inside was some sort of thick, gooey paste.

"Smear it all over his boot," Vidar instructed. "It should enable him to shimmy free."

I was about to ask what the substance was when Anders said, "You don't want to know."

Snapping my mouth shut, I knelt near his foot. Lifting two fingers, I prepared to scoop the goo when Anders swiftly sat up and grabbed my hand. "Don't touch that stuff," he said, squeezing my fingers. "There's probably a leaf or something to use so it doesn't come into contact with your skin."

There was a large, green leaf attached to the side of the basket. Wrapping it around my fingers, I mumbled, "Here goes nothing." I scooped up a glob of the substance and smeared it all over Anders's boot. "This stuff smells like a rotten body."

"You're not far off," he responded. "My boot is going to permanently stink."

"See if you can wiggle it free."

"It's moving a little bit, but not enough."

Scooping up more of the goo, I rubbed the pungent-smelling stuff on his boot. "What about now?"

Anders jiggled his leg, trying to free his foot. His face turned red.

"Are you hurt?" I asked.

"I'm fine," he replied, not meeting my eyes.

Throwing the leaf on the ground, I sat next to him, taking his hand in mine. He didn't pull away. "Please be honest with me. Did you injure your foot when it got wedged in the crevice?"

He leaned back, lying on the ground, his hand still clasped with mine. "I think my ankle is sprained."

No wonder he couldn't get it out; it was probably swollen. "Why didn't you tell me?"

"Because it's not important." He propped himself up on his elbows. "Listen, you need to get yourself out of here."

There was no way I was going to leave him.

"Kaia," he whispered, "it's almost nighttime. You need the protection of Vidar's necklace." His face had a few days' worth of stubble. "I'm sure my foot will be able to slip out once the swelling decreases." He squeezed my hand.

"Let's try one more time." Releasing his hand, I grabbed his calf and pulled. His boot didn't budge. Perhaps if I were positioned above him, instead of on his side, the angle would be more conducive to freeing him. Swinging my leg over to straddle him, I placed my hands below his knee, yanking upward.

Anders grunted, and his boot came free. I fell backward,

landing on top of his stomach. He wrapped his arms around me, holding me in place so I didn't topple to the rocky ground. "Are you okay?" he asked, his voice right next to my ear, sending shivers down my spine. He slid his hands to my hips, and my heart hammered. We were too close. I nodded, and he released me.

Standing, I was unable to meet his brown eyes as I yelled up to Vidar, letting him know Anders was free. The vine rope dropped down.

Anders got to his feet and hobbled over. "Let's attach this to you."

"No, you first." I grabbed the vines and handed them to him.

"You will not stay down here alone," he said. "You will go first."

"You're the one who's injured," I argued. "And I'll only be alone for a moment."

"Will you two stop bickering like an old married couple?" Vidar yelled. "Kaia, grab hold, I'm pulling you up."

These two men drove me nuts with their overprotectiveness. Anders wrapped the vines around my waist and securely tied them. I attempted to undo the knot, but he shouted to Vidar who immediately started hoisting me up.

"I'll get you back for this!" I said to Anders.

He smiled. "I sincerely hope so."

Vidar had lined the hole with large, green leaves so when he pulled me up, the vines didn't fray or break. Once I was safely out, he threw the rope down to Anders. After he was out, we decided to head to the nearest cave for the night. Unfortunately, Anders's ankle was sore and swollen. He had to wrap his arm around Vidar for support.

I led the way, careful to stay acutely aware of my hands. If there was any sort of pain, no matter how minor, I steered us in another direction in order to avoid potential danger. Once we reached the cave, I remained with Anders while Vidar left to gather firewood.

Anders slid to the ground and removed his boots. I handed him the water sack. When he was distracted drinking, I gently touched his ankle to see if it was broken.

"What are you doing?" he asked, yanking his foot away.

"Investigating." I grabbed his foot and laid it on my lap. "Stay still so I don't accidentally hurt you."

He grunted but complied. I carefully removed his sock, exposing a very swollen and bruised ankle.

Vidar returned, dropping a large pile of branches on the ground. "How does it look?"

"I need catnip and sage."

"Glad someone knows what they're doing," he replied. "I'll be back as soon as I have them." He ducked out of the cave.

"What do you know about catnip and sage?" Anders asked. "You're from the city."

His intense scrutiny made me uncomfortable. "Catnip reduces swelling and sage reduces inflammation. I've tended to my father's wounds more than once." Since Papa was a guard in the mines, he often came home with a swollen eye or bruised ribs from a scuffle.

Anders's face remained unreadable. Reaching for his sack, I pulled out a blanket, folded it in half, and shoved it under his ankle so his foot was propped up. "Do you need anything else?"

"No. You've already done more than enough."

"Friends help friends." I shrugged as if it wasn't a big deal.

"In case you haven't noticed, I don't have many friends."

"Me neither," I whispered, fidgeting with the end of my sleeve.

"When I was a slave, I had friends." Anders's voice was soft, barely audible. I remained quiet, hoping he'd share more about his childhood. "One day, my best friend's shoes were stolen. He saw a fellow slave wearing them, and when he asked for them back, the kid started punching my friend. I jumped in and defended him. We got the shoes back." A ghost of a smile flitted across his face.

"Unfortunately, our fight had been witnessed by my master who knew the value of someone with my skills. He sold me later that day to an assassin. I never saw my friend, or my family, again. All because I helped someone.

"The assassin took me far away. I spent years training, honing my skills, learning hundreds of ways to kill or maim a man in less than twenty seconds. I studied poisons, weapons, and human anatomy. My value lay in my ability to kill from the shadows, unseen. I was taught to never trust anyone. And that is what has kept me alive." He leaned his head back against the wall of the cave.

"My father taught me the same thing," I whispered. "About not trusting anyone." I didn't realize how much we had in common. "But you trust Vidar."

"I do."

"And I trust you." The weight of my words hung heavy in the air. He tilted his head, and our eyes met. My heart pounded in my chest. I wanted to say more, but couldn't find the right words.

Vidar entered, and I jerked back, away from Anders.

"I have the items you requested," Vidar said. He handed them to me, and I quickly got to work. If he noticed the awkward tension between Anders and me, he had the decency not to say anything.

After we ate, Anders nodded off to sleep. Vidar arranged his bedroll near the fire. "I don't know about you," he softly said, "but I'm not tired."

"Me neither." My conversation with Anders was still fresh in my mind.

Vidar pulled out a stack of cards. "Want to play?"

"Yes." A game of cards sounded like fun, and it would be a nice distraction from thoughts of the sleeping assassin.

Vidar dealt us each five cards. "It has been quite an eventful day."

We must be playing Stolen Moons. It was a game I knew well. I put one down and drew another from the stack. "Yes," I replied. "It has."

Vidar laid two cards down and picked up one more. Anders's eyes were still closed, his breathing steady. I discarded another card. Vidar didn't have anything to play, so he was forced to draw five.

I had three moons and was ready to reveal my winning hand. "What are we playing for?"

He fought a smile. "I assume you have a good hand?" I didn't answer. "How about we play for information?"

"Deal." I placed my cards down. "I win."

"Unless I have the same three cards." There was no way he could have managed that. He laid down three identical ones. "I win."

I wanted to strangle him. "You must have cheated."

"Nope," he said, chuckling. "I've been playing this game a lot longer than you have."

I folded my arms, fearing what he'd ask.

"So," he mused, gathering the cards and putting them away. "I want to know something personal about you."

Relieved his request was so simple, I opened my mouth to

say something when he cut me off. "No you don't. I choose the question you'll answer. Who was the last person you kissed?"

"Easy. My father."

"That's not what I meant."

My face went beet red. Of all the things he could have asked me, he chose to discuss this? I was mortified.

He laughed at my discomfort. "Come on," he said. "You promised."

"Fine. I've never kissed anyone." I covered my face, wanting to shield myself from his scrutiny. Technically, Anders had kissed me in the brothel. Although, I hadn't kissed him back, and it didn't mean anything.

Vidar burst out laughing. "You've never kissed a man before? How is that possible? You're sixteen! Most people marry around your age."

"I'm not most people," I mumbled. "Now leave me alone."

"Sorry," he said, still laughing. "We can fix that right now if you want."

"Absolutely not." I moved closer to the fire to make sure Vidar didn't do anything to embarrass me—like kiss me out of jest.

"Oh, come on. I'm only teasing you."

I ignored him, not wanting to make a big deal out of this.

"Kaia, I'm sorry." He sat next to me, our shoulders touching. "You know I wasn't serious."

"What did you do?" Anders demanded, causing me to jump.

"Nothing," Vidar said. "Go back to sleep. I was just teasing Kaia, and she took it personally. I'm trying to apologize." He nudged my shoulder.

"You're lucky my ankle hurts," Anders said. "Otherwise I'd come over there and pummel you."

Vidar laughed. Afraid he'd tell Anders what we were talking

about, I said, "I'm fine. Please let it go."

"I'm serious," Anders said. "Kaia tended to my injury, now I'm in her debt." He winked at me.

"Maybe I'll get hurt so she can fawn all over me," Vidar said.

I had the sudden urge to be out of the cave. "Excuse me," I said, lurching to my feet. "I'm going to step outside for a couple of minutes." Without waiting for a response, I turned and left.

"What did you say to her?" Anders asked.

I rested against the rock outside the cave, listening.

"Nothing," Vidar responded. "I was just teasing her; trying to get her to loosen up."

"Why?"

Vidar sighed. "I need to talk to her about something, and I don't think she's going to take kindly to the news."

"What is it?"

"Something Grei Heks told me." There was a moment of silence before Vidar continued, "What do you think of Kaia?"

Anders didn't hesitate to respond. "She's intelligent, tough, and has excellent survival skills. Why?"

Not wanting to hear any more, I walked away from the cave. The trees towered above me, shielding the sky. Sitting at the base of a tree trunk, I inhaled the frigid air.

Why couldn't I stop thinking about Anders? Why did he make me so uncomfortable? Did it even matter if we were friends? Once the Krigers killed Morlet, I'd be back in the capital with my father. My breath caught. I couldn't think about Papa right now. All my energy and focus had to be on getting my weapon.

The wind whirled around the trees, rattling the leaves. My head pounded. Morlet was searching for me. Perhaps communicating with him while I was awake would afford me more control over severing our connection. As stupid as it was to seek him out, the

146

desire to know more about him before I killed him consumed me. Closing my eyes, I let myself relax and forced my power out. *I entered Morlet's bedchamber. He stood in front of a window, staring outside. His cape lay nearby, draped over the back of a chair. His hands gripped the window ledge, and his shoulders hunched forward. "You came," he said, his voice ragged.*

*"Yes," I replied. "Can we talk?"*

*He straightened and turned around to face me. I'd forgotten how intimidating and handsome he was. Clasping his hands behind his back, he asked, "What would you like to discuss?"*

*I took a tentative step toward him. "I've heard stories of what happened and how you came into power, but I'd like to hear your version."*

*"How will you know if I'm being honest?" He strolled over to the fireplace, staring at the flames.*

*That was the problem—I had no way of knowing; yet, I was willing to take that chance.*

*"If I tell you my story, I want something in return."*

*Of course he did. "What is it?"*

*Morlet motioned for me to move closer. We now stood only a foot apart. His bright blue eyes reflected the dancing flames, mesmerizing me.*

*"Come to the castle so we can end this together."*

*Did he honestly think I'd willingly go to him so he could kill me? "Tell me your story, and I'll consider it."*

*He grinned. "No you won't."*

*"Never mind." I turned to put some distance between us.*

*"Wait." Morlet grabbed my arm. "Please don't go. I need you."*

*I glanced at his hand, surprised by his touch. He released me, his blue eyes revealing emotions he kept hidden from the world. Maybe he would open up and trust me, and then we could find a way to fix this mess without a fight or anyone dying.*

*Morlet reached out, cupping my cheek in his hand. "What is it about you that I find so appealing? You're by no means elegant or a great beauty," he whispered. "You're a Kriger—a warrior. Yet, I feel a desire to be near you."*

*I swatted his hand away. "If you're not going to tell me the truth, then I have no reason to stay."*

*Two soft hands touched my neck, startling me. "Kaia," Morlet whispered. "I've longed to tell you the truth, but I'm afraid of your reaction."*

*We were only a couple of inches apart. His hands slid to my shoulders, sending a soothing warmth through me. "If you stay, then I will tell you everything."*

*I stood on the edge of a great cliff. One step forward, and I'd fall to my death. I couldn't remain on that ledge, always wondering, and never moving. Taking a deep breath, I said, "Okay."*

*Once the word was out, there was no going back.*

# Chapter Thirteen

*M*orlet's hands dropped from my shoulders, and he moved to the window, staring outside into the night. In the distance, tall apartment buildings were crammed together, lights flickering in a few of the windows.

"I've never shared this story with anyone," he said, his voice barely audible. "No one has ever asked or cared before."

Sitting on the chair next to his bed, I patiently waited for him to tell me what happened all those years ago.

"Quite simply, I'm Morlet Forseve—the dark force—because I fell in love with a girl." He turned around, leaning against the window ledge, watching me closely. "Not what you expected, is it?"

I shook my head, unable to utter a single word.

A ghost of a smile flitted across his face. "I met a commoner and fell in love. We wished to marry and have a family. When I sought permission from my parents to wed her, they refused. They said she was beneath me and not befitting for someone of my station." He closed his eyes, lost in the painful memory. "Their reasoning didn't make *any sense. After all, I was only a second son, and my older brother was set to inherit everything. Why did it matter who I married? So we ran away," he whispered. "I planned to defy my parents and marry her." His eyes met mine as if he expected me to criticize him.*

*"What happened?"*

*"We fled to the Forest of a Thousand Lakes and stumbled across a small hut. Not knowing who lived there, we knocked on the door, seeking shelter for the night. An elderly woman invited us in, fed us dinner. We told her our story. She said she could help by taking care of my parents so I could marry the girl I loved." He rubbed his hands over his face. "I was hesitant to accept her offer. It seemed as if my mind was clouded by something brewing over the fire. However, my betrothed encouraged me to take the deal. I was young and naive, so I agreed."*

*Morlet's eyes glossed over, and he moved to the hearth, facing the fire. I watched his back, hoping he'd continue to speak.*

*"The elderly woman was Skog Heks—the evil witch of Nelebek who wields dark magic. The witch hired an assassin from a neighboring kingdom to hunt down and kill my parents and brother. When word came that they were dead, I was devastated. I went straight to Skog Heks and confronted her. When we made our deal, she never said anything about killing them—she was supposed to change their minds. She laughed in my face and cast a spell to force me to do whatever she wanted." His shoulders were tense as he spoke. "I fought her, and somehow her magic left her body and ended up inside of mine." He raised his arms and then let them fall to his sides. "I have Skog Heks's magic stuck in me." He slowly turned around and faced me. "I live in darkness. Never aging, never changing, until the evil magic is transferred back to its rightful owner."*

*I moved closer to him. "How did you become the king?" A sick feeling rose in my stomach.*

*"My parents were the king and queen of Nelebek, and I was*

*Prince Espen. That's how I became king of this forsaken land."*

*It seemed as if the room spun around me while I stood there, horrified by this revelation. Morlet was indirectly responsible for his parents and brother's deaths. All because he loved a girl who his parents deemed unworthy to stand by his side.*

*"You want nothing to do with me," Morlet said, his head hanging low, dejected.*

*"No," I gently replied. "That's not it."*

*A snarl flickered across his face. "Kaia—Skog Heks has your father. She will kill him unless you come to the castle. She needs you in order to get her magic back."*

*Fear shot through me. I couldn't let my father die. "Will she release Papa if I come?"*

*"Yes," he replied. "But she'll kill you and all the Krigers."*

*I didn't have my weapon yet, so my power couldn't connect with the other Krigers. Morlet must not realize my bo staff wasn't in my possession. "I have to save him." It was a risky move on my part, but worth it.*

*He nodded. "My elite guard is in the forest looking for you. If you tell me your location, I can guide you to them. They'll escort you to my castle unharmed."*

*"I'm not sure where I am."*

*Morlet placed his hands upon my shoulders. "Kaia, look into my eyes and let me help you."*

*I did as he said, and my vision blurred. "What are you doing?"*

*"Don't fight it," he purred. "Let me in."*

*I relaxed, and something slithered inside my head.*

*"Good. Now bring your mind back to your body. I will be with you and lead you to my men."*

I opened my eyes and found myself sitting against a tree trunk. What had just happened?

*"Look around so I can see through your eyes in order to determine your location," Morlet spoke in my mind.*

I stood and turned in a slow circle, observing my surroundings. *"I know where you are. Go to your right. Keep heading in that direction. I need you to hurry. The spell I cast will only allow us to stay connected for an hour or so."*

I started walking, my mind in a foggy haze. I thought I heard Vidar call my name. Stopping to listen, my head started to ache with acute pain.

*"Keep walking, my dear Kaia," Morlet spoke in my mind. "You need to save your father."*

I ignored Vidar and did as Morlet commanded. The pain in my head immediately went away. I stumbled onto a narrow dirt path.

*"Follow this trail," Morlet said. "Whatever you do, don't deviate from it."*

The fogginess in my mind withdrew. It took me a minute to remember I was on my way to save Papa. I walked for hours through the dark forest.

Eventually, there was a soft glow up ahead, and I ran toward the light, entering a clearing filled with a dozen *soldats* dressed in black. The ones around the perimeter held torches while the others held swords, bows, and spears.

I had just willingly walked into enemy territory. My hands throbbed with pain. Taking a step backward, I tried calling on my power. Something hard hit the side of my head, and I lost consciousness.

\*\*\*

When I came to, my body was tied to a wooden board being carried by four armed *soldats*. My hands were covered with some sort of coarse fabric. Curling my fingers into a fist, I punched the board.

"Don't even try to use your power," the man near my shoulder said. "Those gloves block magic."

In the dim light of dawn, we traveled along the outside of the wall surrounding the capital. A *soldat* opened a wooden door in the ground, and my body was lowered into a tunnel.

"Where are we going?" I demanded. "Morlet said I'd be brought safely to the castle."

One of the men near my feet glanced back at me. "That's where we're taking you. And the *king* instructed us to bring you in alive—that's all."

They carried me down a damp, narrow corridor. The urge to kick and scream filled me, but I needed to conserve my energy. We stopped before an iron door built into the rocky tunnel. A *soldat* pulled out a ring of keys and unlocked it. They took me inside a dark room, lowering me to the floor. They left without a word and closed the door, the bolt sliding into place.

Excruciating fear shot through me as I lay there in complete darkness, tied to the board. The only sound was my rapid breathing.

\*\*\*

After what seemed like hours, someone began untying my arms and legs.

"I'm so sorry, my dear Kaia," a voice whispered near my ear. "But I had no choice."

When the last binding loosened, I scrambled to a sitting position. Something creaked behind me, and I spun around. The door opened, casting a thin ray of light into the dark room. A cloaked figure exited, closing the door behind him and plunging me back into solitary darkness.

My breathing sounded heavy echoing off the stone walls of the dungeon. I needed to escape and save my father. On two separate occasions when I was angry, Anders and Vidar both said that if they hadn't been wearing the medallion, they would have been hurt. Maybe I could project my power toward the door and open it.

Removing the magic-blocking gloves, I took a deep breath and concentrated on my inner power. I didn't feel anything. I tried again. Nothing at all. An emptiness filled me, and I hunched over, wanting to cry. Perhaps this room had some sort of spell cast on it that blocked magic, similar to the medallion and the gloves.

Sitting there, I tried to remain calm and conserve my energy.

\*\*\*

Someone yanked me to my feet, startling me. The *soldat* roughly shoved me out of the room and led me down a dimly lit hallway lined with iron doors. Occasionally, someone moaned or chains clanked. We climbed a set of narrow stairs and came to a locked door. The man banged twice, and the door swung open.

He grabbed my arm and took me into an enormous hall, the ceiling at least three or four stories above my head. Tapestries lined the walls, and rugs covered the gray stone floor. Torches lit up the massive room, reflecting off the stained glass windows near the top, which allowed in the gray light of day.

The *soldat* kept a tight hold on me as we crossed the room and stopped before an arched door where two sentries stood on either side.

"Inform His Highness the prisoner is here."

One of the sentries disappeared inside the room. He returned a moment later and granted me entrance.

I stepped inside a large, elegant dining room, the door clicking shut behind me. A table stretched the entire length of the room; heavy curtains covered the windows, blocking the daylight, and torches hung on the walls illuminating the room in a soft glow.

At the head of the table sat Morlet wearing his black cape, concealing his face in shadow. No guards or servants were present.

"Greetings," Morlet said. Even though this was the first time I had ever spoken to or seen him in person, he was exactly as he'd been when we communicated through my dreams. "I didn't think you'd come."

"I didn't have a choice," I answered, unable to believe he stood only a few feet from me.

"You always have a choice," he said. "Whether you make the correct one is another matter entirely." Two plates of food sat untouched on the table. "Care to join me?" He pointed to the chair on his left.

"Tell Skog Heks to release my father," I demanded, feigning confidence.

Morlet chuckled. "She doesn't have him," he admitted. "I only said that to get you here."

Skog Heks didn't have my father? Morlet tricked me? Anders and Vidar had warned me not to trust him. Shame washed over me at how gullible I'd been. I would never make that mistake again.

"My guards tell me you didn't have your bo staff with you." His words were short and clipped, as if upset.

"I was on my way to retrieve it when you brought me here."

He slammed his hand on the table, making me jump. "I thought you already had it."

The only exit in the room was the door through which I'd entered.

"Sit down," Morlet growled.

I hesitated. Should I try to escape?

"Oh, my dear Kaia," he purred. "You're not going to be shy now, are you?" He stood and glided over to me. There were at least two *soldats* outside the door. Was it possible to outsmart Morlet and fight off his men?

"Well?" he asked.

I shifted my weight from foot to foot. Stay and see what he had in store? Or make a run for it? "Why are you wearing your cape?"

He placed his cold hand against my cheek, and I flinched. "My cape is always on unless I'm alone in my bedchamber," he whispered. "You are the only one who has seen me without it." His hand warmed, and a sense of calm melted through me.

"Why do you hide behind it?" My head started to feel heavy. He had to be using magic on me. I took a step back, away from him, breaking our physical connection and immediately felt better.

His hand dropped to his side. "It's easier this way," he mumbled as he turned and went back to the table, taking his seat. Morlet ate his food, his face hidden. "I suggest you eat while you can."

My stomach growled because I hadn't eaten since yesterday. Inhaling the scent of honey bread, I took a seat and picked up a spoon, taking a bite of the porridge sprinkled with cinnamon. It was delicious. Before I knew it, my plate and bowl were empty. Morlet tilted his head revealing his chin and a sly smile.

"Since I don't have my weapon, are you going to release me?" There was no reason to keep me here without it.

"No." He stood, the chair scraping against the stone floor. "Killing you is the only way for the dark magic that resides inside of me to be returned to its rightful owner."

"Then what?" I asked, wiping my mouth with a napkin and leaning back on my chair.

"I'll be free from this wretched curse." His fist pounded on the table, rattling the eating utensils.

"That's not what I meant." I stood to join him. "What are you going to do with yourself once you're free from magic? Will you start ruling justly?" If the Krigers were going to die so balance could be restored, he'd better plan to right the wrongs of Nelebek.

Morlet laughed, the sound dark and menacing. "If I have my way, the rest of my days will be spent alone in the forest, away from the capital."

"Who will rule in your place?"

"I don't care what happens to Nelebek," he spat.

Was he so self-centered that he couldn't see or understand what he was doing to the kingdom? "In your obsession to capture the Krigers, you've completely neglected Nelebek. You dishonor the memory of your parents and brother. If you became better acquainted with your people, you'd see they're working like animals yet starving to death. I'd hoped that once you were free from your *burden*, you would become the ruler this kingdom needs. Clearly, that's not the case. You're rotting away just like Nelebek."

He turned away from me, his cape floating around his legs from the sudden movement. "I should never have become king in the first place." He snatched a candlestick from the table and hurled it across the room. The metal clanged against the stone wall before tumbling to the ground.

I moved closer to him. "Didn't you just say we all have a choice?"

He swiveled around to face me. "Don't lecture me," he snapped. "I didn't ask for this magic."

"No, you didn't. But you certainly can choose how to wield it."

"You know nothing," he spat. "The magic wields *me*." His shoulders hunched forward. "I am but a tool. The day I fell in love, I lost my free will."

"No, you didn't." Love didn't take away your choice. It wasn't supposed to work that way.

"Kaia," he whispered. "You have no idea. You shouldn't even be here." He shook his head.

A *soldat* entered the room. "Your Highness," he announced. "She is ready for you."

# Chapter Fourteen

Morlet yanked me out of the dining room, through the great hall, and into a dark sitting room. Two sofas and several chairs were situated in the center of the space. The only light came from the fire in the hearth. Incense hung heavy in the air, making my head spin. I wanted to run from the room, but Morlet gripped both my arms, holding me firmly in front of him.

"Here's the last Kriger," he said in a bitter voice.

I didn't see who he was speaking to. Suddenly, a shadow detached from the wall and glided toward me, morphing into a hunched over human-like figure. As it neared, it appeared to be an elderly woman with long, knotted gray hair hanging down her back. She reminded me of Grei Heks.

"*Gha,*" the old woman said, the menacing sound making my skin prickle. Her eyes were solid black, and I took a step away from her, bumping into Morlet.

He kept hold of my arms, squeezing tightly. Sweat dripped

down my forehead.

"A girl?" Skog Heks crackled. "All these years searching. No wonder we couldn't find all twelve Krigers."

My head felt heavy, as if I were about to fall asleep. Incense smoke swirled around me in the hot room. Morlet's right hand slid down my arm to my wrist. As soon as we had skin-to-skin contact, the fogginess receded, and I could focus again.

"How old are you?" she asked while her plump, wrinkled fingers played with a string of beads.

"Sixteen," I replied.

Her black eyes narrowed. "Your power must be strong." Skog Heks closed her eyes and tilted her head back. "I can feel your strength," she purred. "It will be a pleasure watching you squirm." A devilish smile spread across her face. "Take her to my play room."

"I got her here—she's mine," Morlet said.

She fingered her beads. "Do you want to find out where her weapon is, or should I?"

Morlet stiffened behind me. "I'll do it."

"Then by all means," she said. "Get to work."

He led me from the room, back to the great hall. I inhaled the cool air as Morlet dragged me along after him. "Where are we going?"

"The torture chamber."

Fear shot through me. *Torture?* I couldn't wait to be united with the Krigers before attempting to flee. Six *soldats* marched behind me. After escaping Morlet, I'd have to deal with them. Since they were the king's personal guards, they were probably lethal fighters.

I needed to act quickly while still on the ground floor. Fabric hung on the wall to my left concealing the windows. Pretending to trip, I fell, tugging Morlet down with me. Caught off guard, he didn't have an opportunity to use his magic. I rolled, hauling him on top of me so his back was to my chest. Wrapping my right arm around his neck, I squeezed. The men surrounded us, drawing their swords and pointing the tips at me.

"Stay back!" I shouted, pressing harder. "Or he dies."

After a long, excruciating ten seconds, Morlet's body went limp—he'd passed out. I reached above me, grabbed the nearest *soldat's* leg, and let my power surge through me. He screamed and tumbled to the ground. I shoved Morlet off me and jumped to my feet, my hands outstretched.

Everyone backed up, clutching their heads in pain. I continued to release my power. Once they were far enough away, I picked up one of the dropped swords and yanked down the nearest curtain. Light burst into the corridor. Using the hilt of the sword, I whacked the lead glass, shattering it. After shooting one last burst of power toward the men, I dropped the sword and climbed out the window, falling ten feet to the ground and landing on brown weeds.

Scrambling to my feet, I took off sprinting along the side of the castle knowing men armed with bows would be after me at any moment. I needed to make it past the wall that surrounded the castle grounds and into the city to hide. When I reached the end of the castle, I ran across the open field heading straight toward the wall. There were a few large oak trees, but not enough to conceal me.

My entire body became paralyzed, and I collapsed to the ground. Cold liquid slithered through my limbs. Pounding footsteps quickly approached from behind, and *soldats* surrounded me.

"Remember," Morlet said, "don't kill her." Black fabric came into my line of sight. "That was a very stupid thing you did." He crouched beside me. His blue eyes glistened with malice beneath the hood of his cape. "How could you do that to me?"

Still frozen, I couldn't speak. Morlet touched my wrist, and my body warmed, movement gradually returning.

"What did you expect?" I said. "For me to go quietly to your torture chamber? I thought you knew me better than that."

Morlet stood, pulling me up with him. He yanked my arms behind my back and bound them with rope. My vision blurred, and standing became difficult.

"You used too much power," he whispered in my ear. "You're going to pass out. Wonder what will happen to you when you're unable to fight back."

I wanted to punch him but instead, sank into his arms and into a dream.

***

Blackness surrounded me. Something cold and hard pressed against my body. My breathing sped up, and fear cascaded through me. Whatever contraption I was in was meant to instill fear. I had to remain calm.

But I couldn't.

My heart thundered as if it were going to burst out of my chest. There wasn't enough air to breathe. I wanted to scream and pound against the device I was in. But that was what Morlet wanted. When he was ready, he'd let me out of this thing.

Closing my eyes, I imagined my father reading to me. When that didn't calm me down, I pictured walking in the forest with the towering trees. Anders's face appeared before me.

"Kaia," he said. "You have to be strong. You can survive this. You're the toughest girl I know." He smiled, filling me with confidence.

Something banged above me, and I heard people talking. Light suddenly gleamed into my eyes, making me squint. Rough hands grabbed my arms, pulling me to a sitting position. I was in a rectangular box that looked like a coffin. I jumped out and stood staring at the sadistic contraption I had just spent an hour or so in.

"Ever wonder what it would feel like to be buried alive?" Morlet asked from behind me. "Put her on the table."

Scattered throughout the room were various instruments I'd never seen before. To my right was a wooden rack with chains attached to either side. The chains were connected to a crank. In the corner of the room was a pointy metal instrument covered in blood. My stomach twisted violently, and I lifted my hands in the air, trying to gather my power in order to protect myself.

"Oh, my dear Kaia," Morlet purred. "I've taken precautions so you can't do that in here."

He must have cast some sort of spell on the room in order to render my power useless—which meant that he couldn't use his magic, either. Two *soldats* clasped my arms, dragging me over to a flat wooden table in the center of the room.

"Please don't do this," I begged Morlet. "What do you want? You already know I'm the twelfth Kriger."

One of the men lifted me, but before he could set me on the table, I twisted my body, clutched his shoulders, and slammed my knee into his stomach. He dropped me, and I kicked my leg out, knocking him over.

The other *soldat* wrapped his arms around me from behind.

"Stop fighting," he said, holding me tightly, "or you'll go on the rack. Trust me, the table is a far better option than having your limbs torn off. It is the least violent contraption in this room. I suggest you start cooperating before she gets here and punishes you."

Tears poured down the sides of my face.

The man picked me up and put me on the table, holding me in place while the other one locked my wrists and ankles to it. Morlet leaned over me, his penetrating blue eyes focused on mine. I stared back at him, challenging him to hurt me.

He rested his hand on my cheek, his thumb gently brushing away the tears. "Don't cry, my dear Kaia."

"Then don't do this to me."

"You have information we need. This is the only way."

"No, it's not."

"Tell me who has been assisting you." He removed his hand and placed it on the table next to my body.

Didn't he want to know where my weapon was? "Why do you think someone has been helping me?" I needed to keep Anders and Vidar's identities from Morlet.

"You never would have made it out of the capital otherwise."

A valid point. "I'm resourceful."

He tapped his finger against the table. "When I first saw you in the Town Square, a man was with you. I didn't see his face, but it was clear, based upon his actions, that he is no ordinary person."

I had to stay as close to the truth as possible. "There was a man there, but that was the first time I saw him as well." It would be so easy to say Anders's name. Morlet probably didn't even know him, and if he did, it wasn't as if he could hurt him. The assassin was hidden in the forest, far from here. However, he was my friend, and I would protect him at all cost.

An uncomfortable silence stretched between us. When I didn't elucidate, Morlet leaned down, his face only inches from mine. "You're keeping things from me," he whispered. "You're making the choice, not me." He took a step back. "Just remember, I never wanted this."

The door flew open and Skog Heks entered, wobbling over to me. The putrid smell of rotting flesh filled the air. "Where's your weapon?" she demanded, her voice grating on my ears.

My bo staff was hidden in a cavern. As to its exact location, it was a mystery to me. Turning my head so Skog Heks could see the fury in my eyes, I spat, "Like I'd tell you."

She chuckled. "Morlet, you said you had her wrapped around your finger. Apparently, you aren't the only one playing with her heartstrings. And your antics aren't nearly as effective as you think."

Her cruel words were like a slap across my face. Was Morlet that heartless? Had he been toying with me all along in an attempt to lure me here? It made sense—after all, he'd used my father as well. Of course he'd manipulate me, make me sympathize with him.

"Raise it," Skog Heks ordered. The *soldats* came forward and used the crank under the table, slowly lifting it until I was upright. "Get me the horn."

One of the men went to the corner of the room and picked up a metal horn, filling it with water. When he was done, he came over.

"Wait," Skog Heks said. "Morlet will do it." She pointed at him. "Take the horn, and fill her with water until she's ready to cooperate."

Morlet gave a curt nod and took the horn. The evil witch

snapped her brown, crooked teeth an inch from my face. "This is the part I love," she said, her hot, rancid breath wafting over me.

"Hurting people?" I asked, panic swelling inside of me.

"No," she replied. "Watching humans suffer. After all, you are the ones who came to our land, trying to kill us. It seems only fair that we return the favor and destroy your kind."

Morlet lifted the horn to my mouth and tried shoving it inside. I squeezed my lips shut. He nodded to one of the *soldats* who pinched my nose. Desperately needing air, I gasped. It was all Morlet needed, and he thrust the end in my mouth. He pushed a lever on the side of the horn, and water poured inside me. The opening was so large that I couldn't spit the water out. It gushed down my throat, forcing me to swallow. I started gagging, but the water didn't stop. I was drowning.

My heart raced, and my head started pounding. Morlet tilted the contraption to get the remaining water into me. His eyes glistened, and a single tear slid down his cheek.

Once the horn was empty, he removed it. My stomach cramped; I was going to vomit.

"When I come back," Skog Heks sneered, "I'll ask you again. If you refuse to tell me, you'll undergo another round of this, then I'll throw you in the coffin for the night." She hobbled toward the door, the two *soldats* trailing behind her.

Morlet stood next to me, his arms folded across his chest.

"Are you coming?" she barked.

"In a moment," he responded, his voice cold and menacing. "I have a few of my own questions for the prisoner."

She left the room, the door slamming shut behind her.

Morlet took a step closer to me. "Why?" he whispered, pushing his hood back, revealing his crestfallen face. "I can't protect you. Just tell her where your weapon is." He reached forward and gingerly wiped the tears from my cheeks.

"Don't touch me," I said, my voice coated with venom. "I hate you."

His shoulders dropped. "If you won't tell her where it is, will you at least tell me who is helping you?"

"I thought you had Skog Heks's power?" He nodded. "Then why is she controlling you? It should be the other way around. You have what she desires. You should be the one giving orders."

He turned away from me. "You don't understand," he mumbled. "It's not that simple."

My throat burned. "Then know this: I will never tell you where my bo staff is."

"She's searching for your father right now," he revealed. "We know he's a guard in the mines. It's only a matter of time until we find him. When she puts him in front of you and tears his skin off bit by bit, you'll tell her whatever she wants to know."

His voice revealed a deep sadness, but I didn't care. He'd just tortured me, and he'd lied before. I couldn't trust anything he said.

"You have one hour until we return." He pulled his hood back on and glided from the room.

# Chapter Fifteen

Someone gently patted my shoulder, rousing me awake. "Your father is safe," a man whispered.

Relief filled me like a warm stew on a frigid day.

"I'm sorry, but there's nothing I can do to help you," he said. "Skog Heks knows who my wife and child are."

"I understand." My voice was coarse and gravelly. "Thank you for telling me about my father."

He glanced at the door. "They're coming. Skog Heks is furious you haven't cooperated. She'll be more aggressive this time." His back stiffened, and he took his post near the door.

Footsteps echoed in the corridor, and I shuddered, not wanting to endure another round of water torture.

Skog Heks stormed into the room, Morlet trailing not far behind. The witch's eyes shot daggers of hatred at me. "I think we need to change it up a bit," she snidely said.

Panic filled me. What form of pain would she choose to

inflict upon me this time?

She clapped her hands. "Maybe I'll gut you."

"You can't kill her," Morlet said, taking an imposing step forward so they stood side-by-side. "At least, not until she links with the other Krigers."

She looked up at him, her black, beady eyes pleading. "It may be worth it."

"I'm not waiting another two decades to find the new Kriger." He clasped his hands behind his back.

"If only I had my magic." A cruel smile formed on her lips. "Oh, but *you* do. There are things you can do to her." Skog Heks's eyes gleamed with excitement.

"I would love to use your magic on her," he said. "However, this room is encased with a spell which prevents magic from being used."

"We could take her to my secret chamber," she suggested, making a bizarre noise with her mouth, like an animal salivating before a kill.

"No. Then she could use her own power to defend herself." He strode through the room, briefly stopping before each contraption. "Move her to the rack," Morlet ordered the two *soldats*. "That shouldn't do too much damage as long as we don't pull hard enough to rip her limbs from her body." He laughed, the sound making my stomach twist. Why had I felt sympathy for this man?

The men untied me from the table. Even though my body was weak, I swung my fist, punching the man to my left. He didn't even flinch. They dragged me over to the rack, pulling my arms up and attaching them before locking my ankles in place.

"One rotation," Morlet said. The *soldats* each took hold of the rollers and turned.

My arms stretched up, my legs down. I screamed—my limbs were about to pop out of their sockets.

Skog Heks came before me. "Where is it?" she demanded. Her plump fingers grabbed my chin, squeezing hard. She smelled of decaying rats.

I spat on her face.

"Foolish human child," she said, backhanding me across the cheek. My vision blurred. "I can't wait to drain the life from your pathetic body."

"Enough," Morlet ordered. "If Kaia passes out, she can't answer. Let me do this my way. I've torn enough limbs from bodies to know how far to go."

Her eyes narrowed. "Let's take her to the tower and bring the other Krigers up. We can force them to link powers, and then you can enter their minds. Discover where they retrieved their weapons. From that, you should be able to figure out where hers is."

"That will work," Morlet answered. "Since it's easiest for the Krigers to link powers at dawn's first light when the moons are still visible, we'll do it then."

Skog Heks nodded and left the room.

"Quarter turn," he instructed the *soldats*.

They complied, and my body stretched farther apart. I screamed a blood-curdling sound.

"I'm sorry," Morlet murmured. "You are going to die. You might as well live your last hours in relative comfort instead of being tortured." He leaned in so close his breath caressed my face. "My Kaia, why do you have to be a Kriger? I wish things were different."

"But they're not," I said. He reached out and touched my face with the tip of his fingers. "Don't touch me," I begged.

"There's something about you."

"I'm a Kriger who is going to kill you," I growled.

His brows pinched together as if trying to figure something out. "What is your mother's name?" he asked.

"I don't have one. She died when I was born."

Morlet shook his head. "You remind me of someone. She ended up ruining me. I can't make the same mistake twice." He took a step away from me. "I will kill you," he declared, his voice steady and calm. He turned to the *soldats*. "Release her and follow me."

They undid my bindings, and I crumpled to the floor, unable to stand. One of the men lifted me in his arms, and I turned my head toward his chest, willing the excruciating pain to go away.

A few minutes later, he laid me on a soft bed and left. I was in Morlet's bedchamber. "Why am I here?" I demanded as a new fear set in. We were alone in his bedchamber, and in my condition, I was completely vulnerable.

"I couldn't put you back in the coffin," he admitted. "Besides, you need to rest. In a few hours, I'm taking you to the tower. Once my men have retrieved your weapon, we'll end this once and for all." He was a walking contradiction. I didn't understand how he could be so evil, yet show kindness at the same time. He didn't want to hurt me, yet he did it anyway.

Escape was impossible. Tears slid down my face—I'd never been in so much pain before. My body started shaking uncontrollably. Morlet sighed and removed his cape. What did he plan to do? If he attempted to harm me, I didn't even have the energy to summon my power. I was at his mercy, and that scared me more than anything.

"Let me help you," he gently said, sitting next to me.

"I don't want your help." This was probably another one of

his lies meant to gain my trust before he stabbed me.

"You're too stubborn for your own good." He reached for me, and I jerked away, my vision blurring and my stomach cramping. Morlet took hold of my tender arms.

"Leave me alone!" I wished I were somewhere else. Anywhere else. I'd rather die than have him take advantage of me or be tortured again.

"Kaia, look at me."

I squeezed my eyes shut. Morlet mumbled something unintelligible, and then warmth shot through me. My eyes flew open. His brows were pinched together, and his eyes were closed as he continued muttering. My muscles relaxed, and my stomach no longer hurt. His power freely flowed from his body to mine, rejuvenating and healing me.

Beads of sweat covered his forehead, and his breathing became labored. He stopped talking and released me. Swaying, he slowly stood and stumbled over to the fireplace where he knelt on the ground, his back to me.

I sat up, not a single ache in my body. "Why did you do that?" He'd just spent hours torturing me.

Morlet didn't respond. His body shook as he pointed to the nearby chair where a small pile of clothes sat neatly folded. "You can change in there." His head nodded toward a door.

After picking up the clothes, I opened the door and discovered a large washroom. A small bathing pool filled one side of the room, and a dressing area took up the other. I peeled off my disgusting clothes and climbed into the warm water. All the sweat, dirt, and grime washed away. I stayed in there for several minutes, relaxing in the luxurious bath.

Finally, I got out and dressed in the clothes Morlet had provided—black pants and a plain tunic. I combed my hair, wishing it were still long so I could twist it back into a bun off my face.

Rolling my shoulders back, I steeled my resolve. This was my last opportunity to escape. Back in the bedchamber, Morlet hadn't moved an inch. Seeing him there, exposed and defeated, pulled at my heart.

Against my better judgment, I asked, "Are you all right?" Most likely, he'd depleted himself healing me.

"I'm fine. Just tired. The warmth helps."

Squatting next to him, I had no idea what else to say. One second he was inflicting pain, and the next he was helping me. "I don't understand you."

A small smile spread across his face. "Neither do I." His shoulders slumped. "Kaia, I have to kill you."

"Then why did you bother using your magic to heal me?"

"I don't know," he mumbled. "I couldn't stand to see you hurt." He wouldn't look at me.

I stood and prepared to kick him so I could make a run for it. His arm shot out, and he grabbed my ankle, yanking it hard. I tumbled to the ground, stunned.

"Don't make me regret it." He jumped to his feet, pulling me up with him. "Go to sleep. I'll let you know when it's time to leave for the tower."

So much for my great escape.

*✳✳✳*

Morlet gingerly shook my shoulder, waking me. "Let's go."

Getting out of bed, I stretched. Morlet looked vastly different without his cape on. He transformed from a villain into an utterly handsome and regal man. However, there was still a dark sadness hovering around the edges.

"You're staring," Morlet said taking a tentative step toward me. It felt slightly invasive, almost too close, but I didn't move away. His bright eyes studied me. Not wanting to be sucked into a spell, I tried to focus on him without actually looking directly into his eyes.

"I never thought the last Kriger would be a girl," he said, his voice gruff.

I raised my eyebrows. "You have got to be kidding." He sounded like Anders and Vidar. "What has you so upset isn't the fact that you're going to slaughter twelve innocent people, but that one of them happens to be a girl?" I wanted to wrap my hands around his neck and squeeze.

A sly grin spread across his lips. "What I mean is that I'm sorry it's you."

"You should be sorry you're murdering people."

"I've killed so many over the last hundred years that it hardly affects me anymore." He went to the chair where his cape lay. "I imagined being happy when I reached the end. But ... something doesn't feel right."

"Maybe you should be the one to die instead of the twelve of us. Have you ever considered that?"

He slid the cape around his shoulders and pulled the hood over his head, concealing his face once again.

I forged on, "Once you kill us, the magic returns to Skog Heks. Is that what you want?"

"What I want?" He bitterly laughed, the sound dark and foreboding. "I want the curse to be over. I don't care how, so long as it ends."

What would happen if the Krigers managed to kill Morlet? Would the magic die with him? Would Nelebek be free from Skog Heks? If so, how was that possible if everything had to be in balance?

"This predicament I'm in? It's all Skog Heks's fault, and yet, I'm the one who has to kill." He reached his hand out, placing his palm against my cheek. I wanted to move away, but something kept me rooted in place. "I had no idea she planned to kill my family in order to put me on the throne." Morlet's other hand came up, cupping my cheek. "Do you know she planned it the entire time? She wanted to rule through me."

His hands shook. He released me and took a step back. "Do you have any idea what it's like to see your family slaughtered like pigs? In my brother's room, there was blood splattered everywhere. My mother's throat had been slit. My father stabbed in the heart."

I couldn't imagine seeing my father murdered. "Do you know who Skog Heks hired to kill the royal family?"

"No." Is that how Anders was tied into all of this? Was he the assassin who murdered them? The thought made me sick.

"Skog Heks had to know when she used her magic to control you in order to rule Nelebek that the balance of power would be off, and she'd never succeed."

"She didn't realize she could lose her magic," he said. "She still believes she's capable of anything, including outsmarting the *Heks* power source deep within our world."

"Is that why you opened the mines?"

"Yes. She insists she can obtain power if we dig deep enough to find it."

"I think the world would be better without Skog Heks."

"Perhaps, but then the balance of power will be off." He

opened the door, revealing half a dozen guards in the hallway waiting for us. "Now if you'll accompany me, we are going to the tower." He tilted his head down so no one could see his face as he stepped into the corridor, his cape billowing behind him.

We entered the great hall. Skog Heks leaned on a walking stick in the middle of the vast room. She smiled, revealing her decaying brown teeth. "Do we know where it is?"

Morlet reached back and grabbed my arm, pulling me forward. "We're on our way to the tower. I promise we'll have the location shortly." His fingers dug into my skin, and I realized he was afraid of the evil witch.

She wobbled over and backhanded me across my cheek. My head flew to the side from the impact. Instinct took over, and I raised my hands, forcing all of my power at her.

She screamed and stumbled backwards. "Stupid girl!" she chided.

Morlet pinned my arms down, blocking my power with his own. The evil witch ran at me. She shoved her thumbs against the base of my neck, making it difficult to breathe. My vision blurred.

"No," Morlet insisted, "you can't kill her yet."

Skog Heks didn't loosen her grip. Morlet pried her thumbs off, and she reluctantly halted her assault. My knees buckled as I gasped for air. Morlet grabbed me, keeping me upright.

"Let her fall to the ground," the witch said, seething with rage.

He let go, and I tumbled to the floor. Skog Heks kicked me. A searing pain shot through my side. I reached out to grab her foot to trip her, but Morlet stepped on my wrist. The witch jumped on top of me, pulling my hair and hissing at me.

I twisted my hips and flipped on top of her, pinning her

down. Morlet grabbed me from behind, lifting me off her. He held me against his body while I thrashed my arms and legs, trying to break free.

Skog Heks scrambled to her feet, her eyes wild, skin flushed. "I want her in my chamber."

"No," Morlet responded. "I'm taking her to the tower so we can finish this."

Her shoulders rose and fell as she stared at me with hatred in her dark eyes.

"Do I need to remind you that I am the one with your magic? If you want it back, stand down."

Her head jerked back, startled. "You do not order me around," she snapped. "Fine. Let's go to the tower, but I'm going to play with her." Her eyes gleamed with pleasure.

Morlet tensed. This wasn't good. The king dragged me to a narrow staircase. "Why did you attack her?" he whispered in my ear as we started climbing.

I refused to answer. At the top of the winding staircase, we came to a circular room. Twelve open windows revealed the sun hadn't yet risen. Chains were attached to the stones under each one. In the center of the room were black markings I'd never seen before. Morlet shoved me inside.

Six *soldats* entered and spread throughout the room. Skog Heks stalked toward me. I raised my hands, and Morlet wrapped his arms around my body, holding my arms down.

"Let me go!" I threw my head back, head butting him. When his grip loosened, I angled sideways and elbowed him. Hooking my leg around his, I seized his wrist, about to flip him over my shoulder. Something zapped through my body, paralyzing me. I crumbled to the ground.

Skog Heks hovered over me. "My turn." She kicked my ribs,

and I grunted in pain. She laughed as she repeatedly kicked me until something cracked. Grabbing my hair, she lifted my head a foot off the ground and then slammed it down onto the stone floor. Pain exploded and white dots floated around in my eyes. There was nothing I could do to defend myself.

"Enough," Morlet said. "I need her to be able to link power with the others." He knelt next to me, his hand on my shoulder. A slow ebb of warmth seeped into my body. Was Morlet healing me? Maybe he wanted to ensure I didn't die.

The witch spit on my face. "Foolish girl. I will destroy every last wretched human in this kingdom. You are powerless to stop me." She kicked my face, and my world went dark.

# Chapter Sixteen

Frigid liquid filled my mouth, cascading down my throat. My eyes flew open as a jolt of energy surged through me. Anders's eyes loomed above my body. "Am I dreaming?" I croaked.

He held a finger to his lips while slipping his free arm under my back and lifting me to a sitting position. A stinging sensation radiated down my side, but it was manageable.

"The concoction I gave you will only last for thirty minutes or so," he whispered in my ear. "We must be off the grounds before then because your pain will once again become unbearable." Anders wore snug-fitting black material that covered his entire body, including his hands and head, leaving only his face exposed. He carefully pulled me to my feet. Six *soldats* lay on the floor, each with a dart sticking out of his neck.

"Put this on." He handed me black fabric similar to his. "Morlet is bringing up the other Krigers as we speak."

I stripped out of my bloody clothing, not caring that Anders watched. With shaking hands, I slid on the constricting material, pulling the close-fitting fabric over my head, making sure my hair was covered.

Instead of going to the stairs, Anders waved me between two windows. "Outside, next to this window, the tower meets the main section of the castle. We must stay in the corner where the shadows will conceal us." The sun had not yet risen and darkness blanketed the land. "I'll go first," Anders said. "After I'm out, place your feet on my shoulders. I will bear your weight on the way down."

Tears filled my eyes.

"If you're in too much pain, I can carry you."

I shook my head.

"What is it?"

"I'm a fool," I admitted. "I fell for Morlet's tricks."

Anders's face softened. "I think you're incredibly strong. It's your desire to see the good in people that makes you special."

Voices echoed from the stairwell. Anders grabbed the rope nailed to the stone window ledge. He slid his legs over the side and descended. Hopefully, the concoction he gave me was potent enough to hold my body together until I escaped.

I climbed onto the ledge and slid my legs over the side. There wasn't any pain, which was both frightening and comforting. As soon as my feet found Anders's shoulders, he started to descend. I grabbed the rope to keep my body steady.

The sentries on the roof carried torches, but they didn't notice us since we were dressed in black fabric that blended in with the coloring of the castle.

Something oozed into my eye, and I wiped it away. My gloved hand was covered in blood. My head must be bleeding, and I couldn't even feel it. Not wanting to panic and risk falling, I ignored the thick liquid dripping down my brow and focused on putting one hand below the other as we descended the rope. We had one more level to go.

Anders froze as three sentries passed below us. He held the end of the rope over his shoulder so it didn't reach the ground where someone could stumble against it. For once, I was glad he was an assassin and knew how to enter and exit a fortified compound unnoticed. His body shook ever so slightly from supporting my body weight.

He started to lower us again, this time much faster than before. The guards were probably on a rotation, and he knew exactly how long we had until they passed by again. I moved my hands as fast as I could, trying to help. When his feet hit the ground, he reached up and brought me down beside him.

Anders unsheathed a dagger from his boot and threw it toward the top of the rope, slicing it through. The knife plummeted to the ground, and I picked it up while he shoved the severed rope under a nearby bush.

Crouching low, we sprinted away from the castle toward a cluster of rocks. I dropped to my knees, resting against them as Anders surveyed the surrounding area. Breathing became difficult, and my vision blurred. A ragged scream pierced the air. Morlet must have discovered I was gone. His shadow passed by one of the tower's open windows. We didn't have long until his entire army was searching for me.

Anders placed his hand on my shoulder. "Ready?"

I couldn't speak. My stomach and head were throbbing with pain. He pulled me to my feet and pointed to the right. I nodded, and we started running. All of my energy focused on staying upright and following Anders. When we reached a tall oak tree, we stopped. Leaning against the trunk, an odd sensation washed over me.

"Morlet is searching for me," I said. "Do you have the medallion?"

"No. Too risky. Perhaps you can block him."

"I didn't think that was possible."

He shrugged. "The other Krigers can't communicate with Morlet like you can. I tend to think the rules don't apply to you, and anything is possible."

"Do you have any idea how to block him?"

"Instead of projecting your power outward, keep it around you like a shield." He glanced to the left. "Let's go."

We started running.

Reaching inside myself, I coaxed my power to my hands and envisioned wrapping it around my body like a blanket. A wave of dizziness overcame me. Anders grabbed my arm, keeping me upright. I continued to use my power to form a protective layer around me, having no idea if it worked or not. I no longer felt Morlet searching for me, but my body was in so much pain, I couldn't be sure.

We finally reached the wall surrounding the castle grounds. Anders motioned for me to stay put. I nodded, and he slunk away. Three guards fell from the top of the wall, hitting the ground with a horrific thud. I refused to look at their still bodies. A moment later, Anders was at my side with a rope and crossbow.

"I had them hidden under a bush," he explained. He attached the rope to an arrow and shot it to the top of the wall. I heard a soft *ping* as it stuck into the stone. Anders pulled on the rope, ensuring it would hold our weight. Satisfied, he turned to me. "Can you climb?"

I tried to pull myself up, but my arms were like blades of grass.

"Luckily, you're light. Get on." He crouched to the ground,

and I leaned on his back, wrapping my arms and legs around him. He tied the end of the rope around both our bodies, securing me to him. The muscles in his back flexed as he scaled the wall, pulling us up with his arms.

When we reached the top, he flung the rope to the other side, and we quickly descended.

The sun started to rise, turning the sky a dull gray. Shouts rang out, and the sound of a horn blasted through the air. The army was getting into formation. Anders started moving at a frantic pace. The sound of hundreds of boots marching on the ground came from somewhere to the right.

At the base of the wall, Anders untied the rope, and I slid to the ground, my legs mush. He dragged me along, and we stumbled down a small slope until we reached the moat surrounding the outside of the castle wall.

His eyes darted around, surveying the area. "Come on." He lowered himself into the water. "Be careful not to splash. *Soldats* are probably close by." Worry flashed in his eyes.

Attempting a smile to reassure him, I crawled into the frigid water. I tried moving my arms and legs, but pain engulfed me, making it difficult to move. It seemed as if I'd been cut in two and my head had been crushed by a rock. I slipped under the water, unable to swim.

Anders wrapped his strong arm around my chest, just under my arms, lifting my head out of the moat. He swam, hauling me along with him. If we were caught, he would die because of me.

"Take a deep breath," he commanded. I inhaled, and he shoved me under the water, holding me down, my lungs screaming for air. After a few long seconds, he tilted my head back so only the top portion of my face surfaced, allowing me to breathe. Anders did the same, his face right next to mine. *Soldats* searched alongside the moat looking for me. We stayed in that position, with only our noses and mouths above the water, until they moved far enough away. Anders started swimming again, pulling me along with him.

We reached the other side. He waited a few minutes, observing the area, before climbing out of the water and dragging me out behind him. Remaining on our stomachs, we crawled forward through the tall grass. The city was only fifty feet or so in front of us. Several men held torches, searching the open area. The nearest one was only a short distance away. When Anders froze, I froze. When he moved, I moved.

My arms and legs started violently shaking. A sharp, shooting pain pierced my stomach. Curling into a ball, I tried not to scream. Blood continued to drip down my forehead.

"The medicine is wearing off," Anders whispered near my ear. "Climb on top of me. I'll get us to the streets. From there, it will be easy to hide."

I nodded, unable to speak, and shimmied on top of Anders's back. Tears streamed down my cheeks. His muscles tensed as he moved, trying to remain quiet and unseen. Dogs barked in the distance, and he started crawling faster. If the castle hounds were searching for us, they'd lead the *soldats* straight to the moat. From there, it wouldn't take them long to figure out I'd swum across. My head pounded, and my ribs ached. Anders patted my shoulder and eased me off his back.

He stood, lifting me in his arms. We were next to a building at the edge of the city. "I need to get you to a healer." He sprinted alongside the building, turning down the next street.

The pain intensified, and my eyes rolled back. I gasped, the sound wheezy. I was going to die.

"It's not far from here," Anders whispered. He ran, careful

to stay hidden in the shadows of the tall apartment buildings. Occasionally, he would stop or hide in a doorway. I closed my eyes, attempting to use my power to heal myself. I couldn't focus long enough to force my power to do anything.

Anders opened a door and entered a dark room. We descended a flight of stairs. Metal rattled, and then I heard a door open and close. He descended another flight of stairs, the air turning cool and smelling of damp earth.

"Where are we?" I mumbled.

"We're in the tunnels below the capital."

"Tunnels?"

"We have men working in the mines who have dug tunnels under the capital. There are also tunnels from the natural springs that used to flow underground decades ago. We use the tunnels to get in and out of the capital, hide from *soldats*, and communicate with each other."

I remembered the first time I met Anders and the tunnel we used from the tailor's shop to the brothel. "There are others like you?" I asked, trying to distract myself from the pain.

"Well, no, not like *me*. But there are others who wish to help the Krigers. Your father is one of them. Having him work in the mines has significantly aided our cause."

He knew my father? Why had Papa kept all of this a secret from me?

Anders pushed open a door, entering a small room. Soft light glowed from oil lamps hanging on the walls. Two men sat on chairs playing a game of cards. One jumped up and opened another door for us. Anders carried me into the second room, this one much larger and filled with over a dozen men talking animatedly with each other. When they saw us, silence fell.

"I need a healer," Anders said. "Immediately."

One man nodded and left.

"Over here," someone said. "Lay her on this cot."

Anders gently lowered me onto the hay mattress. "Back up and give her room." He carefully pulled the fabric off my head.

"She's covered in blood," one of the men said.

"Get me a basin of water and a washcloth," Anders said.

"What happened to her?" someone else asked.

The pain became unbearable, and I passed out.

\*\*\*

Peeling my eyelids open, my father sat on a chair next to me. Was I dreaming? I blinked.

"Oh thank the moons!" Papa cried. "I thought I'd lost you. You've been asleep since yesterday." Tears glistened in his eyes.

"Where am I?" Pain seared my throat.

"You're safe," he answered. "You've been badly injured. There's a large gouge on your head that the healer had to stitch together. You also have several broken ribs, and you're covered in bruises." His voice broke, and he clutched my hand. "I'm sorry I wasn't there to protect you."

"Why didn't you tell me I'm a Kriger?" I croaked.

"Shh, we can talk about that later. Right now, you need to rest." He lifted a cup to my lips, and warm liquid dribbled down my throat. The steeped listerblossom soothed me, and I closed my eyes, falling fast asleep.

*"Kaia?" Morlet asked, his voice desperate.*

*"I … can't … " I didn't have the strength to answer—to tell him that I was so injured, I couldn't even lift my head.*

*"I'm sorry Skog Heks did that to you."*

*"No ... you're ... not. You ... could have ... stopped ... her."*

*"Open your eyes," he prodded. "I'm in my bedchamber. Let me help you."*

*I didn't want to accept anything from him. However, if I didn't let Morlet help me, it could take months for my body to heal, and I needed to flee the capital and reach the safety of the forest as soon as possible.*

*Opening my eyes, I found myself lying on Morlet's bed with him sitting at my side.*

*"There isn't much time," he said. Raising his hands above me, he moved them in a circular motion while speaking softly. A blue light shone below his fingertips, and then he pointed at my stomach. The light flashed, shot out of his hands, and plummeted into me. I wanted to scream except my body was paralyzed. The light moved through me, cold liquid slithering to my limbs, healing my injuries. My strength gradually increased. Once the light extended to my head, healing my laceration, it shot out of me and returned to Morlet.*

*He collapsed on the bed, motionless, exhausted from using so much of his magic to heal me. I easily sat up, rejuvenated. It was time to return to my consciousness so I could escape out of the capital.*

*Except I couldn't stop staring at the king.*

*It seemed as if there were two personalities trapped inside his body—Morlet, the evil man who tortured innocent people, killed children, and had no mercy; and Espen, the man who made a mistake and had been suffering a century for it, the man who healed me, the man who had compassion. However, it didn't matter that there was good in him because there was also evil, and I had to defeat that evil in order to restore peace to the kingdom of Nelebek. I couldn't afford to feel anything but disgust and hatred for him.*

*So why was I still sitting here next to him? I leaned down and kissed his forehead. "Thank you," I whispered before standing and concentrating on returning to my body in the underground room.*

My eyes opened, and several men I didn't know stood near me.

"You were talking in your sleep," one of them said.

"What did I say?"

"Don't know," another answered. "Couldn't make out any of the words. Your father told us to keep an eye on you, so that's what we've been doing."

Blood was crusted all over the pillow near my head. "Where is my father?"

"Out with Anders. They went to make sure the *soldats* aren't looking in this area for you."

Swinging my legs over the side of the bed, I stood, and everyone's eyes widened. "Maybe you should lie down," a man said.

"I healed myself using my own power." If I told them the truth, no one would understand.

The door opened and Vidar and Anders walked in. Vidar ran to me, a questioning look on his face.

"Healed myself." I repeated the lie easily this time.

He whooped and picked me up, swinging me around in his arms. When he set me down, he kissed my cheek. "I'm so happy you're okay."

Anders's eyes narrowed infinitesimally. Either he didn't believe my lie, or he didn't think Vidar should be so rough with me only moments after my miraculous recovery. "Thank you, Anders. I would have died if it wasn't for your daring rescue."

"Looks like you didn't need me after all," he mumbled as he turned and left the room.

Vidar grabbed my face and kissed my forehead. "I was so

afraid we'd lost you—not because you're a Kriger," he said, sensing I was about to argue with him. "But because I would miss *you*."

My father entered the room, and I bolted over to him, throwing my arms around his neck.

"You're not coughing," I said, relieved.

"No," he replied, his voice filled with joy. He held me at arm's length, observing me. "Anders gave me some more medicine. I'm doing much better. Looks like I'm not the only one, though." He smiled, his face alight with wonder.

"I healed myself with my own power."

He kissed my cheek. "Just like your mother."

"I'll give you two a moment alone," Vidar said. He left the room.

My father and I sat on the cot away from everyone else. "There are *soldats* everywhere," he said, squeezing my hands. "It's only a matter of time before they start interrogating citizens. You need to leave, and we must make sure they know you're gone."

"Of course. I'm strong enough to go right now."

He smiled, the corners of his eyes wrinkling. Papa looked older than I remembered. "It has been decided that Vidar and Anders will take you to the cavern. You need to retrieve your bo staff so you can access your full power. We can't do anything else until you have it."

I didn't want to leave my father again, but he'd never be able to travel in the forest with his failing health. I hugged him. "Thank you."

"For what?" he asked, squeezing me back.

"For everything." The training, keeping me safe, and the tunnels.

Vidar came back into the room. "We need to go. It's almost dawn."

My father kissed my forehead. "Be safe. Remember everything I taught you."

"I will."

"Most of all," he said, tapping a finger to my heart, "remember who you are, and always believe in yourself. You will bring peace to our kingdom. You will save us all."

Tears swelled in my eyes. I stood, blinking them away.

The other men in the room looked like they were ready to leave too. One wore Anders's black outfit and hood. The man noticed me staring at him. "We'll lead the *soldats* in the opposite direction."

"Thank you."

Vidar grabbed my hand, pulling me to the other room where Anders waited for us. "Are you sure you're well enough to travel?" he asked, releasing me.

"Yes. I'm completely healed."

"That is one miraculous recovery," Anders observed. "You were only asleep one day. I'm surprised you didn't deplete yourself for a full week using your power like that."

A week? Would Morlet be bedridden that long while he recovered? If so, it should make our escape a lot easier. When I didn't respond, Anders tossed a bag to me. "Put the commoner clothing on first, the *soldat* uniform on top."

After we all changed, Anders led us up several flights of stairs to a small room. "When we leave this place," he said, "there will be absolutely no talking. Walk with purpose, head up, and shoulders back. Don't shy away from anyone. Understood?"

He opened the door, stepping into a narrow alleyway, Vidar and I close behind him. We walked down the center of the streets in the early morning light. Although there weren't any citizens out at this hour, there were several dozen men from the King's

Army roaming the streets. Luckily, they didn't pay us any heed. Anders maintained a fast pace as we traveled across the capital.

The sound of dogs barking echoed in the distance, making the hair on my arms rise. I stepped closer to Anders. "They'll be able to smell me. We can't outsmart dogs."

"Didn't you notice the man wearing your black outfit? The smell of your blood on the fabric will attract the dogs. He's leading them away from us."

"What about once the animals catch up to him? The decoy isn't a girl. The *soldats* will know they've been tricked."

Anderson tugged at the collar of his snug-fitting tunic. "We better be on the other side of the capital's wall and in the forest by then."

"Stop talking," Vidar ordered. "We're being followed."

I wanted to glace back but knew not to. We continued walking as if nothing had changed. The dogs stopped barking, and an eerie silence fell over the capital. Footsteps pounded behind us, and Anders spun around, a small tube between his lips. The *soldat* who had been following us lay on the ground, a dart protruding from his neck.

"Run," Anders commanded. I sprinted as fast as I could, right behind Vidar, while Anders followed me in order to protect my back. "Go straight. The wall is just ahead."

The dogs started barking again, this time much closer. Without warning, a blast rocked the ground, making everything shake. A plume of smoke rose in the sky a couple of blocks away.

"What happened?" I asked, slowing my pace.

"An explosion," Vidar answered, pulling me along.

"It was a planned distraction," Anders added, a grin on his face. "Now get moving."

# Chapter Seventeen

The wall was only fifty feet away. Thrilled, I sprinted with an extra burst of energy. When we reached it, Anders felt around the stones until he located a loose one. Then he pushed four stone blocks through, just as he'd done the night we escaped out of the capital. After I climbed to the other side, Anders and Vidar joined me, shoving the stones back into place.

"Go!" Anders yelled, pushing me forward.

I ran toward the trees, eager to conceal myself among them. About a hundred feet into the forest, Anders stopped and stripped off his uniform, revealing his plain brown clothing underneath. Vidar and I quickly did the same. Anders dug a shallow hole with his hands and then buried our uniforms. When he was done, we headed north.

"How far is the cavern from here?" I asked.

"If we don't stop, we should reach it tonight," Anders replied.

"Are you sure you're okay?" Vidar asked. "You don't need to rest?"

"I'm fine." Better than fine. I wasn't even winded after all that running.

Anders glanced over his shoulder at me, his eyes lifeless. A pang of guilt hit me for lying to him about healing myself. Somehow, he knew what really happened. I was sure of it.

"If we want to make it there before nightfall," he said, "I suggest we pick up the pace." He started running.

\*\*\*

When we neared the clearing where Morlet's men had captured me, we skirted around it in case anyone lingered there. After traveling several miles, not once stopping to rest, eat, or drink, we reached the base of the rocky mountain range where the cavern was located. Vidar said the entrance wasn't too high up, but we had to climb in order to reach it. Anders led the way, and Vidar brought up the rear. The climb wasn't completely vertical, yet I still avoided looking down. We were higher than I cared to be.

As we ascended, my mind wandered. What would happen when I entered the cavern to retrieve my weapon? How would I be challenged? Would the trials be mental? Physical? Would I be deemed worthy and pass? Had others in my family faced the challenges? Had they passed?

Clutching the rock above me, I hoisted myself up. The rock came loose, and my hand slipped. I lost my footing and slid down, pebbles and stones tumbling with me. My stomach dropped as my hands frantically tried to grab hold, to no avail.

Vidar caught me, pulling me against his body. "Are you okay?" he asked, breathing hard.

"Yes." My hands were scratched and bleeding, but considering all I'd endured lately, it was nothing. Vidar held onto me until I took hold and started to climb once again, ignoring my sore hands and knees. Anders was perched twenty feet above, watching me. When our eyes met, he quickly turned away and continued his ascent.

The sun set, and the sky began to darken. Anders glanced over his shoulder. "We're here." He reached down and pulled me up onto the ten-foot by ten-foot ledge. Turning so my back was to the cave, the view before me was astonishing. The mountain range extended to either side as far as the eye could see. In front of me, the vast forest was below, the ledge I stood on only feet above the treetops. "Come on," Anders said as he entered the cave.

I followed him inside where the temperature dropped. He fumbled with some kindling, and then lit a torch on fire. "We keep supplies here, just in case." He walked around the cave lighting several other torches that hung on the walls. The area was quite spacious—the ceiling a good twenty feet above me. The walls formed a circular space, and there was an archway revealing a dark tunnel toward the back.

"You should sleep for a few hours," he said. "Once you're well rested, you'll enter the tunnel and begin the trials."

Vidar joined us. "Do you want to do a perimeter check to make sure there aren't any *soldats* nearby?"

Anders agreed and ducked out of the cave. I watched him go, feeling an odd tension between us. Ever since I'd lied about healing myself, he'd distanced himself from me.

"He's not much of a talker," Vidar said as he took a couple of logs from the woodpile. He tossed them in a fire ring that had been constructed in the center of the cave.

"Yes, but he certainly notices a great deal." More than I wished he did. Shame washed over me for having lied to him.

After lighting the wood on fire, Vidar grabbed two bedrolls from the supplies stacked against the side of the cave and handed one to me.

I unfolded mine, laid it on the ground, and crawled on top of it, glad to rest after running all day.

"I need to talk to you about something." Vidar placed his bedroll next to mine and sat on it. He fidgeted with his hands, not looking at me.

"What is it?"

"First, let me say that I'm glad you're alive and healed. And not because you're a Kriger, but because I've come to consider you a friend."

"Thank you," I said, pulling a blanket over my body and yawning.

Vidar cleared his throat. "I want to ask you a question."

"Sure," I mumbled, my eyelids growing heavy.

"Have you ever been in love?"

"No." He knew I'd never been courted or kissed, so why was he asking me about love?

"I have," he said in a soft voice. "I've been in love a few times. I know the difference between love and friendship."

"Not to be rude, but it's late and I'm tired. What are you getting at?"

"The spell that was cast which created the Krigers is the same one that cursed Anders and me." He dropped his head onto his hands, rubbing his eyes. "I'm not sure how to say this … but Grei Heks told me something." He hesitated. "She said your blood and my blood are destined to be together."

"What are you saying?" I asked, suddenly wide awake.

"Grei Heks told me that when Morlet is killed, if our blood hasn't mixed to produce an offspring, all will be lost."

"What does that mean?" I sat up and faced Vidar.

"We're meant to marry one another and bear a child together."

"Are you certain?" Why would Grei Heks cast such a spell? "Is this why it's always a female from my family?"

"I believe so." He scooted closer to me. "I know we're only friends, and there is nothing romantic between us. However, we must marry and have a child, as Grei Heks foretold, so we can ensure the curse will end along with Morlet and his tyranny."

I sat there stunned. Marry? Have a child?

Anders ducked inside the cave. "All clear." His eyes darted between Vidar and me. "Did I interrupt something?"

"We're just discussing our future." Vidar seemed unsettled and not his usual confident self.

"I … uh … " I stumbled, trying to find the right words.

Vidar reached out and took hold of my hands. The gesture felt awkward, so I pulled free. "I need some fresh air." I scrambled to my feet.

"You shouldn't be out there alone," Vidar said. "We can't let Morlet kidnap you again."

"I won't go far." I shouldered past Anders and ran outside the cave to the ledge. Not wanting to climb down the mountain in the dark, I leaned against the rocks next to the opening, inhaling the cool air.

"What did you say to her?" Anders's voice drifted out to me.

"I told her what Grei Heks foretold," Vidar answered.

There was a long pause before Anders asked, "About the two of you marrying?" There was an odd hitch to his voice.

"Yes. I'm sorry."

It had been a long day, and I didn't want to deal with this

right now. The idea of marrying Vidar and having a child with him seemed ludicrous. We were just friends, and I wasn't ready to marry.

"She has to retrieve her weapon tomorrow," Anders said.

"You should've kept your mouth shut until afterward."

Yes, Vidar should have. I wanted to applaud Anders.

"I couldn't wait. I needed to do it now, before she develops feelings for someone else."

"What's that supposed to mean?" Anders bitterly asked.

"If we have an agreement in place, it will prevent problems from arising."

Anders said something that I couldn't hear.

"Why are you so mad?" Vidar asked. "You knew this was coming."

"I'm going to go and find Kaia before she is captured again."

Anders walked out of the cave and immediately spotted me leaning against the rocky mountainside.

"Are you okay?" he asked, his voice low.

"I'm fine." I felt like there was a brick wall between us—a wall that arose from my lie. I very much wanted to tear down that wall and to explain what really happened. But would he understand? Or would he belittle and chide me?

"You should go back in and get some sleep."

"Just a few more minutes," I whispered. How could I explain my relationship with Morlet when it didn't make sense to me?

"What did you tell him?"

"Don't worry, I didn't tell him anything about you or Vidar."

"What?" Anders's eyebrows pulled together.

"When Morlet demanded to know who's been helping me, I refused to tell him. Skog Heks tortured me because of it."

He ran his hands through his hair, leaning against the rocks next to me. "You met Skog Heks? And she tortured you?" I nodded. His fingers curled into a fist. "I'm sorry," he said, his voice ragged. "I knew you'd been severely injured. It never crossed my mind that you were tortured because of me."

I didn't want to tell him about being locked in the coffin, or strapped to the table, or the water being forced down my throat. I especially didn't want to remember Morlet paralyzing me so Skog Heks could beat me to the brink of death.

"If you ever want to talk about it, I'm here. I … I know what it's like to be tortured." His words were like a knife sliding over my skin. I wanted to ask him about it. However, if I didn't want to talk about my own experience, he probably didn't want to relive his either. "What I meant was, did you give Vidar an answer?"

"No." Was it really even a marriage proposal? The chilly air whipped around me, and I folded my arms across my body, trying to stay warm.

"Why did you assume I meant Morlet?"

"All you care about is freeing the Krigers and killing the king. I assumed you'd be more concerned about what happened to me while imprisoned than my response to Vidar's odd proposal."

"You think his proposal is odd?" The corners of his mouth rose as he fought a smile.

I rolled my eyes. "I hardly think now is the time to get engaged, even if Grei Heks foretold it."

Anders kicked a loose rock, sending it flying off the mountain. "Is something else the matter?" He reached out and took my hand, squeezing it.

"I didn't heal myself," I blurted, staring at our joined hands.

"I figured as much."

The wall between us crumbled. Anders's calm presence, his fierce determination, and his steady disposition empowered me. His hand was a lifeline. An owl hooted in the distance. The treetops below swayed in the wind.

"Did Morlet heal you?"

"Yes." Admitting it lifted a huge weight that had been crushing me.

"I don't understand. Why did he torture you, then turn around and heal you? Especially after you had already escaped? To make sure you didn't die? Or is there another reason?"

"I'm not sure." While running through the forest today, I'd gone over and over it, trying to figure Morlet out. He healed me knowing the physical toll it would take on his body. There was only one reasonable explanation: to ensure my survival so he could kill me with the other Krigers.

"What sort of a man did you find Morlet to be?" Anders asked.

The king was a man of contradictions. Nice one minute, evil the next. I didn't know how to answer.

Anders peered into my eyes. "Be careful," he said. "Morlet is a conniving man. Don't be fooled by an act of kindness. I'm sure it was simply a means to an end—serving only to further his agenda, not yours."

He was right. Even though my heart felt torn, I needed to be logical about this and not let my emotions get in the way of common sense. I'd made that mistake once; it wouldn't happen again.

\*\*\*

Taking another bite of cooked rabbit meat, my temper got the better of me. "There better be something hanging from my chin,"

I snapped. Because having Anders and Vidar sit there watching me like I was about to explode was annoying.

"I'm just nervous for you, that's all," Vidar said, exasperated.

"Staring at me is not helping."

Anders shook his head, grinning at my outburst while Vidar stood and started pacing. Thankfully, there hadn't been any more talk about getting married. For now, I was going to pretend the conversation didn't happen.

"The other Krigers never talked about what they encountered in there," Vidar said.

"I'd rather not know." Either I was worthy of being a Kriger, or I wasn't. Knowing the challenges ahead of time wouldn't help.

"What if something bad happens?" Vidar squatted before me, pursing his lips.

"She'll be fine," Anders insisted, speaking for the first time since our conversation last night.

"Plenty has happened to me, and I've managed to survive," I assured Vidar. "This will be no different."

He reached for my hand, so I jumped up, pretending not to notice. Normally, I wouldn't have minded. If anything, it would have been welcome. However, knowing he thought we were supposed to marry—even though we didn't care for one another that way—I didn't want to encourage him or show I agreed in any way.

"Do I need to take anything?" I asked Anders, swinging my arms and stretching.

"No. Just go through that archway. With any luck, you'll be back in a few hours." He smiled encouragingly at me. The simple gesture stirred something inside me that I didn't recognize or understand.

"Okay," I said, pushing my hair behind my ears. "I'm ready."

"Good luck." Vidar forced a grin on his face. He had waited so long for this moment. Once I had my weapon, the Order of the Krigers could rise.

Turning to Anders I asked, "Any last instructions?"

"Trust your instincts and you'll do fine. Now get going— we have a kingdom to save." His eyes were bright, shining with excitement. I couldn't help but smile.

Walking into the dark tunnel, unable to see, I stuck my hands out before me to make sure I didn't smack into a rocky wall. After a dozen feet, a soft glow emanated ahead of me. Nearing the light, it got brighter and morphed into a ball, floating in front of me. The center of it was white, the outer portion a soft blue. The ball rose above me and then circled my body before drifting down the corridor.

I followed it, knowing it was leading me to my first challenge. The floor abruptly ended. The ball of light zoomed down thirty feet, hovering above a pool of green water. The light glowed brighter, beckoning me. What if the water was too shallow? Perhaps my courage was being tested. Steeling my resolve, I took a big breath and jumped. Falling through air, my stomach did a somersault before I crashed into the frigid water.

Kicking, I rose to the surface, relieved.

The light circled above me and then plunged into the water. Not wanting to overthink it, I took a deep breath and went under, following the ball as it sank lower and lower. Then it shot into an underwater tunnel. Swimming as fast as possible, I followed it. Leaving the tunnel, it bolted upwards.

I broke the surface and gasped for air, my heart beating wildly. The light flew to the shoreline and disappeared. I swam over, my arms weak and shaking, and climbed out of the water. This was a small cavern. The walls glowed a soft gold, giving the illusion of sunlight. Lying on the ground, I basked in the warmth. Had I passed my first challenge?

The ground beneath me rumbled as part of the rocky wall slid open. Scrambling to my feet, I tentatively headed over and peered inside. It was a room filled with half a dozen *soldats*. My father was kneeling in the center of the room, a sword pointed at his neck.

"Kaia!" my father yelled. "Get out of here!"

I ran straight for the man who held the sword to my father. He prepared to strike me, so I slid on the ground, ramming my feet into his shins. He fell backward, his head hitting the ground. I rolled and reached for his dropped sword, springing to my feet. Another *soldat* lunged at me, and I swung the sword up, blocking his strike. When he came at me again, I grabbed his shoulders and thrust my knee into his groin. He fell to the ground.

My father engaged two men in combat. Another one came up behind me and wrapped his arms around my torso. I flung my head back, banging his face. He released me, and I spun around, punching him. He dropped to the ground. Another one came at me and I ducked, missing his blow. Flipping my sword around, I flung the hilt toward the man's head, rendering him unconscious. My father managed to knock the remaining two men out.

There were six men on the ground—not a single one dead. My heart pounded and adrenaline coursed through me. As I turned to my father, his body vanished, and the blue light appeared in his place. Had that been my challenge? It felt real, even if it wasn't entirely logical that *soldats* would have been here with my father.

The light moved to the opposite wall, and the rocks parted, revealing yet another room. Keeping a firm grip on the hilt of my sword, I followed the light, wondering what was next. The blue light disappeared, and the entire room glowed pinkish red. The room contained twelve alcoves, eleven of them empty. My eyes landed on the twelfth one where my bo staff rested. Mesmerized, I moved toward it.

A laugh echoed behind me. "You'll never get it," Morlet said. I spun around to face him.

"Surprised to see me?" he asked. "I always show up for this part of the trials." He pushed his hood back and folded his arms, intently watching me.

He couldn't be real. He had to be a figment of my imagination, like my father in my last challenge. "What do I have to do? Kill you?" I gripped the hilt, ready to wield the sword if necessary.

"Yes," he murmured, "if you can."

"Put your hood back on." He needed to look like Morlet, not a normal person.

He shook his head, his blue eyes sparkling with amusement. "You have to look me in the eyes when you stab me in the heart."

Beads of sweat covered my forehead. He made no indication he was going to defend himself as I neared. "Do you plan on using magic?"

He shook his head. Raising the sword, I prepared to strike.

"Kill me," Morlet said, his voice gentle, almost pleading.

I swung the sword toward him; he didn't block me. I pulled back at the last second, barely missing him.

A smile spread across his face. "Can't do it?"

I lowered the sword. "I want to. Especially after all you've done. You've killed innocent people, you tortured me. You deserve to die."

"But I also healed you." He took a step toward me.

"Only to keep me alive so you can kill me when it benefits you."

"Is that what you think?"

"It's the only reason that makes sense."

"You should kill me because when I get the chance, I won't hesitate to take your life. There is nothing worth saving nor is there anything redeeming about me."

"I think there is," I whispered. At least a sliver of who he used to be before Skog Heks's evil magic consumed him. If only there was a way to help him, to save that part of him, instead of killing him.

"My dear Kaia." He removed his cape, the black fabric puddling on the ground around his feet like water. He reached out to me, resting his palm on my chest, directly over my heart. "Never change."

His face contorted in pain as his body turned into smoke, melting into thin air. I dropped the sword, and it clanged to the ground.

What had just happened? Had I failed the challenge since I couldn't kill him? The blue light reappeared in front of me. It slowly drifted over to the bo staff. Before I could get too close to my weapon, the light darted away and went to the wall on my right.

A wooden door slowly opened, revealing yet another room. The light went inside, so I followed. Stepping through the archway, an elderly woman was sitting on a rocking chair, mashing leaves in a bowl with the handle of a wooden spoon. This was Grei Heks's hut.

She looked up at me. "Hello, dear. Have a seat." She pointed to the chair at the table.

I sat down. "I failed." My shoulders slumped forward. She kept mashing the leaves, not answering. "I'm not well suited to being a Kriger, seeing as how the one thing Krigers are supposed to do is the one thing I can't."

Grei Heks put the bowl aside and looked at me. "My dear child, you did not fail."

"I didn't?"

"No."

"But I didn't kill him."

Grei Heks slowly stood and walked over to me, placing her hand on my shoulder. "The only way to regain balance is with Morlet's death. I sense your feelings are torn on the matter. I'm sorry—it wasn't supposed to be like this. I had envisioned another way, a better way. But Skog Heks destroyed her and changed everything."

"I don't understand."

She pulled me up, and we headed toward the other room, our arms linked together.

"You don't need to worry about Morlet right now. Nothing can be changed. The spell is cast, the curse is underway." We stood in front of my bo staff. "All the other Krigers have a small seedling of *Heks* power deep within them. When a Kriger dies, the seed moves on to the next male human child born so that there are always eleven Krigers. The only way for each of them to access their power is with their individual weapon."

"Is it magical?"

"It is infused with *Heks* power. It only works with the right Kriger. You're different. The *Heks* power inside of you is stronger. None of the other Krigers can use their power without their weapon like you can." She pointed to my bo staff. "Yours is also more powerful than the others. Before you can even think of going up against Morlet, you must learn to control both so they do not control you."

My bo staff was made from a beautiful, dark red wood. I reached out and took hold of it. It was taller than me by about a fist and felt perfectly balanced between my hands. Toward the top, there was a strange marking.

"That means *choice*. All of them have a different saying engraved on them."

"Did you create them?" I asked.

"Yes. Once things fell out of balance, my magic increased so I could cast spells in order to undo the evil done."

I slid my hands up and down the smooth wood. Power pulsed through it, and my hands tingled with energy.

"You must go," Grei Heks said. "You have much to do."

"Thank you," I said, wrapping her in a hug.

She placed her soft hands on my arms. "You are the twelfth Kriger for a reason. You passed the trials not only because you showed compassion where it was due, but also because you thought for yourself. You didn't fight or kill blindly."

"When we kill Morlet and the evil magic returns to Skog Heks, will everything be as it should?"

"Skog Heks's power won't return to her. It will die with Morlet."

"Won't the kingdom be out of balance?"

She smiled, the look grim instead of happy. "The spell I cast all those years ago ensures that once Morlet dies, both Skog Heks and I die as well."

"Why?" And how was that even possible?

She kissed my forehead. "Some things you are not meant to understand. But know this: you are special, and I expect great things to come from you."

Overwhelmed, I had no idea how to respond. She motioned for me to leave the room. She waved goodbye and the door slid shut.

There had been so much more that I wanted to ask her, that

I wanted to say. Her words echoed in my mind: *You are special, and I expect great things from you.* Holding my bo staff, a sense of calm spread over me. This was my destiny, and I would end the reign of terror and save Nelebek.

The blue light appeared before me. Instead of going into the water as I feared it would, the light went over to the other side of the cavern, revealing a wooden ladder built onto the side of the rocky wall. The light shot upward, so I started climbing. My arms and legs felt like mush, but I kept at it until I reached the top, coming to a small room.

The light disappeared, and a door opened, leading to Anders and Vidar who were sitting in the cave waiting for me. I entered, and both men glanced up. Relief washed over Vidar's face, and a slow smile spread across Anders's.

"Congratulations," Anders said. "You did it."

"Was there ever any doubt?" I asked.

"Never."

# Chapter Eighteen

"Spread your feet shoulder width apart," Anders instructed.

I huffed, annoyed that he insisted on telling me what to do. My father had trained me to fight since the day I could walk. If Anders bothered to look at my feet, he'd see they were already in the correct position, my weight balanced. It was insulting he thought otherwise. Gripping the bo staff with both hands, I felt the smooth wood hum with power.

"You feel it, don't you?" he asked.

"Yes." I held the weapon parallel to the ground while a subtle vibration pulsed through it. "It's amazing."

"From what the other Krigers have told me, the trick is to send your will or desire to the weapon, and that in turn will unleash its power." Anders stood before me holding a long, thin tree branch about his height. "I've never seen a Kriger use the bo staff before, but I imagine the power can be unleashed from either end." He angled the tip of his branch toward my torso,

showing me what he meant. "So then the power would hit you." I imitated him and he jumped back. "Don't point that thing at me!" he yelled. "You don't know how to control it yet."

I'd been able to use my hands to wield my power; the bo staff couldn't be that different. "I'm not willing it to do anything right now, so you don't need to worry." It quivered, and then blue light shot out of both ends, startling me. The tree to my right burst into flames while a boulder to my left exploded, sending thousands of rocks raining down. "Oops." I held the weapon still, shocked at the sheer power it had just produced. It was like nothing I'd ever experienced before. "Didn't mean for that to happen."

Anders stuck his head out from behind the trunk of a nearby tree. "All clear?" I nodded. He slowly came around and observed the damage. "So, as I was saying—"

"I need to learn to control the power in it."

He folded his arms and looked pointedly at me. "Yes. Others have found it helpful to learn how to use the weapon first, and then channel the power afterward."

"Yes, I think that's a wise idea." I tried not to laugh at Anders's stern expression as he stood between the rocky rubble and the blackened tree.

"I was trained to use many weapons, including this one." He gingerly took it from me and placed it on the ground. "Let's go over some basics. You should use a long stick until you're ready to harness your power."

After finding a fairly straight tree branch on the ground that was approximately my height and one inch in diameter, I stood next to Anders, ready to work.

"This suits you well," he began. "Since you're small, it allows you to attack your enemy without getting too close." He grabbed another branch from the ground and broke it in half, holding one of the pieces before him like a sword.

Taking a deep breath, I pretended he was a *soldat* from the King's Army. When he raised his sword to strike, I angled the branch upward, blocking him.

"Excellent," Anders said. "See how much room we have between us? Use that to your advantage." He attempted to hit me from the side. I spun the branch, blocked his sword, and then turned one of the ends toward his chest. The branch was unbelievably fast and easy to control.

"When you have it in that position," he said, "thrust it here." He snatched the end and shoved it against the top portion of his stomach. I nodded, understanding that there was no reason to kill the guards with magic—they just needed to be rendered unconscious.

"If someone comes up behind you," he said, moving around to my back, "you have a few options." Something sharp poked me. "Pretend I have a dagger."

Instinctively, I twisted to my left, dropping the branch while locking my left arm around his arm. With my right hand, I punched him, slammed my elbow into his face, and then pulled his body down, ramming my knee into him.

"Good job," Anders squeaked, trying to right himself and catch his breath. "Do you always practice with so much enthusiasm?"

"Usually more." When I sparred with my father, I struck with much more force.

"Your bo staff is unfortunately on the ground. Someone could grab it, and then where would you be?"

He had a valid point. Anders motioned for me to pick it up and turn around. "This time," he said from behind me, "use your weapon."

After I picked it up, his warm hands clutched my arms, just above my elbows, startling me. Since he was so close, I wasn't sure how to disarm him.

"Pull it in vertically, next to your body," his gruff voice spoke near my ear, sending chills down my spine. I did as he said. "Good. Now you'll want to be quick so you have the element of surprise." His deft hands slid up my arms to my shoulders, and he turned me around so we were face-to-face.

I blinked several times, surprised by the nearness of him.

"Angle it back, and jab me in the face."

I angled it on the side of my body, and then pretended to ram the end into his chin. We stood there for a minute, staring at each other, neither one of us speaking.

Anders abruptly took a step back. "Excellent job," he said. "You catch on quick." He retrieved a longer stick from the ground. "Let's go over some basic forms."

We spent the rest of the day working on various ways to hold the bo staff, how to strike an opponent in order to cause the most damage, and thrusting techniques. He also showed me blocks, parrying, deflecting, and sweeping. By the time we'd gone over everything, my muscles ached, and the sky had already turned dark.

Anders told me I had three days to train. Then we were going to free the Krigers.

***

Early the next morning, I woke up before Anders and Vidar. Excited to work with my weapon again, I left the cave and climbed down the mountain to the forest floor. I breathed in the heady smell of the pine trees and listened to the sound of birds singing as the wind rushed through the leaves. I loved it out here and found the forest preferable to the overcrowded capital.

Grabbing the long stick from yesterday, I started going over the moves Anders had taught me. I closed my eyes, imagining it was an extension of my arms, and went through the various forms a couple of times. Comfortable with the movements, I started speeding them up, going faster and faster, the stick whipping through the air.

"Morlet should be scared," Vidar said. "You look deadly—and that's only a twig. Imagine what you'll be like with your actual bo staff."

I finished the form and held the branch still, not even winded. "Where's Anders?"

"He'll be here in a minute." Vidar twirled a pine needle between his fingers. "If you want, I can teach you to control the weapon's magic."

I glanced at the charred tree. "I'm not quite ready for that yet."

He threw the pine needle on the ground. "Of course you are." He took my hand and led me over to a boulder where he ordered me to sit. "I've worked with all the Krigers," he bragged, standing before me with my stick. "You should be able to feel you power humming through it. The key is using that power effectively." He pretended to parry a blow and then pointed the stick at his imaginary attacker. "In this case, you could wound or kill, depending upon the amount of power you release."

"How do I know how much that is?"

"With practice you'll get it." Vidar sat next to me on the boulder, still holding the stick. "You probably noticed the marking at the tip." I nodded, recalling Grei Heks telling me it meant *choice*.

"When you're with the other Krigers fighting Morlet and your powers connect to one another, somehow that will play a factor."

"What are the other markings?"

"Unity, direction, leadership, and strength—to name a few." What choice would I encounter during the fight? Would it be the ability to kill Morlet when the time came?

"Have you given any thought to my proposal?" Vidar fidgeted with the stick.

"No," I admitted. "All of my time and energy is focused on rescuing the Krigers and defeating Morlet. Everything else can wait."

"But Grei Heks said that all will be lost if we don't produce an offspring."

"Can we at least rescue the Krigers first? Once that's done, I'll consider it."

He drummed the stick against the side of the rock. "Very few are lucky enough to marry for love. Marriages are political alliances, insurance policies, or money driven." He threw the stick on the ground. "I want to end the curse and free Nelebek. I won't take any chances of something going wrong."

"I get that. But you must understand that I've only thought of you as a friend and not in any other capacity."

A small smile spread across his face. "Is the thought of marrying me really so unappealing to you?"

"That's not it. If Grei Heks says it will happen, then won't it happen naturally?" Although, I couldn't see our friendship developing into something more.

Vidar laughed, the sound bitter. "Kaia, there is nothing natural about the life I've lived for the past hundred years. No one is going to alter the course of my life again. I'm going to make sure things happen the way they're supposed to from here on out. If that means we have to marry and have a child, so be it." He stood and stormed away.

When I first discovered I was a Kriger, deep inside of me it felt right, as if a missing piece of my life was finally in place. The idea of marrying Vidar seemed as if I was falling over a cliff to a jagged, rocky valley below.

\*\*\*

The rest of the morning, Anders and I practiced various moves. After a midday meal, we sparred with one another until I was comfortable using the bo staff in a fight. By changing my grip, I could tailor it for use in either close quarter or long-range combat. Before long, it felt like an extension of my limbs.

"You're ready," Anders said. "Tomorrow you'll focus on connecting your power to the bo staff's magic."

With any luck, the task would come to me as easily as using the weapon had. I didn't want to burn down half the forest in the process. Or worse, hurt someone.

"You need a break," Anders said. "Are you up for a little adventure? Or would you rather head back to the cave?"

"I could use a little fun." The idea of returning to the cave and facing Vidar wasn't very appealing right now.

"Follow me." We headed deeper into the forest, the trees becoming denser, blocking out the sunlight. The sound of pine needles swaying in the wind sounded all around us. After walking about half a mile, the trees abruptly ended, revealing a small lake. A fifteen-foot waterfall fed into it. The water flowed quickly, splashing through a narrow channel at the other end, dumping into a lake below.

Anders stripped off his leather vest, shoes, and socks while I did the same.

"Um," he awkwardly said, running a hand through his hair. "Would you mind if I removed my undershirt? I don't want to get it wet."

Oh. The water was clear, and he wouldn't be concealed. My body felt like it was suddenly next to a fire as heat coursed through me and my face turned red. The prospect of seeing him half-naked made me uneasy. If this were Vidar, would I feel the same way?

"Kaia?" he asked, waiting for my answer.

"No, I don't mind." I shouldn't mind, couldn't mind. This was Anders, an assassin, and Vidar's best friend.

In one swift motion, he pulled his shirt above his head, tossing it to the ground near his boots. He went to the edge of the water, and the sun glistened off his back, exposing crisscrossed lines that permanently scarred his body. A sick feeling emerged in the pit of my stomach.

He dove into the water, surfacing a minute later. "It's rather cold," he said. "Definitely not fed by a warm spring."

The image of his scars was seared into my mind. Did he get them from his years as a slave? Or when he trained to be an assassin? Or was it something else? I knew very little about him.

"Are you coming in? Or are you just going to stand there?" he asked.

I fidgeted with the end of my sleeve, shifting my body weight from foot to foot. "Turn around," I demanded. Anders raised his eyebrows and complied. I removed my pants and jumped in the chilly water.

"Can I look now?"

"Yes."

"What did you do?" he asked as he examined me. His eyes widened. "You don't have pants on."

"No." I went under the water again. It was utterly clear and several fish swam by. I resurfaced and said, "Pants are hard to swim in."

He shook his head, and then started swimming toward the shore.

"Where are you going?"

He grinned. "Wait and see." After climbing out of the water, he headed into the cover of the trees. A few minutes later, he appeared at the top of the waterfall. I waved to him, and he jumped, plunging under the water. A moment later, he came up with a huge smile plastered across his face. "You should try it."

It looked fun, but I didn't want to climb up there with my bare legs exposed.

Sensing my hesitation, Anders taunted me, "What? Kaia— the mighty Kriger—afraid of heights?"

"Oh, please. It's not that high."

"Then what's the problem?"

I bit my lip and glanced at my clothing sitting near the shore.

"You're worried because you don't have pants on?" I nodded. "Don't forget, we've already bedded and swum naked together." He winked.

Shock rolled through me—did Anders, the straight-laced assassin, just make a joke?

He laughed and swiped his arm on top of the water, splashing me in the face.

The episode at the brothel when he swatted my bottom, saying we'd just bedded, seemed like a lifetime ago. Same with the warm spring pool when we both swam utterly naked. I bit my bottom lip. Why was I so self-conscious now? Was it because back then we didn't know each other?

"Kaia," Anders gently said, swimming closer to me. "You have nothing to be ashamed of. We're friends." He placed his hand on my shoulder, sending a jolt of warmth through me.

*Friends.* I mulled over that word, not quite sure how I felt about it. Well, since he only considered me a friend, then there was nothing to be embarrassed about. Taking a big breath, I swam to the bank and pulled myself out of the water.

After making sure my shirt covered my undergarments, I headed up the rise to the lake above and climbed in. The bottom was coated with slippery moss-covered rocks, so walking across them was slow going. At the top of the waterfall, there were several large boulders. I climbed on the one with the flattest surface.

Standing tall, the sun warmed my face, and the gentle wind caressed my skin. Freedom, peace, and contentment filled me.

"Jump!" Anders yelled.

I counted to three and jumped, my body falling through air and plummeting under the water. I swam to the surface. Anders's warm, brown eyes were staring expectantly at me.

"You were right," I said. "That was fun." When was the last time I'd done something simply for the sake of enjoyment?

"Let's do it together."

"We should probably get back to the cave soon." I didn't want to have to climb up the mountain at night.

He got out of the water and stood, waiting for me. "This is the last jump, and then we'll head back so you can rest. Tomorrow you'll be harnessing your power, and that will take a lot of energy."

Trying not to stare at his bare torso, I climbed out of the water. Anders led the way up the rise. I pulled my undershirt down and held my arms in front of me to ensure nothing could be seen through the thin, white fabric. We climbed into the smaller lake and made our way to the top of the waterfall.

We stood on the same boulder, side-by-side; our shoulders brushed. Anders was staring at me, his expression unreadable. The tips of his fingers touched the back of my hand, making me shiver. The setting sun shone behind him. His head leaned down ever so slightly.

And then he abruptly jerked back, blinking, as if suddenly realizing he'd been about to kiss me.

"Ready?" he asked, his voice gruff. I nodded, unable to speak. "On the count of three. One … two … three!" We jumped at the same time, diving into the water below.

When I surfaced, Anders was already afloat smiling at me. "Beat you." He splashed water at me, diffusing the tension between us.

"Only because you weigh more." I splashed water back at him, laughing.

"What are you two doing?" Vidar asked. He stood at the edge of the lake with his arms crossed, intently watching us. How long had he been there?

"We're taking a break," Anders answered. "Why don't you join us?"

Vidar turned his attention to me. "I came to see how you were faring. Only, I couldn't find you and feared you'd been kidnapped. Clearly, you're doing just fine." He turned to go.

I started swimming to the edge of the lake in order to run after Vidar so I could speak with him. However, Anders stopped me. "Let me talk to him."

"Are you certain?"

"We're best friends." He climbed out of the water, grabbed his clothes, and chased after Vidar.

I ducked under the water, trying to clear the memory of my almost kiss with Anders. A few minutes later, my body shook from the frigid water, so I got out and put my clothes on, slowly making my way up the mountain. At the flat area outside the cave's entrance, I paused and listened. Inside, Vidar and Anders were engaged in a heated discussion.

"You know I've proposed to her," Vidar said.

"I do," Anders answered.

"Then why were you in such a compromising situation with her?"

"We were practicing all day. I was sweaty, tired, and wanted to cool off. Nothing is going on between us. We're friends; that's all."

I sat on the ground and picked up a small rock, twirling it on my palm. Of course we were just friends. What else could we be? But … why did his words sting? Why did they feel so wrong? Why did I have tears in my eyes?

"You two looked like you were enjoying yourselves," Vidar said.

"We were. I think she finally feels comfortable around me. At least she doesn't look like she's afraid I'll kill her in her sleep anymore."

Vidar chuckled. After a few minutes of silence, he said, "I want you to keep your distance from her."

I dropped my rock. The sun had set, and the sky was turning dark.

"You and I have been friends for quite some time," Anders said. "Have I ever given you reason not to trust me?"

"No."

"You have my word. I will maintain an appropriate relationship with Kaia. You are my best friend, and I would never do anything to jeopardize that."

I lined up three rocks in a row, wondering why I didn't have any say in this conversation. After all, it was about me.

"I'm sorry," Vidar said. "I just want to make sure we do everything right. If that means I have to marry Kaia, so be it."

His words were like a kick to my stomach.

"Since Grei Heks said the two of you are destined to be together, then it must happen."

"I think I know why," Vidar admitted. "Morlet is in love with Kaia." Anders didn't respond. "She is the key to defeating him. If we can use those feelings against him, it might give us the advantage we need."

"I must be missing something," Anders said, his voice low and deadly. "Why would Morlet be in love with her? He captured her, tortured her, and nearly killed her."

"Trust me when I say he loves her."

"Did Grei Heks really say you and Kaia are destined to be together? Or did you make that up so you could use her against him?"

"Grei Heks told me I'm destined to be with her. It must be because of Morlet's feelings for her."

His reasoning didn't make any sense to me, but Anders wasn't questioning it. There was a long pause. I stood, about to enter when Anders spoke. "He can't possibly love her."

"I assure you, he does. And we will exploit that weakness."

Making noise so they'd hear me and stop talking, I walked into the cave, pretending I hadn't heard a word of their conversation.

\*\*\*

It felt as if a feather lightly brushed against my arms. I rolled over, hoping the sensation would go away. My head started to pound.

Was it too much to ask for a few hours of sleep?

"Something wrong?" Vidar mumbled from the other side of the dying fire.

"No."

He peered over at me. "Morlet is trying to find you, isn't he?" I nodded. "Come closer to the medallion."

I couldn't face Morlet right now. Usually, being in the same vicinity as the medallion was enough to protect me. Morlet must be using a tremendous amount of his magic to attempt to contact me. I placed my bedroll a couple feet away from Vidar. His hand shot out, and he pulled it right next to him.

"Vidar," I started to protest.

"Humor me," he replied. "I won't be able to sleep worrying about that monster trying to reach you. I don't want him anywhere near you—not even in a dream."

Anders was sound asleep. Lying down, I pulled the blankets over me and closed my eyes, thankful the closer proximity to the medallion was already working.

Vidar slid his arm around my torso, and I stiffened. "Humor me," he mumbled again, drifting back to sleep.

After a few minutes, I lifted his arm off me and scooted a couple of feet away, not wanting Anders to get the wrong idea when he woke up.

\*\*\*

Anders ducked behind a large boulder. "Okay," he yelled. "Pick up your weapon."

The beautiful bo staff rested on the ground waiting for me to use it. However, I didn't want to accidentally hurt someone. My father's words came back to me: *Fear—although real and valid—can only hold you back. Take all your fears and insecurities and lock them away. Focus on your strengths. You can, and you will, do this. All you have to do is believe.* Taking a deep breath, I picked it up and radiated calmness just as Anders had instructed.

"Are you okay?" he asked from behind the boulder.

"Yes."

"Good. Now go through your forms."

Pretending it was the stick I'd been practicing with, I started moving it, surprised at how strong and solid it was.

"Set anything on fire?" Anders hollered.

"Not yet." I twisted the bo staff over my head, brought it down, spun it on the side of me, and then crossed it over my body. "Why don't you come out from behind there?"

"I'll stay here for a little bit longer. Just keep running through your forms."

I rolled my eyes, but did as he said, knowing he was right. I crossed the weapon over my head and brought it down to a shoulder strike. When I finished the last form, Anders was standing right in front of me.

"Impressive," he said, folding his arms across his chest. "Now it's time to use your power."

Taking a deep breath, I waited for him to tell me what to do. He didn't say anything. "Well?"

"Well what?"

"How do I use my power without killing you or setting a tree on fire?"

He shrugged. "I don't know."

Didn't he want me to radiate calmness? Because right now, I wanted to punch him. "You don't know?" I said, taking a step toward him.

He raised his hands. "Take it easy." His eyes darted from me to my bo staff. "All I'm saying is that you need to do what you've been doing with your hands, except with the weapon. I think."

"If you don't know how to use its magic, then why are you even here?"

"Moral support." He smiled wryly.

I shook my head in disbelief. "How about I use you as a target?"

His smile vanished. "I'll take cover behind that boulder while you figure it out."

A wise decision. Once he was out of sight, I pointed at a small rock near my feet. Focusing on my inner power, I projected it out, through my hands, and to the bo staff. It began to vibrate. I imagined power shooting out of the end and hitting the rock. Instantly, a blue light burst out, obliterating the stone into a thousand pieces. The force threw me backward onto the ground.

Anders was immediately at my side. "Are you all right?"

"I think so." He pulled me to my feet. "That was a lot more powerful than I'd expected." I brushed the pine needles and dirt off my clothes.

"The key is learning to control the amount of power you release," Anders said. "Try it again, but think of the power in quantities and only allow a small thread out. Does that make sense?"

"Why didn't you say that before?" I muttered.

"No one has managed to do it the first time. Besides, I didn't realize someone so small could unleash so much power."

I whacked his arm. "Go hide again before I zap you."

Once he was out of sight, I did as he suggested and pulled my power through my hands and to my bo staff. When it responded,

I imagined a large bowl of grain, releasing only a tiny portion of it, and then I closed the bowl, keeping the remaining grain inside. Suddenly, the weapon felt contained, and I knew beyond a doubt it would do what I commanded. Not far away, there was a moss-covered rock the size of my foot. Aiming at it, I released a small tendril of power. The rock blasted into several pieces, but much gentler than before.

Anders peered out from behind the boulder. "Unbelievable," he said as he came over and patted me on my back. "I've never seen a Kriger do that so easily before."

"Watch this." I pointed to a single leaf hanging from a branch. Like before, I pushed a small amount of my power to the weapon, connecting to its magic. The leaf burst into flames and then died out, leaving nothing but white ashes.

Turning to Anders, I couldn't hide my smile. He stood there staring at me, his eyebrows pulled together. His reaction caught me off guard. "What?" I asked, my smile fading.

"Nothing. It's just that ... you're amazing." Before I had time to respond, he said, "Now that you can accurately strike an inanimate object, let's see how you perform in a combat situation."

Although I enjoyed sparring with him, I wasn't ready to do so with my bo staff. The last thing I wanted was to accidentally injure my friend. My hands started sweating when someone approached from behind.

"Ready for me?" Vidar asked.

"She is," Anders responded.

"Why is Vidar here?"

"He is wearing the medallion, so you can't harm him."

Vidar picked up a stick and casually stood in front of me with a wicked grin.

"Are you sure I won't hurt you?" I asked him.

"I'll feel a small sting or jolt, but that's all."

Anders moved to a nearby boulder and climbed on top where he sat watching us. Vidar started to circle me. "Let's see how well Anders trained you," he taunted. He swung the makeshift sword toward my feet, trying to knock me over.

I stepped back, swung my bo staff in his direction, and shot a wisp of magic out toward his stomach. Vidar doubled over.

"Are you okay?"

"I'm fine," he said, righting himself. "Just didn't expect you to get in a hit so quickly."

"You're sure it doesn't hurt?"

"It's only a small sting," he said. "My pride hurts more than my stomach."

I glanced over at Anders, who had a smug expression on his face.

Vidar came at me again, this time more aggressive. I parried his blows, trying to find a way to use my power on him. However, he never let me point either end at him. Running out of options, I pretended Vidar hurt my arm. I grabbed it as if in pain, crying out. The second he stopped his attack, I lifted my bo staff, pointed it straight at his thigh, and shot him with a jolt of power.

"I win."

Anders started laughing. "That was brilliant."

Vidar blinked. "What just happened?" he asked, looking down at his leg. "You weren't hurt?"

"No. I simply exposed your weakness."

"Apparently Anders taught you well," he huffed. "I don't think you need me."

Confidence swelled inside of me. Controlling the weapon and its power was exhilarating. However, if there was one thing my father drilled in me, it was that one could never train enough. "I'd like to keep practicing. After all, we leave tomorrow morning for the capital."

Vidar smiled. "Excellent. More opportunities for a sixteen-year-old girl to make me look incompetent."

Anders burst out laughing.

# Chapter Nineteen

"You have got to be kidding," I said, staring into the black hole.

"It'll be fine," Vidar assured me. He sat on the ground and slid his legs inside. "I'll be there to catch you. I promise." He dropped down and disappeared. "Ready!" he called up.

"I've gone in this way hundreds of times," Anders said. "We'll only be in the tunnel for two miles. It leads directly to the back end of the mines where we're meeting up with some men who are helping us."

We'd already been traveling all day, and night was quickly approaching. However, the forest seemed safer than the dark, rocky underground tunnels. "Can't we go in the same way we exited the capital last time? Through the loose blocks in the wall?"

"Let's go!" Vidar yelled up.

"This way is safer," Anders said. "Trust me."

I nodded and sat at the edge of the hole. Turning on my

stomach, I slid my legs down. Anders grabbed my wrists and lowered me until Vidar had hold of my ankles. When Anders released me, Vidar set me on the ground. After my bo staff was handed to me and Anders joined us, Vidar lit a small torch. Anders led the way through the narrow tunnel. He warned me when the ground raised, lowered, or veered one direction or the other. He'd traveled this route so many times, he had its nuances memorized.

Being belowground made me anxious, and my hands began to sweat. It was hard to relax and trust that everything would be okay. That the ground wouldn't cave in and crush us. That we wouldn't get lost. The sound of our footsteps echoed off the rocky walls along with my labored breathing.

After thirty minutes or so, we stopped. Anders went on ahead to let the others know we were there and to make sure it was safe for us to enter into the main section of the mines.

"Are you okay?" Vidar asked.

"I'm a bit nervous."

"Me too," he admitted. "But neither Anders nor I will let anything happen to you."

Little did he know, getting hurt or captured was the last thing on my mind. I was worried about running into Morlet while trying to free the Krigers. The tip of my bo staff was engraved with the marking *choice*. I had to remind myself over and over again that I was in charge of my future—it was my choice to be here, to free the Krigers, to face Morlet, and to kill. My life, my choice.

Yet, sometimes I felt trapped, as if there really wasn't a choice—at least, a good one. I didn't want to kill, but it was the only way to defeat Morlet and undo the terror he created. My choice was to save the kingdom of Nelebek, no matter what. The people deserved a better life, and it was in my power to give it to them.

Anders returned and motioned for us to follow him. The

tunnel curved and then opened to a cavern so large that neither the top nor the bottom was visible. Keeping close to the rocky wall, I inched my way along the narrow path etched into the side of it. Luckily, after twenty feet we went into another tunnel, which took us to a small cave-like room where a dozen men dressed as miners stood waiting for us.

No one spoke as the three of us were handed uniforms, which we put on over our clothes. The workers started leaving via a tunnel at the opposite end of the cave.

My bo staff stood out, since we were supposed to be miners and they never carried weapons. Vidar took it from me and slid it down the back of his shirt and down his pants, concealing it beneath his clothes. He raised his eyebrows at me, asking permission. I nodded; it was safer with him. We followed the workers, Vidar trying to walk as naturally as possible with a long stick against his leg and back.

When we started ascending, a *soldat* blocked our path. "Your group is working awfully late," he said.

"Yeah," one of the men responded. "But we're done for the day. Finally met our quota."

"You're the last group," the man replied. "Go ahead."

I kept my head down as we passed him and went up the steep incline toward the exit. The slope leveled out and fresh, cool air greeted us. When we walked out of the mines, it was almost dark out and close to curfew. We didn't have much time to seek shelter in order to avoid being arrested. The group quickly split up into smaller groups of two or three, everyone heading home for the night. *Soldats* stood on the street corners closely observing the citizens hurrying about. They were probably keeping an eye out for me, but they didn't expect I would be dressed in a mining uniform. Anders's plan was brilliant.

The three of us swiftly made our way along the streets, not talking. Anders stopped before a nondescript apartment building and opened the door. We went inside, down a dark hallway, and entered the last doorway on the right. It was an unfurnished, dimly lit room filled with a dozen men I didn't recognize.

Everyone's eyes immediately went to Vidar. He pulled my bo staff out from under his clothing and handed it to me. It felt good to have the wood between my hands again. He smiled and addressed everyone in the room. "Thank you for coming. It's going to be a long night of planning. First, allow me to introduce Kaia, the twelfth Kriger."

I nodded my head once, wondering who these men were.

"Please give me a moment, and then we'll begin." Vidar gingerly took my hand and led me to an adjacent room with a single cot and nothing else. He closed the door.

"What's going on?" I asked.

"The men out there are the leaders of our organization. We're here to plan the Krigers' rescue. Then they'll pass the information down the line. This is the most effective way since gathering in large numbers is dangerous."

Vidar pulled off his uniform, tossing it in the corner. I did the same.

"You can come out and listen to us, or you can use this time to rest for a few hours." He pointed to the bed. "It's up to you."

Exhaustion consumed me, but I wanted to hear what these men had to say. "I'll go with you."

We rejoined everyone, and Vidar took control of the meeting as if he'd done this a hundred times before. One man laid designs for the interior of the castle on the floor. Everyone gathered around the papers and started brainstorming ideas on how to sneak in and free the Krigers. Sitting on the outskirts, I watched as the men spoke passionately with one another.

Anders sat on the ground next to me, handing me a loaf of bread. "Sorry it's a little hard. It's all I have."

"Thank you." Leaning against the wall watching everyone, I yawned, trying to stay awake.

Anders's leg nudged mine. "How are you holding up?"

"I'm fine."

He studied me a moment before scooting closer and speaking in my ear. "Each of these men is in charge of a different section of the capital. Those two over there," he pointed to two guys who had beards and were warmly dressed, "are from nearby cities. They snuck in for this. When we're done, they'll send runners back to their hometowns to report and gather forces if necessary."

"You communicate with other cities in Nelebek?"

He nodded. "It's one of the main reasons Vidar and I live where we do. We are only a few days' journey to all the major cities in the kingdom."

"Are the two of you the leaders?"

Anders grinned. "Vidar is. Like I've said before, I'm bound to him."

"What does that mean?"

"That is a conversation for another time." He reached out and squeezed my hand, sending a smidgeon of warmth through me. I turned my head toward him, and my breath caught—our faces were mere inches apart. I'd never wished to kiss a man before. However, sitting here next to Anders, I wanted to kiss him. My face warmed, and I leaned forward. One little kiss wouldn't hurt … just the feel of his skin, his lips.

"What do you think, Kaia?" Vidar asked, making me jump. Several men turned and looked at me.

I hadn't heard a word that had been spoken in the past five

minutes. "I don't know. Please explain it one more time."

Vidar's eyes narrowed. I gave him my full attention, ignoring Anders and the expression of shock written across his face.

Vidar said, "We'll send in men here, here, and here." He pointed to the map. "Then you and Anders will enter through here." He pointed to another spot on the map. "The two of you will make your way to the dungeon while everyone else keeps the *soldats* distracted. Once the guards are neutralized, you'll use your power to break the magical ward keeping the Krigers there."

"What if Kaia is captured?" Anders asked, his voice low.

"Aren't you the one who's always telling me how strong and capable she is?"

"The plan sounds simple enough," I said, interrupting them. "Let's do it."

Anders stiffened beside me. "Are you certain?"

"You'll be there with me. What could possibly go wrong?"

***

"Kaia," Vidar said, gently shaking me awake.

"Where'd everyone go?" I sat up and looked around the empty room. My back was stiff from having slept on the hard floor.

"After finalizing plans, everyone left. It's just you and me." He pulled me to my feet.

"What about Anders?" I'd fallen asleep with my head on his shoulder and his arm wrapped around my lower back, holding me tightly against him.

"He has a few things to take care of before tonight."

"Is there time to practice?" I stretched my arms above my

head. My bo staff rested against the wall, calling me.

Vidar smiled, and his eyes sparkled with mischief.

"What is it?" I asked.

"Your father wants to see you before tonight."

I ran for the door. The thought of seeing Papa during this trip hadn't occurred to me.

"Wait," Vidar said, laughing. "You can't walk on the streets carrying a bo staff."

"I'm not leaving it here."

"Fine," he mumbled, taking it from me. "I'll put it under my shirt and pants like before." He slid it under his clothing.

"Thank you."

His finger tilted my chin up so I was forced to look into his eyes. "Do you not want to marry me because you have feelings for another man?"

My breath caught—he couldn't possibly think I was in love with someone else because that was preposterous.

"Kaia?"

"I'm only sixteen and not ready to marry."

"Are you refusing me?" he asked in disbelief. "Knowing that Grei Heks said all will be lost if our bloodlines aren't mixed to produce a child before Morlet is killed?"

"We need to focus on the Krigers right now."

His hand dropped from my face. When I was around Vidar and he pressured me about getting married, it felt wrong. It couldn't possibly be because I was developing feelings for another man, could it? Because if Grei Heks said Vidar and I were supposed to be together, then surely it would feel right—like using my bo staff did.

"Let's go," he muttered.

We left the apartment building, neither one of us speaking.

I kept my head down as we traveled from the south end of the capital to the western sector. Vidar led me to a gray four-story building. We entered and climbed two flights of stairs, went down a hall and into a small, musty room. Several beds were shoved haphazardly against the walls, a table stood in the middle of the room, and shelves filled with food and books took up the remaining wall space.

Situated in the corner of the room, my father was sitting on a chair. When he saw me, he slammed his book shut. I ran over and wrapped my arms around his neck.

He kissed my head and held me at arm's length. "You look good." He smiled. Vidar cleared his throat, and my father glanced at him. "It's good to see you, too. Thanks for taking care of my girl."

"It's my honor," Vidar replied as he removed my weapon from his clothing.

The three of us sat at the table. Papa reached his hand out, and I clasped it. Although faint, the wheezing was still there, and his skin had a sheen of sweat on it.

"How are you?" I asked. "Are you being well cared for here?"

He attempted a smile. "My dear, sweet girl," he muttered. "I just wanted to see you one last time. And here you are." His eyes filled with tears. "I'm sorry I won't be there to see the Krigers rise."

I shook my head, refusing to believe Papa was going to die. "You looked good the last time I saw you. What happened?" His pocket was bulging with a bloodstained handkerchief.

My father patted my hand, wheezing. "Although the medicine has helped, it's not a cure. My lungs are failing."

"I hate that working in the mines has done this to you." Anger and pain warred inside of me.

A ghost of a smile flitted across his face. "Please don't be sad."

Tears slid down my cheeks, dropping onto the table. "Don't leave me. I need you." My heart constricted as if someone were crushing it.

Papa's eyes darted to Vidar and then back to me. "I'm sorry I didn't tell you about being a Kriger sooner."

"You were just trying to keep me safe." I released his hand and wiped my cheeks.

"Your mother would be so proud of you. You've turned into such a beautiful, strong woman."

At a loss for words, I hugged Papa, resting my head on his chest, wishing we could stay like this forever.

"I have one request."

"Anything."

"End this," he said, wheezing. "Kill Morlet, and restore peace to Nelebek. You must save our family from this wretched curse."

"I promise."

He kissed the top of my head. "I know you can do it."

"If I could be so bold," Vidar said. "I know you're concerned about your daughter's future—especially since you won't be there to protect her." My father's jaw quivered at the truth of Vidar's words. "I have a solution. Give me your blessing to marry your daughter. I promise to take good care of her. She will want for nothing."

It felt as if I'd been punched in the stomach. My father was going to die—now was not the time for marriage proposals.

"This is a dream come true," Papa whispered. Another punch to my stomach. I looked at my father and saw the unspoken words in his eyes. He wanted this for me. "To know she'll be loved and taken care of." His smile softened the lines around his eyes as his body relaxed with relief.

"Do I have your blessing then?" Vidar asked.

"I would be honored to give my daughter to you, but she has no dowry, no money."

"Your daughter is more than enough."

"It is too good to be true," Papa said. "Then yes, you have my blessing." My father shook Vidar's hand.

"Thank you."

"It is I who should thank you," Papa said.

Balling my hands into fists, hurt filled me. I was a person, not a piece of property. Yet, seeing how happy this made my father, I couldn't deny him that. "Thank you, Papa." I forced a smile.

"We need to go," Vidar gently said.

"I'll be in the mines tonight to make sure you have a clear path to the dungeon," my father said.

"You should stay here and rest," I urged him.

He shook his head. "I will be there protecting you." There would be no changing his stubborn mind.

I stood and hugged Papa. "I love you."

"Be safe," he said.

I nodded and hurried out of the room, unable to look back.

Before leaving the apartment building, I stopped and glared at Vidar. "I can't believe you just did that."

"We'll talk about it later. Come on, we're going to be late."

"Where are we going?"

"A local tavern," he responded. "We're meeting some people there." He peered out at the main street. When it was clear, we exited and started walking. Vidar hunched over and leaned on the bo staff for support as if he were an elderly man.

"Aren't you going to hide my weapon?"

"It's my walking stick," he said. "When we arrive at the tavern, I can't very well sit with it under my clothes." He gave me a lopsided grin, and I wanted to hit him. He was far too chipper over the stunt he just pulled with my father.

"We're here," Vidar said as he shoved a wooden door open, and we stepped inside a dark tavern. The long, lacquered bar at the front, the round tables, and the scantily clad women were all familiar. Of course, it made sense we'd come to this tavern since there was an entrance to the underground tunnels here.

We went to a table at the back where Vidar nonchalantly slid my weapon on the ground next to my feet. A serving wench brought us two mugs of ale.

"I've been here before," I said, pulling my mug closer to me.

"You don't strike me as a tavern sort of girl."

I snorted. "I'm not. Anders brought me here before we escaped from the capital. This is where we bedded."

Vidar spit out his drink. "Where you *what?*" he shrieked.

I chuckled. "Didn't he tell you the story? That's how we managed to get past the *soldats*. We pretended I worked here as a harlot, and he was a patron."

Vidar cocked an eyebrow. "I don't picture either one of you pulling that off."

A young woman entered the tavern. Vidar turned his head, watching her glide across the room. She headed our way, tossing her blond hair over her shoulder and walking tall, exuding confidence. She appeared to be in her early twenties and wore a nice dress indicating she was from a merchant family. Her eyes briefly scanned me before resting on Vidar. He smiled, and she winked as she passed by, sitting at a nearby table.

"Do you know her?"

Vidar tore his eyes away from the beautiful girl. "Her father is one of the leaders," he softly replied. "She's meeting us here with two other men."

"Then why is she sitting over there?"

"So she doesn't draw attention to us."

I traced my finger along the top of my mug, not drinking any of the strong-smelling ale. I may not have had any experience courting or flirting, but that didn't mean I was blind. Vidar obviously had feelings for that girl. "Can we talk about that stunt you pulled with my father?"

"You mean our engagement?" His eyes strayed to the beautiful girl once more.

"Yes," I replied. "I'd like to speak to Grei Heks so she can sufficiently explain all of this to me."

"When I talked to her, she told me that your blood is tied to all of this. When I asked her to explain, she patted my cheek and said that love is fickle and makes us do crazy things. She told me that when all of this is said and done, your line will carry on with mine." He stared down at his full mug. "We don't have a choice. Now that we have your father's blessing, we're officially engaged."

He chugged his ale. "At first, I teased and flirted with you because I thought Anders liked you." He slammed the empty mug on the table. "I thought if I showed an interest in you, it would force him to act on his feelings. He's never taken notice of a woman before." He glanced over at the blond girl at the next table and then back to me. "If you are to be my wife, I don't want to see you with another man. I want our engagement announced. However, we can wait and have the ceremony after you've spoken with Grei Heks on the matter."

My father's face invaded my thoughts. He had looked so happy with the idea of Vidar marrying me. I folded my arms. "Fine. You can announce our engagement tomorrow. After we've rescued the Krigers." He opened his mouth to argue, but I held my hand up. "This is not negotiable."

He bit his lip. "No one argues with me like you do." I wrapped my hands around my mug, waiting for him to agree. He scratched the back of his neck. "Okay. We'll wait and announce it tomorrow."

Two men walked into the tavern. One sat down at our table, and the other sat with the blond girl.

"This is a friend," Vidar informed me. "He's here to tell us what's going on in the castle. The other man will help us navigate the tunnels. The girl will report to her father, so he can inform the others."

It felt as if everyone in the tavern was watching us. It had to be my imagination playing tricks on me. I kept thinking *soldats* would storm in at any moment and arrest us. I'd be taken before Morlet, tortured, and killed.

The man cleared his throat. "Reports indicate that the king hasn't left the castle," he said. "There are rumors he's sick. He has men scouring the capital for the last Kriger. Whoever captures her will be rewarded a bag of gold."

I knew Morlet wasn't sick—he was recovering from healing me.

Vidar's eyes narrowed. "Have patrols been going door-to-door?"

"No."

"Something's not right," he mumbled.

"I agree," the man said. "The king should be tearing the capital apart searching for her, and he's not."

"Regardless," Vidar said, leaning forward on his elbows, "we're still on for tonight."

"Very well," the man answered. "I'll give the word." He stood and left without saying goodbye.

"Interesting fellow," I commented.

"He obtains information quickly. He's an asset to our organization."

"Now what?"

"Follow me."

Reaching for my bo staff, I grabbed it and followed Vidar up a flight of stairs. The girl and the man she'd been sitting with casually trailed behind us. Vidar went into the room with the entrance to the underground tunnel. The man stood watch outside the door while the girl and I went in.

When the door closed, the girl asked, "The two of you are engaged?" She carefully pronounced each word, indicating she was cultured and well educated.

"We are," Vidar answered, giving no indication he was going to introduce me to her.

Shock flittered across the girl's face, but she quickly hid it. "My father said as soon as it's dark, he'll get men into position. No one will move until the signal is lit. If nothing happens by midnight, he'll call off his men."

"Excellent," Vidar said.

She pulled on knit gloves. "Anders said to tell you he'll meet you at the blacksmith's shop near the mines' entrance. Make sure the girl—I mean your fiancée—has her weapon." She briefly glanced at me. "And don't return to the original apartment."

The lines between Vidar's eyebrows deepened. "Has the room been discovered?"

"Anders saw *soldats* watching the place."

I don't know why, but the idea of Anders talking to this girl irked me. My hands tingled with power, so I loosened my grip on my bo staff, not wanting to accidentally hurt someone.

"Does he think our plans have been compromised?" Vidar asked.

"No," she responded. "I need to tell him you're on your way. Be careful, and good luck." With her chin raised in the air, she spun and left.

"Wait here," Vidar said to me while rushing out of the room after her.

Crossing my arms, I paced back and forth. How well did Anders know this girl? Were they friends? Vidar and the girl— whose name I still didn't know—were arguing on the other side of the door.

A sharp searing pain exploded in my head, and I tumbled to the ground, dropping my bo staff.

*"Kaia!" Morlet cried.*

I forced myself to remain in that room, so we didn't fully connect to one another. Pain swirled around in my head and extended down my body. I focused on the wooden floor beneath my palms, my vision blurring and my arms shaking.

*"You can't escape me," he purred. "I will have you. It's your destiny—you don't have a choice."*

"No! I have a choice," I ground out through gritted teeth.

"Kaia!" Vidar said, placing his hand on my back. The pain instantly disappeared. "I thought I was close enough for the medallion to protect you." He pulled me to a sitting position.

"I didn't fully connect with him."

"You're shaking," he said, hugging me.

I wrapped my arms around him, thankful for his presence.

"We need to get moving. We're on a tight timeline." He helped me stand.

I was anxious to be on our way in order to get my mind off Morlet because when he had yelled my name, his voice had been filled with utter desperation. I envisioned him on his knees, pleading for me to return to him. And sympathy was something I couldn't afford to feel toward the man I was going to kill.

# Chapter Twenty

Clutching my bo staff, I descended the ladder to the dark tunnel.

"The name's Askel," the guide said, lighting a torch. "If you must speak, whisper. Let's go."

I followed him, Vidar behind me. We walked in silence about a quarter of a mile before turning into another tunnel. The ceiling of this particular one felt lower, and it was rounded. The sides and ground were polished, smooth rock. This tunnel had to have been carved by water. We continued in silence. After a mile or so, we turned into yet another tunnel. The sides of this one had uneven chisel marks and it was more square-shaped, indicating it was manmade.

When we came to a ladder, Askel stopped. "This leads to the blacksmith's shop," he whispered. "The blacksmith told me he'd close early for us."

He placed his torch on the ground, then kicked dirt on the

flames. At the top of the ladder, he opened the square door an inch and peered out. Satisfied with what he saw, he threw the door open the rest of the way and climbed into the shop.

Vidar went up next, and I followed him. Pulling myself into the blacksmith's shop, I noticed my hands and bo staff were warmer than usual.

Glancing around, there was a brick fireplace with an anvil and a large metal bucket of water sitting next to it. The room was stuffy; the only light came from the roaring hearth.

"Where's the blacksmith?" I asked. No one answered.

A *soldat* emerged from the shadows behind Askel. I started to raise the end of my weapon when the man violently shoved a longsword into Askel's stomach. I screamed as he tossed him to the ground. Dark blood pooled around Askel's lifeless body.

"Just who I'm looking for," the man said. "There's a large bounty for you." He yanked his sword free.

Vidar stepped in front of me. "You won't touch her."

He laughed and swung his sword, just missing Vidar's chest. Vidar turned, grabbed a hammer sitting in a pile of unused tools, and swung toward his attacker.

I tried to focus in order to channel my power and wound the *soldat* without burning the entire building down or hurting Vidar. The man kicked Vidar's leg. Vidar gracefully twisted his body as he fell, clipping the man's thigh with the hammer. I aimed for the man's feet, wanting to render him unconscious and not kill him. I released a small sliver of power and he stumbled, falling over and clutching his leg. In one swift move, Vidar swung the hammer down, smashing the man's head. A bone-chilling crunch echoed through the shop.

I dropped to my knees, stunned. "You killed him." My bo staff hummed with power, responding to my anger. Taking a deep breath, I tried to calm myself down.

"This is war," Vidar said. "It's kill or be killed."

The door to the blacksmith shop clicked shut. "Where's the blacksmith?" Anders asked.

"Don't know," Vidar responded. "Most likely dead."

I scrambled to my feet. Anders wouldn't look at me. There was a coldness to him that made my skin prickle with fear. He hurried over to Askel and pulled his lifeless body into a dark corner, then he did the same with the *soldat*. Vidar helped him rearrange a few things to make sure the dead bodies were concealed.

"We're at war with Morlet—not his army," I said. Both Anders and Vidar turned to look at me. "That man was probably forced to work for the king. He could have been a father, like mine. You didn't have to kill him."

Vidar grabbed my arm, his eyes alight with rage. "Morlet is the king. He controls the army. You must understand that. I need to know that you're ready—that you can fight and kill if necessary. I won't risk other men's lives if you're not capable of doing this."

Staring into his blue eyes, I honestly didn't know. Could I kill another person?

"If you're not ready, we can postpone this," Vidar said. "However, you did promise your father you would end it."

The kingdom of Nelebek needed the Krigers. Morlet's tyrannical reign couldn't continue. "I can do it," I said, making my choice.

"Good," he said, releasing my arm. "I need to go. Anders will take you to the dungeon. I'll meet you there." He kissed my forehead and left.

"I have an idea," Anders said. "Give me a moment to prepare." He went to the corner where the dead bodies were hidden. When he disappeared from sight, I started pacing. The next time I faced a *soldat*, I'd have to act quicker. There was no reason to kill. I could knock him out instead. We'd be in such a hurry that Anders wouldn't be able to check if they were alive or not.

"Let's go," Anders said. He was wearing the dead *soldat's* uniform. We left the blacksmith's shop. Outside, the air was crisp and the sky quickly turning dark. "Use your bo staff as a walking stick," he instructed. "If anyone asks, I'm escorting you to the dungeon for questioning."

"Even though we're going the wrong direction?"

"Yes," he said, pulling the hat low on his head. "I'm just doing another round before I take you in."

He avoided looking at me. "Fine," I said as we headed toward the mines.

"Why did you agree to marry him?" Anders asked.

My shoulders stiffened. The girl from the brothel must have told him. I wanted to explain that I didn't want to marry Vidar, that I was only marrying him because my father wanted me to, and because Grei Heks said it was inevitable. Instead, I said, "Now is not the time."

We neared the end of the jam-packed apartment buildings and hid in the shadowy alcove of a doorway. The entrance to the mines was located approximately fifty yards away.

"Keep your weapon at your side, so it blends in with your body," Anders whispered in my ear. "I'm going to hold your arm like I'm escorting you."

"We're going to walk out in the open?" I asked, horrified. The land from here to the mines was flat and void of any structures. *Soldats* watching the area would easily see us.

"Yes," he replied. "It's the fastest way. Make sure you stay by my side."

Before I could respond, he took hold of my arm and dragged me from the doorway. We headed straight across the open land to the large, cave-like entrance of the mines dug into the side of a small hill. It was almost completely dark out except for a soft glow coming from the entrance.

Being so exposed made my skin crawl. At any moment, someone could scream that I was the Kriger Morlet sought. However, we reached the mines without incident.

"That was easy," I said as we neared the twenty-foot by fifteen-foot entrance. Several torches hung on the dark gray rocky walls. The floor sloped downward as we made our way into the mines.

The usual sounds of metal chiseling and men talking were absent. I held my bo staff before me, ready to use it. All the workers had gone home for the evening since the citywide curfew was in effect. However, my father had told me *soldats* were stationed near the entrance the entire night.

Anders glided alongside me without making a sound. His eyes roamed over every inch of the cave looking for trouble. I opened my mouth to speak, but he held a finger to his lips and froze. A second later, he shoved me into a crevice in the wall, shielding my body with his. He took my weapon and held it flat against me. The black uniform he wore blended in with the gray rocks.

"Someone's coming," he whispered in my ear. "Whatever you do, don't move."

Holding perfectly still, I tried to calm my breathing. My hands started to throb with pain, so I clenched them into fists, working through the awful burning sensation.

Anders grunted from my power. "Slide your left hand to your bo staff," he whispered.

I moved my hand between our bodies, and my fingers

immediately found the smooth wood of my weapon. The pain went away, and my body instantly relaxed.

Voices drifted toward us. Anders went rigid, and I did my best to stay still, curled between the rocky wall and him. Someone in the distance yelled, and the sound of boots pounded past us. After a few minutes, they faded away.

"We need to get into one of the smaller tunnels," Anders whispered. "We're too exposed here." He peeled away from me and stepped out of the crevice. He nodded for me to join him. "Stay close to the walls and move fast."

We ran deeper into the mines. When the ground flattened, we came to a circular area with half a dozen tunnels that jetted out. Anders picked one to the left and I followed, wondering if he knew where he was going since we didn't have Askel to guide us.

Torches hung every thirty feet, providing light. The last time we were in the mines, the tunnels had been pitch-black. The sound of boots faintly echoed around me. After a minute, the sound intensified. There weren't any places to hide.

Anders glanced at me. "Be prepared," he mouthed.

I nodded and clutched the bo staff with my sweaty hands, ready to face the *soldats*. Shadows of men carrying swords danced on the stone walls, growing larger the closer they came. Channeling the power from the core of my body, I forced it down my arms and to my weapon. It responded, humming with power. I envisioned a cup of water, planning to slowly pour a little bit out. If I could control the amount of power I unleashed, these men wouldn't die.

Lifting my bo staff, I held it before me, ready.

Six *soldats* came into view. The first dropped to the ground. The remaining men scrambled to unsheathe their swords. Four more collapsed. The last man standing turned to run. He couldn't be allowed to alert others. I was about to zap him when he, too, fell.

Anders lowered his blow dart. Each one of them had a dart sticking out of his neck. He squatted and retrieved his darts.

Six men lay unmoving on the ground. "Did you kill them?"

Anders paused a moment before answering, "Yes."

"How can you kill so many without remorse?" I tried to keep my voice low so others wouldn't hear me. "I was going to knock them out, but you didn't even let me try. Do you always go around killing for no reason?"

His face reddened, and his eyes narrowed making him look dark and furious. I took a step back, away from him, dropping my bo staff. He swiftly grabbed my neck, jerking me toward him. I shoved his chest, but his grip tightened. He lowered his forehead to mine, our noses brushing, the heat of his breath caressing my face.

"Let me go," I demanded.

"Not until you stop acting ridiculous."

"Did it ever occur to you that these men have families? They're doing what they have to in order to survive. They probably hate Morlet as much as you do."

"I know," Anders said. "You forget I've been around a lot longer than you have."

Our foreheads were still touching, and his skin was hot against mine. He infuriated me, and I wanted to clobber him.

"Is this what you think of me? That I'm a cold-hearted killer?" he demanded. "Is that why you agreed to marry Vidar?"

"What does Vidar have to do with this?"

He chuckled, the sound harsh. His lips moved to my ear. "I had to kill those *soldats* to protect you. If I didn't, when they woke up, they'd hunt you down," he whispered. "If you knew me, understood me, you'd know I detest killing." Anders released me and stormed away.

I ran after him. After several silent and uncomfortable moments, I asked, "Couldn't you have given them a stronger dose of medicine so they'd sleep longer? Allowing us to escape?"

"No," he replied in a clipped voice.

"Why?"

"The sleeping medicine only lasts an hour at most," he said. "That isn't enough time for us to rescue the Krigers and flee the castle." He sighed. "I don't kill for the fun of it. There is always a calculated reason."

I had tried numerous times to get him to open up to me, but he was always so withdrawn.

"This is war," he continued. "People—on both sides—are going to die tonight."

That was true—deaths were inevitable in war. However, I wished he didn't kill as a first line of defense. Yet, he hadn't killed out of hate or spite. He'd killed to protect me. Although I didn't like Anders's methods, we both wanted the same thing—to end Morlet's reign.

We came to another circular area where six tunnels jetted off. Anders motioned for me to follow him, and we headed into one of the dark ones where I bumped into him. His hands gripped my arms.

"Something is wrong," he whispered in my ear. We stood only five feet or so from the tunnel's entrance.

"What do you mean?"

"The tunnel we need to take to reach the dungeon is the only one lit. Morlet must know we're here."

"Do you want me to try and contact him?" I didn't want to

speak to Morlet, but I would do it to ensure our safety.

Anders's hands tightened. "No," he said. "That's not necessary."

"What are we going to do?"

"We're going to take the tunnel we need to. Stay behind me and be prepared to fight. I'll do my best to protect you."

We went back to the mouth of the tunnel and stayed there for a moment, watching the open area. Once Anders was certain it was safe, we headed into the only lit tunnel.

There was a rumble, and then dust floated from behind us. Anders jumped on top of me, pinning me to the ground. We stayed that way until the dirt settled.

"Was that an explosion?" I asked.

"They just blocked one of the ends to this tunnel."

The idea of being buried alive or trapped underground scared me more than facing Morlet did. "So we can't go back that way?"

He shook his head. "Which means we're walking into a trap." Anders rolled off me and pulled me to my feet. "We're going to have to fight for our lives," he said, still holding my hand.

Which meant I was going to have to kill.

"It's never an easy choice to make," Anders said, squeezing my hand and releasing it. "But you can do it."

My stomach felt queasy, and my arms shook. The bo staff warmed, sending a wave of soothing calmness through me.

Anders led the way and we continued on, listening for sounds of an ambush. When we came to an intersection, he pushed me against the wall while he peered at the three other tunnels. "If someone is going to attack us, it'll be here. I'll go first. Once I make it to the tunnel directly across, you go."

I wiped my sweaty palms on my pants and lifted my weapon, preparing to protect Anders when he made his way across to the other tunnel.

"Kaia," he said, his voice soft. "If anything happens to me, do whatever you can to save yourself."

"Nothing's going to happen," I insisted.

He stepped closer to me, almost touching. "I wish things were different," he whispered. "If only you weren't engaged to Vidar."

I was about to question him when he abruptly stepped back, unsheathed a pair of daggers, and exited the tunnel. Two arrows sailed directly toward his torso. He jumped to the side, and the arrows narrowly missed him. A dozen *soldats* stormed into the intersection with their swords drawn.

I raised my bo staff and released a sliver of power, hitting one of them in his stomach. He dropped to the ground. Leaping over him, I swung at another one, striking his head and knocking him out. Spinning my weapon on the palm of my hand above my head, I unleashed a bit of power, hitting several men at once. They fell to the ground. Anders threw his daggers into his two opponents' chests. They toppled over. Every single *soldat* lay unconscious or dead.

"Are you hurt?" Anders asked.

"No," I answered, gasping for air. My weapon warmed, and my breathing evened out as my strength replenished.

The corners of his mouth rose into a devious smile as he surveyed the damage. "You're a lethal little warrior."

During the fight, I hadn't even hesitated once; it was as if the bo staff and the power inside of me had guided me through it.

Voices echoed from one of the tunnels.

"Which way do we need to go?" I whispered.

Anders pointed to the tunnel that the voices were coming from. My heart sank. We were going to have to fight more men. The sound of marching resounded from the other tunnel. We were trapped.

"Ready yourself," Anders said as he raised his bloody daggers before him. "I'll need you to release enough power to strike down as many as you can right away—otherwise we won't stand a chance."

I lifted my weapon, pointing the end toward the tunnel with the voices. It hummed, ready to be used.

My father stormed out of the tunnel, his eyes wild. "Run!" he yelled. "The King's Army is down here searching for you. They have orders to kill anyone you're with and to take you alive." He coughed, blood splattering on the ground. "There are six men pursing me."

Anders wrapped his arm around my father, pulling him back into the dark tunnel. I ran over to help, but Papa shoved me away.

"Get out of there," he said, wheezing.

"We can't leave him," I cried as Anders dragged me to the intersection.

"The only way to save him is to fight." He clasped my shoulders, looking into my eyes. "Killing blows."

I nodded, and he released me.

Six *soldats* ran out of a tunnel. Anders turned and slashed one across the chest with his knife while throwing his second knife at another. I aimed my bo staff and unleashed a chunk of power, killing the remaining four at once. My arms started shaking.

Papa crawled into the intersection. "Kaia," he wheezed. "Get out of here. Don't risk your life for me."

"I can't leave you here," I cried, dropping to my knees and hugging him.

"Please," my father begged. "You are the only one who can end this. Rescue the Krigers, kill Morlet, and save Nelebek. Do it for me."

I shook my head, unable to leave him. The sound of boots marching down one of the tunnels was so loud, it was hard to hear my father speak.

"They're almost here," Anders said, his hands clutching his knives. "There's only one tunnel that's clear right now."

I stood, prepared to fight to save my father. We weren't leaving without him.

"I love you, Kaia," Papa said. "Know that I am doing this for you." He pulled out a dagger and plunged it into his chest.

"No!" Everything around me spun, and the air was knocked out of me. I collapsed on the ground.

Anders's strong hands grabbed my shoulders, steadying me.

My father looked at him. "Get my daughter out of here," he mumbled, blood dripping from the corner of his mouth. "Promise me you'll take care of her."

"I promise," Anders responded, his voice gruff. My father's eyes fluttered closed as the life drained from his body.

"Papa!" I shook him. He couldn't be dead. He just couldn't. "I love you. Please don't leave me here all alone. I need you."

Anders wrapped his arms around me, dragging me from my father's lifeless body and down the only empty tunnel. "I'm sorry," he said. "But we need to go."

*Soldats* stormed into the tunnel behind us in close pursuit.

"Please, Kaia," Anders said. "I need your help."

A dagger flew past my head, narrowly missing me. The man aimed a second knife. I lifted my bo staff, striking him with my power. There were at least a dozen men behind him. I wouldn't let them kill Anders. Raising my weapon at the ceiling, I released a bit of magic, hitting the rock and collapsing the tunnel between us and the *soldats*. Anders and I ran, trying to escape the dust and rubble.

When we were far enough away, I fell to the ground, unable to continue. The image of my father's dead body was seared into my mind. Anders knelt by my side, looking me over for injuries. Not finding any, he sat and gently rubbed my back.

"I'm sorry," he whispered. "I know how you feel, but I need you to get up. Those men will dig through the rubble in a matter of minutes. Don't let your father's sacrifice be for nothing."

The tears wouldn't stop. I felt as if someone had reached inside my chest and torn out my heart.

"You feel like you have nothing left," he continued. "That your life is over; that you'll never recover from this loss."

"How could you possibly know what this feels like?" I sobbed.

"When I was sold to the assassin, I didn't want to leave my family. So he bought them, lined them up, and one by one, slit their throats right in front of me, while I watched, tied to a post, unable to stop it from happening." His voice caught. "I live with the pain every day."

Anders's teary eyes revealed incomprehensible grief. Reaching up, I placed my hand on his cheek. The two of us were connected in a way I couldn't explain or understand, but I felt it in the depth of my soul. His strength radiated from him, pouring into me. He was right; my father's sacrifice couldn't be in vain. I had to shove the pain away. Once we defeated Morlet, I would allow myself to grieve. But for now, I had to be strong.

I stood.

"Are you ready?"

"I am. Thank you for everything."

"Of course," he said. "We need to put as much distance between them and us as possible."

We ran for a solid mile before stopping. Anders pulled me to the side and put my hand on the rungs of a ladder. I climbed to the top where I felt around for a latch and threw the door open, entering a dimly lit room, Anders right behind me.

We stood staring at one another, both breathing hard and covered with dirt. This man, who had once seemed cold and hard to me, now appeared steadfast, compassionate, and a piece of me was reflected in his eyes.

"What are we going to do now?" I asked, ignoring the desire to kiss him. My father's death was making me confused. It was making me feel things I shouldn't be feeling.

"I have a backup plan if you're up for it. Or, we can call this off and regroup."

Morlet was the reason Papa was dead. I wasn't going to sit around crying. It was time to end this. "I want to tear the king apart." Anger was easier to deal with than pain.

"In order to do that, you must free the Krigers. The edge of the capital is three blocks from here. We'll need to make our way there so I can observe the castle grounds to determine the state of things."

"Then let's get to it." If I saw Morlet tonight, I'd kill him. Gripping my bo staff, I was ready to face my destiny.

# Chapter Twenty-One

I hid in the shadows while Anders easily scaled the building. When he reached the top, he laid on the roof, observing the castle. After several minutes, he came back down and joined me.

"There are *soldats* on patrol," he whispered. "Fewer than usual. The grounds are dark, so it's feasible to avoid them."

"What exactly is this backup plan of yours?"

"That we go through the main gate and to the front door."

"What?" I asked in disbelief. "Do you want to be captured?"

Anders's eyes narrowed. "No, of course not. What I'm thinking is that the safest route is the one Morlet least expects."

I held the bo staff between my hands, squeezing it. Anders wanted to walk right in the front door. The idea seemed crazy, absurd, and maybe, just maybe, it would work. "Fine. We'll do it your way. You obviously have more experience with this sort of thing."

He rubbed his chin. "There's another part to this idea," he

said. "But you're not going to like it."

"What is it?" I asked.

"Do you trust me?" he countered.

"Yes," I replied without hesitating.

"Excellent. I'm taking you in as my prisoner."

\*\*\*

Crossing the bridge over the moat, at least a dozen men on top of the wall had their bows trained on me. "This is never going to work," I mumbled.

"Have a little faith," Anders whispered. "And remember the plan. You're responsible for stopping anyone who runs."

"Got it." Hanging my head low, I played the part of a dejected captive. My arms were behind my back making it appear my wrists were bound together.

"Who's there?" A *soldat* from the guardhouse next to the gate in the wall called out.

"Someone of interest," Anders said with a gruff voice. He was using my bo staff as a walking stick.

Two men approached. "Who is it?" the one on the right asked.

"The twelfth Kriger," Anders answered, pretending to be a member of the king's personal guard since he was dressed as one.

"I'll take the prisoner from here." He reached for me.

My hands itched to hit him, but I kept my arms behind my back. We couldn't do anything until the gate opened.

"I want my reward," Anders said, yanking me closer to him. "You're not taking her until I'm paid."

The man laughed. "How about we split the reward?"

Anders snarled. "In case you forgot, fool, I am one of the king's personal guards. Do not try my patience."

"Just let him in," the other one said. "I don't want to lose my head if the king hears about this."

"Fine." He raised his arm in the air and made a fist, signaling the *soldat* in the guardhouse. Metal groaned as chains lifted the spiked gate.

Anders shifted closer to me. "Remember to keep moving so no one has a clear shot at you."

Once the gate was raised, he slid the bo staff to my hands and put his blow dart to his lips.

I swung my weapon in an arc, releasing a wave of power and knocking out every single guard on top of the wall.

"Go!" Anders yelled.

I sprinted for the gate, knowing he had already blown darts into the *soldats* on the ground and in the guardhouse. Since there was no way of knowing what lay on the other side of the wall, I remained connected to my bo staff's power, ready to unleash it.

When I passed through the open gate, someone dived for my legs, knocking me down. I dropped my weapon and swung my legs around his head, flinging him to the side and pulling his arm. He screamed. I squeezed my thighs; his body went limp, passing out from a lack of oxygen. I let him go.

"Nice move," Anders said, wiping his forehead. An arrow sailed between us. He cursed. There had to be men in the watchtower at the top of the wall.

Swinging my bo staff in that direction, I released my power, hitting the stone corner and obliterating it. Rocks flew everywhere. Anders covered my body with his until it stopped. Three men armed with bows stood with their hands raised in the air on the now exposed tower. Freeing only a small tendril, I hit each of them. They fell over, hopefully unconscious and not dead.

"Well," Anders said. "That didn't go quite as smoothly as I had planned." Two dozen men now lay on the ground.

"Are we going to just leave them here?" I asked. "It's a bit conspicuous."

"If we had time to hide the bodies, we would. But after you blasted the watchtower open, our chances of being subtle are nonexistent."

I hadn't meant to blast the tower open—I'd simply wanted to protect Anders. "Let's go before more *soldats* arrive."

We ran toward the castle's front entrance. Since Morlet had his army searching for me in the tunnels, it wouldn't take them long to realize I wasn't there. Not only that, but he'd be able to sense my presence since I didn't have the protection of the medallion at the moment. We didn't have long to rescue the Krigers.

Nearing the castle's main entrance, I saw two sentries standing guard on either side of the large double doors. There were probably a few more on the rooftop. Anders pointed to me and then to the one on the right. He mouthed, "Go," and we sprinted. When I reached the sentry, his hand fumbled for the hilt of his sword. Before he could unsheathe it, I swung my weapon, hitting his head. He fell to the ground, and I jabbed my bo staff at his stomach, releasing a tiny bit of power. Anders had already struck the other sentry with a dart. He quickly pulled both unconscious men against the castle wall, out of sight from the guards above.

Slowly opening the door, we entered the great hall and stealthily made our way across the room. I kept waiting for someone to descend the grand staircase and stop us, but no one did. We headed down one of the hallways. The place was strangely void of servants and *soldats*. The torches hanging on the walls were dim. Anders led the way along several corridors that all looked the same. Dark, sterile, and void of life. The walls were confining, stifling, and I wanted to leave.

Turning a corner, Anders froze, and I bumped into him. The sound of chain mail clinking resonated off the plain, stone walls. He threw open the closest door and shoved me inside a dark room. After softly closing the door behind him, he lay on the ground, watching through the slit under the door. The thumping of boots marching on the ground neared.

My hands pulsed with pain, so I connected to my power, prepared to use it if we were discovered. Several shadows flickered by. I held my breath, afraid to move. After a few excruciating minutes, the hall quieted and Anders stood.

"That was a squad of twenty-five men," he whispered. "All of them armed and headed to the mines."

"How do you know that's where they're going?"

"Down this hallway, there's an entrance to the mines on the left." He opened the door and peered out. Waving me on, we tiptoed in the direction the men had just gone.

The hallway came to a T. Anders leaned down and whispered in my ear, "To the left is the entrance to the mines. To the right is the dungeon. Stay here."

Without waiting for me to respond, he went around the corner and out of sight. As I stood all alone, my heart hammered. I heard two grunts followed by a soft thump.

A moment later, Anders poked his head around the corner. "Come on."

To the left was a fifty-foot long hallway. At the end, a black iron door was propped open. We headed to the right. This corridor was about half that length. At the end, two sentries lay on the ground, not moving. Anders grabbed a ring of keys from one of them and unlocked the iron door, hoisting it open. An eerie, reddish light illuminated a steep staircase leading into the dungeon.

Anders pocketed the keys and went first down the narrow, stone steps. As I descended, the air turned stifling hot. Nearing the bottom, two *soldats* stood guard with their backs to us. Anders pointed to the one on the right. I raised my bo staff, hitting him with a jolt of power. He fell to the ground just as Anders shot the other one with a dart.

We stepped around them and entered a long corridor lined with cells. Locked inside were haggard men with long unkempt hair, torn clothing, and skin covered with black soot. The putrid smell of fecal matter permeated the air making me gag. Were these prisoners unjustly held? Or did they deserve to be here? Should we release them?

Anders was already at the end of the first corridor, motioning for me to hurry up. Not looking at any of the prisoners in the eyes, I jogged and caught up with him. We went down two empty corridors, the torches casting a blood-red glow.

We came to a stop. "Beyond this door is where the Krigers are located," Anders whispered.

My bo staff pulsed with an energy that radiated joy and excitement. Even if Anders hadn't told me, I still would have known the Krigers were there.

"The hallway is heavily guarded by large, burly men who have spent years working down here. They won't show you mercy or compassion—they'll rip your arms off without a thought. It's a small space, and we need to neutralize the *soldats* before reinforcements show up. I'll go in first, and you come in right after me. Don't be afraid to unleash your power."

"Okay, killing blows." I readjusted the bo staff in my hands, preparing to fight.

"Make sure your aim is true. I don't want one of the Krigers accidentally hurt." He unsheathed several knives and stretched his neck. "Are you ready?"

Panic swelled inside of me. What if they overpowered me? What if a Kriger died? What if something happened to Anders? My weapon warmed, and a sense of calm melted into me.

"Kaia," Anders gently said. "If I didn't think you could do this, I wouldn't take you in there."

"I'm ready." I connected to my power, and certainty filled me.

Anders nodded toward the door. I grasped the handle, took a deep breath, and swung it open. The hallway was narrow with cells along the right side. A dozen armed men turned to face us.

Anders started throwing knives faster than I thought possible.

Raising my bo staff, I aimed at the first *soldat*, freeing my power and not holding back. He burst into flames. Another one ran for me. I aimed at his chest and struck him. He disintegrated into thin air. A third man threw his sword at me. I shifted to the side and pointed my weapon at him, releasing my power. He fell to the ground and shriveled up.

All the *soldats* were neutralized.

"Excellent job," Anders said, wrapping his arms around me. "You're not injured, are you?"

"No. What about you?" There weren't any scratches or cuts visible.

"I'm fine," he said, bending to retrieve his knives.

In the cells, eleven wide-eyed men stood intently watching

me. They were just as decrepit as the other prisoners with unkempt facial hair, body odor, and torn clothing.

"Let me introduce all of you to Kaia," Anders said, "the final Kriger."

"If I hadn't seen her use that bo staff with my own eyes," one of the older men said, "I wouldn't believe it possible."

The others mumbled their assent.

Hot pain radiated though my hands, making me yelp. I gripped my weapon tighter, trying to alleviate the feeling. Anders's eyes widened at something behind me. His knuckles turned white as he clutched his knives, still red with fresh blood. I spun around.

Skog Heks closed the door, locking us inside.

"Stupid girl," she spat, waddling toward me. "Who do you think you are, coming into my home? Trying to steal my pets? It's time I kill you and end this nonsense."

Anders tried to push me out of the way, but I stood firm and blocked the hallway.

"You can't kill me," I said. "If you do, you won't get your magic back."

Her lips curled into a smile. "I've already waited a hundred years. What's a few more? Especially for the pleasure of tearing you apart." She grabbed my arm with her chunky hand, her nails digging into my flesh. "Torturing you wasn't enough? Had to come back for more?" Her hot breath assaulted my face.

A dart embedded into her neck. She swatted it away with her free hand as if it were a fly. "Your poison won't work on me, boy."

"Get out of the way, Kaia," Anders said.

I didn't want this evil, vile woman to touch him. *"Don't give fear a chance,"* my father's voice whispered in my ear. *"Attack it head-on."* Years of training kicked in and my hand came up, hitting her arm. She let go, and I took a step back. Her lips twisted, and she snarled an animal-like sound and jumped at me, wrapping her fingers around my neck and squeezing. I dropped my bo staff, brought my hands together between her arms, and then I shoved them outward, breaking her hold. I kicked her. She stumbled but remained upright.

"What happens if I kill you?" I asked, trying to catch my breath. With my weapon on the ground, my hands hurt, and I felt overly vulnerable.

She smiled revealing her pointy, brown teeth. "You can't kill me. I'm a *Heks*."

One of the Krigers laughed. "A *Heks* with no magic."

There was a reason it took all twelve Krigers to link together in order to kill Morlet since he was consumed with magic. But Skog Heks … she no longer had her magic. She darted forward, tugged my hair, and yanked me toward her. Placing her hands on either side of my head, she smiled, about to snap my neck. I punched her stomach, but she only laughed.

"Let me," Anders said, coming up behind her. "You need to free the Krigers."

He tossed my weapon at me while simultaneously flipping his dagger around and swinging the hilt at Skog Heks's head. She released me, and I caught my bo staff.

Dark blue blood dripped from the gash on Skog Heks's forehead. "Foolish, idiotic human," she spit. "I will kill you."

Anders crouched low, ready to attack.

Aside from Morlet or a *Heks*, I was the only one capable of removing the ward placed on the cells. As much as it pained me to do so, I turned my back on him and faced the weary Krigers. "Tell me what to do."

One of the younger men pointed at the bars. "The magical

enchantment is on the iron. You have to counteract it."

"You mean I have to release my power and hit the iron?"

"Precisely."

Realizing the implications, I rubbed the bo staff between my hands, calming my nerves. Each cell was only six feet by six feet. If I missed and hit the person inside, he'd die.

Anders made an odd noise and Skog Heks screamed. They were on the ground grappling, Anders on top, his hands covered with her oddly colored blood. "Focus, Kaia," he said, his voice deep with emotion.

"There's an empty cell at the end," one of the Krigers said, pointing down the hallway.

The twelfth cell—my cell. I ran to it and pointed my bo staff at the iron, allowing my power to connect with and flow from it. Blue light shot between the bars, striking the wall, sending rocks flying through the cell.

"Try again," Anders insisted, his voice strained. Skog Heks was now on top of him.

Moving closer to the cell, my legs shook as I wiped my sweaty palms on my pants. I took a deep breath and pointed at a single iron bar, this time only a few inches away. Concentrating on hitting only a small section, I released my power. A blue light flew from my weapon, striking the iron and causing all the bars to disappear.

"Yes!" I yelled. In the next cell, the Kriger moved to the right corner in case I missed.

Pointing the bo staff at an iron bar on the left, I released my power. It effortlessly flowed out and struck the bar. Again, they all disintegrated.

The Kriger rushed to me and kissed my head. "Thank the moons!" he cried.

Relieved, I went to the next cell, doing the same thing.

"Hurry," Anders said. He had Skog Heks in a headlock. Unsheathing a dagger from his waistband, he placed the tip against her throat.

Our eyes met for a moment.

Would there be any repercussions for killing her? Would it throw the balance of power off since she didn't have any magic?

Skog Heks reached up to push the dagger away. There was something shiny in her hand. She looked at me and smiled as she readjusted the knife so she could plunge it into Anders's side.

"No!" I screamed, aiming at her and releasing all my power. Her body flew against the wall and she slid to the ground with a dull thud, the knife still clutched in her hand. Dark blue blood trickled from her mouth. The Krigers cheered.

The evil witch was dead. What if I wasn't supposed to kill her? What if this changed everything?

Anders looked at me with wide eyes. "You saved my life."

"Now we're even." A wave of nausea rolled through me from using so much power. I held onto my bo staff; the feeling gradually passed.

The two freed Krigers rushed to Anders, patting him on his back in greeting like old friends.

"Kaia, free the remaining Krigers while we make sure no one else is coming."

I easily destroyed the remaining wards. Once the last Kriger limped out of his cell, we all stood there for a moment, staring at one another. This was the first time all twelve Krigers had ever been together. Even though I didn't know any of these men, there was a sense of familiarity to them.

"We need to leave," Anders said, standing near the door. "Follow me." He led us through several dark corridors to another section of the dungeon, stopping before a large iron door without a handle.

"There's a ward on it," he explained. "Can you disable it?"

"I'll try." Taking a deep breath, I aimed at the door, releasing a sliver of power so it wouldn't ricochet off the iron and harm someone. Nothing happened. I tried again, this time releasing more power. The door glowed soft blue for three seconds, and then turned black again.

Anders pushed on the door, but it didn't budge. "Maybe there's a handle hidden somewhere," he mumbled, feeling around the edges of the door.

"Stand back." Once again, I aimed for the door. I let my power freely flow to the bo staff. Light shot out of the end, hitting the door. It glowed bright blue, and then the entire door disappeared. The Krigers rushed inside.

My head became heavy, and my vision blurred. Fear crept through me—this could only mean one thing. "Morlet is trying to find me," I croaked.

"Hurry," he called to the Krigers. "The king knows she's here."

The eleven Krigers came out carrying their weapons. There was a longsword, crossbow, dagger, javelin, misericorde, pike, spear, ax, broadsword, seax, and a short bow. Each beautiful, gleaming, and polished—a stark contrast to the men holding them.

Anders led the way. I hoped we made it out of the dungeon before being attacked again. I wasn't sure any of us had the strength to fight right now. We traveled through several hallways before we reached a stairwell. The *soldats* we had previously incapacitated were still on the ground, unmoving.

"I'll go first," Anders aid. "Kaia, bring up the rear. Make sure no one falls behind."

Several of the men had difficulty climbing the steep stairs. One man stumbled, so I wrapped an arm around him, helping him up the steps. Anders stood at the top, waving everyone forward.

"Thank you," the Kriger said when we reached Anders. "I can walk on my own from here." He smiled kindly at me.

"Vidar is here," Anders said. "Let's go." We hurried down the hall, passing the Krigers, to where Vidar stood.

"You did it!" He hugged me. "And all of my friends are here, safe and sound." His smile lit up his face.

"Not yet," I said. "We still need to get everyone out of the castle. Many of the Krigers are weak or injured."

"We've cleared a tunnel," Vidar said. "I have a dozen men ready to help us get everyone to safety." He pointed to the open door Anders had said led to the mines and instructed the Krigers to enter. A staircase led downward into darkness.

"Is it secure?" I dreaded returning to the underground labyrinth and running into the King's Army.

"For the time being." Vidar instructed everyone to remain silent and at the bottom of the stairs, to enter the tunnel on the left. About half the Krigers had started to descend when pounding boots and voices neared from the adjacent hallway.

"Hurry!" Anders herded the remaining Krigers forward.

Men rushed in the hallway from behind us with their swords drawn. One sliced his sword down, nicking a Kriger who didn't move out of the way fast enough.

Vidar unsheathed his sword and charged toward the *soldats*, Anders next to him. Three Krigers hesitated, one reaching for the injured Kriger.

"Leave him!" I ordered. "Get yourselves out of here. I'll protect him." When a *soldat* neared me, I jabbed my bo staff at his stomach. He lifted his sword in order to hit my side, but I spun around and brought my elbow up, smashing his face. Another man jumped on me from behind. I fell forward onto my stomach. A second later, Anders yanked him off me. We couldn't let any of the *soldats* run for help, alert Morlet of the Krigers' escape, or follow the Krigers. If these two dozen men weren't neutralized soon, there was a high likelihood the three of us would die.

I raised my weapon and released a chunk of my power, hitting the remaining men at the same time. They were all blasted backward, crashing to the ground. I had no idea if they were alive or not. My arms started to shake.

"Why didn't you do that in the first place?" Vidar asked, wiping a trickle of blood from the corner of his mouth.

"Because she doesn't want to kill anyone unless she has to," Anders answered for me. Our eyes met for a moment.

"Well," Vidar responded, "if we encounter anyone else, please just do that so we don't have to fight. I'd rather not get a broken nose if I don't need to."

The Kriger who had been nicked slid to the ground, passing out. I gently pulled his shirt away from his side, revealing a deep wound and blood covering his torso.

"He's not going to make it," I said, glancing up at Anders and Vidar. Vidar grabbed his hair, about to scream. If the Kriger died, we'd have to wait eighteen years for another one to come into his power. I had no intention of waiting that long to kill Morlet. "I can heal him."

"It's too risky," Anders said, shaking his head.

"Do you even know how to heal someone else?" Vidar asked, kneeling next to me.

Morlet had healed me, so I had a vague notion of what to do.

A rebel came in through the door leading to the mines. "We have ten Krigers," he said, gasping for breath. "Where are the last two?"

Vidar went over to his man, speaking softly to him.

There wasn't much time. I closed my eyes and pulled on my own inner power. It immediately responded, begging to be released. I sent it to my fingertips and willed the power to enter the injured Kriger. Something warm slithered out of my body, leaving me cold. I envisioned the Kriger's skin closing and his wound healing. Darkness surrounded me, and I violently shook. How did I get my power to return to me? My head exploded with pain, and I lost consciousness.

# Chapter Twenty-Two

I opened my eyes. Anders was staring down at me, his hands gently holding either side of my face, my head resting on his lap.

"What happened?" I asked, my voice weak, vision blurry.

"You healed him," he said, his eyes glowing with pride.

"How long have I been like this?"

"Only about ten minutes."

"All the Krigers are safely in the tunnel," Vidar said from somewhere close by. "I sealed it up behind them."

"We're not going with them?" I asked.

Vidar came into my line of sight. "No. We're going to lure the *soldats* away from them. Too many of the Krigers are weak and injured to survive an encounter with the King's Army."

My arms and legs were numb. There was no way I'd be able to stand, let alone walk. How would I help lead everyone away from the Krigers?

Anders stood with me cradled in his arms. A tingling sensation radiated through the core of my body. "Morlet is searching for me."

Vidar took a step closer, and I reached out, touching the medallion. Calm poured over me like warm water.

"Here, you carry her." Anders handed me to Vidar and my fingers curled around the medallion. Anders picked up my bo staff, and we made our way down the hallway.

"As soon as you're feeling better," Vidar whispered, "we'll announce our presence and lead the *soldats* on a merry chase through the capital."

I was still weak and lethargic, but the dizziness and cold sensation were gradually improving. "How will we make our presence known?"

He chuckled. "We'll blow something up and allow Morlet to connect with you for a moment."

We reached the great hall and Vidar came to an abrupt halt. One lone figure strode across the room. When he saw us, he froze.

Morlet.

Dressed in his usual black cape, he looked from me to Vidar, and then back again. He slowly glided forward until we stood a mere ten feet apart. "I take it this is who has been helping you," he curtly said.

Vidar gently set me on my feet, and Anders slid my weapon to my hands. I clutched onto it for support.

"Kaia," Anders murmured, "I want you to run. We'll take care of him."

I shook my head, wanting to yell at them to run so I could deal with Morlet on my own, but they'd never listen. There was no way possible for Vidar and Anders to fight Morlet and survive.

I couldn't let them sacrifice their lives for mine. I was the one with the power and the one who had to face the king.

"Kaia," Anders said. "Go."

"No," I replied. "We stay together."

"Such hatred in your eyes," Morlet purred, taking a step closer.

"You tortured me." I took a step toward him. Both Anders and Vidar tensed. My bo staff hummed with intense power, begging to be unleashed on Morlet. The book about Krigers that Vidar had given me warned against such foolishness. I couldn't kill him on my own. His magic was far greater than mine. Yet, I had to find a way to get Anders and Vidar safely out of here.

Morlet reached his black gloved hands up, removing his hood. "Kaia," he whispered, his beautiful face twisted in agony. "What have you done?"

I prayed the Krigers were deep in the forest by now and the *soldats* wouldn't be able to catch up with them. "I had to set them free."

He shook his head, his blue eyes penetrating into mine. Our bodies linked together—his power flowing into me. Gut-wrenching emotions of complete loss and utter devastation bombarded me. I fell to my knees, willing the assault to stop.

"Kaia!" Anders screamed. "Don't look into his eyes!"

Morlet waved his hand and a blue glass-like dome went up around the two of us. Anders banged on the dome, unable to reach me.

"You killed Skog Heks," Morlet whispered, kneeling next to me and taking my free hand in his. "I can't return my power to her." He squeezed my hand. "I'm stuck with dark magic forever." His pleading eyes sought mine. "What am I to do? Now there's no chance of salvation. No hope."

"I'm sorry." His feelings of depression and self-loathing filled me, and I hunched over. His cold hand touched my cheek, and warmth filled my body as he gave me some of his magic.

Two strong hands yanked me away from him. Vidar lifted me and my bo staff, walking right out of the dome.

"Impossible," Morlet said. "How did you do that?"

Vidar set me on my feet next to Anders. "I'm only going to do this once," he said, "so pay attention." He removed the medallion and handed it to me.

Morlet's eyes widened, and his face drained of all color.

Vidar grabbed the medallion and put it back on. "This has been protecting me the entire time."

"I thought you died, *brother*."

"I escaped."

They were brothers? That didn't make any sense. Morlet had told me he was the prince and his parents—the king and queen—had been killed by someone Skog Heks hired. But … he had also told me that he had an older brother set to inherit everything. A brother who had been murdered, too. Was Vidar that brother? And if so, then Vidar was the rightful heir to the throne. How could he have kept this from me?

"You made a deal with Skog Heks for what? Power? Lust? You killed our parents! How could you do that?" Vidar's arms trembled with rage.

Morlet shook his head. "I saw your room!" he cried. "There was blood everywhere."

"Not mine. The assassin you hired couldn't kill me. After he murdered our parents, Grei Heks put a protection spell on me and instead, I escaped."

Morlet turned to Anders as if seeing him for the first time. "You killed them."

"I haven't aged either," Vidar continued, bringing Morlet's attention back to him. "I, too, am stuck until the evil you unleashed is gone."

*Soldats* barged into the room, surrounding us. The king replaced his hood and ordered them to hold their position. At least two dozen swords were pointed at us.

Anders slowly pulled me toward him. "Do you trust me?" he whispered.

I glanced sideways at him. He had killed the king and queen. He had known Vidar's identity and kept it a secret from me. He squeezed my arm, waiting for my answer. Uncertainty and sorrow filled his eyes. Against all common sense, I replied, "I trust you."

His face softened before going void of all emotion as he whipped out a dagger and placed it at my throat. His arm wrapped around my torso, my back to his stomach. "Morlet," he yelled, immediately gaining the king's attention. "You're going to let us walk out of here." The tip of the blade dug into my skin, drawing blood, and I cried out in pain. I didn't know how far he'd take this charade in order to free us.

"I'll allow the two of you to leave," Morlet said, pointing to Vidar and Anders. "But Kaia stays here with me."

"Kaia leaves with us, or she dies," Anders said.

"You'd kill her?" Morlet asked, cocking his head, revealing a portion of his face. "Knowing she's a Kriger?"

Anders shrugged. "If she dies, a new one will be born." He grabbed a chunk of my hair and yanked it. I screamed.

Morlet's face paled. "Don't hurt her," he snarled.

"Why do you care?" Anders spit. "You nearly killed her."

"You need her just as much as I do," Morlet said. "It seems we're at an impasse."

"Tell your men to stand down."

"If you don't hand over Kaia, I'll kill all three of you." Morlet folded his arms, awaiting Anders's next move.

Vidar nodded to Anders, who shifted his weight, preparing to fight.

"Wait!" I yelled. There was no way Anders and Vidar would survive Morlet's magic. "I'll go with you," I said to Morlet. "But you have to let them go."

"I won't leave you here with this monster," Anders said, holding me tightly.

Morlet smiled—he knew Anders had only been bluffing when he said he'd kill me.

"I'm sorry," Anders whispered.

Before I had time to react, Anders plunged the dagger into my stomach. Excruciating pain rippled through me as blood leaked out of my body. Anders held me upright in front of him. "If you want her to live," he said, "tell your *soldats* to stand down. She only has about three minutes until she takes her last breath."

Morlet shook with unsuppressed anger. "I'll kill you." His face darkened, and I feared he would use his magic on Anders.

Vidar took a step closer to me, but there was only so much the medallion could do. It would protect Vidar, but it wouldn't do a thing for Anders.

Anders put his lips close to my ear. "Do you have enough energy to use your bo staff?" he whispered. I nodded slightly. "When we leave, strike the castle above the doorway and collapse it so no one can pursue us."

He loudly said, "Vidar and I are going to walk out of here with Kaia. No one is going to follow. Otherwise, I'll gut her. After all, I'm just a ruthless assassin." He slowly moved backward toward the door, keeping me with him. "In exactly one minute, you can use your magic to heal her if you want her to live. If you don't, you can collect her corpse by the moat."

The room started to spin. I was going to die.

"Almost there," Anders whispered.

Morlet's eyes narrowed, watching us. "I wish I could say it was nice seeing you, brother," he said, his voice clipped. "But seeing as how you're leaving with Kaia half-dead, I think it's safe to say any love we once shared is long gone. You are now my enemy. As for you, assassin," Morlet snarled. "I will kill you. Even if it's the last thing I do. And Kaia, dear, you are *mine*."

"Okay, do it now," Anders said.

Using the last of my strength, I forced my power to my bo staff and unleashed it, striking the stones above the door, collapsing it.

Anders picked me up and started running. "Allow Morlet to connect to you."

I was so weak I couldn't even breathe.

"Kaia," Anders said, his voice pained. "Don't you dare die on me. Let Morlet help you."

He wouldn't help me—he hated me. I closed my eyes. This was the end.

*"I'm here," Morlet whispered. "Come to me."*

*I didn't have the strength to do anything. Darkness descended.*

*A powerful jolt shot through my body, and I gasped. "You're not going to die," Morlet said.*

*I opened my eyes and found myself lying on his bed. Like before, he sat next to me, his hands hovering above my stomach. Blue tendrils of light poured out of his fingertips and into me, healing my knife wound. Breathing became easier, and my strength returned.*

*Morlet mumbled something, and his power left my body, returning to him. He collapsed on the bed. I moved his hood off his face and ran my fingers through his thick, dark hair. He didn't say anything as he lay there heaving deep breaths, working through his exhaustion. In this state, he appeared kind and peaceful, a hint of the person he could be if things were different.*

*"Thank you," I whispered, even though he was forced to save me because of the stunt Anders pulled. It wasn't out of kindness but out of necessity.*

*My hands and arms started to dissolve—Vidar must be close by with the medallion. Morlet reached up to touch my face just as I disappeared.*

# Chapter Twenty-Three

My eyes fluttered open. I was lying on the ground in a small, dark room. Vidar lingered above me, my hand clutching his medallion.

"She's awake." He moved back, allowing Anders to sit by my side.

"I'm so sorry I did that to you," he said, his voice strained. His eyes were red and glassy.

"Don't ever pull a stunt like that again," I said.

"Then don't ever offer to give yourself to Morlet to save Vidar or me."

The truth was, I'd do it again in a heartbeat, so I didn't promise him anything. I sat up, my stomach not even sore. "Where are we?"

"We took cover in a friend's apartment so you could heal," Vidar answered. "Since you were so injured, we didn't lure the *soldats* after us. We narrowly escaped the castle grounds. Luckily,

Morlet was too busy worrying about you that he didn't have time to organize his army."

Anders pointed to my stomach. "Are you healed?"

"Yes." Although, I was still covered with blood. Anders pulled me to my feet, kissing my forehead, shocking me with the intimate gesture especially in front of Vidar.

"The two of you have been lying to me," I said.

Vidar ran his hands over his face. "Technically, not lying so much as concealing the truth."

"Why?" Didn't they trust me?

"I wanted you to like me for who I am—not my position. I was also afraid you'd think I only cared about retaking the throne."

"What's your excuse?" I asked Anders.

"Vidar ordered me not to say anything."

"Do the other Krigers know?" Vidar scratched his chin and shrugged. "I'm the only one who didn't know?"

"It's also hard to stomach the reality of being related to Morlet," Vidar said.

It went deeper than that. "He's your brother." They shared the same blood. Was that why Morlet felt familiar to me? Because he was Vidar's brother? I wanted to get out of the capital so I could have some time to myself to think about everything that had happened today—my father's death, rescuing the Krigers, and Vidar's true identity.

"Espen and I may have been brothers once, but Morlet is no kin to me. He is my enemy."

"I think there's still a part of Espen in him."

Three loud thumps sounded on the ceiling. "That's our cue to go," Anders said. "*Soldats* are getting close to the building."

"We're in a hidden room below a friend's apartment," Vidar explained, sensing my confusion. "He's keeping watch for us.

This room has an escape route he uses for emergencies."

"What sort of escape route?" As much as I hated the tunnels, they were preferable to running through the streets when the army was actively searching for us.

"Well," Anders said, "you're not going to like this, but it's the fastest way." He handed me my bo staff.

Taking my weapon, I rolled my eyes. I never liked any of his crazy ideas, but they always worked, even if they didn't go as planned. He led us to the corner of the room where there was a door in the rickety, wooden floorboards. "Another tunnel?"

"Not exactly," Anders said with a wry smile. He opened the door. Cool air and a loud noise greeted us.

It sounded like a river flowed below. "This is a tunnel filled with water?" I asked with disbelief. "We're not swimming out of the capital are we?" My venture through the underground cavern when I was forced to take the water tunnels to escape hadn't been particularly fun or easy.

Anders laughed. "The tunnels are only half full of water." He pointed inside the opening. I peered down—there was a boat. He reached below the floor and unlatched several hooks. "When I undo the last one, we won't have much time before the boat is carried away. I'll jump first, Kaia second, Vidar—close the door and jump last."

"Wait," I said, "maybe we should discuss this."

"There isn't time." Anders undid the last latch, and a loud boom sounded below.

"How far down is it?" Panic swelled inside me.

"Not far." Anders jumped.

I leapt. Luckily, it was only a five-foot drop. When I landed in the boat, Anders pulled me to the side. Vidar gracefully hopped next to me.

I slid the bo staff near my feet and held on while Anders released two long oars that had been holding us in place. The boat took off, gliding along in the strong current. We didn't speak as we traveled through the dark tunnel. Anders used the oars to prevent us from slamming into the walls and breaking apart.

The rushing underground river flowed out of the rocky tunnel, spitting us into a lake outside the capital. Anders grunted as he used the oars to steer us to the nearest shore. When we hit the bank with a soft *thunk*, Vidar and Anders got out, pulling the boat onto dry land. I climbed out, and Anders dragged the boat away from the lake, hiding it next to a fallen tree.

Vidar pumped his fist in the air, and then wrapped a smiling Anders in a hug. "We did it!"

"Thanks to Kaia," Anders said.

"And we didn't lose anybody."

"Except for my father." The only thing that made the pain bearable was knowing we rescued the Krigers, just as he'd wanted.

"I'm sorry," Vidar said. "It's not easy losing a parent. The pain never truly leaves."

Anders cleared his throat. "Vidar, the Krigers, and me—we're all here for you. We're your family now. You can count on us." A lump formed in my throat. "You are not alone."

"Speaking of which," Vidar said, "let's go join the other Krigers."

Anders led the way deeper into the forest. We traveled all night until we reached the mountain range west of the capital. Vidar had sent the Krigers to the cavern where we obtained our weapons. Exhausted, I pulled myself up the rocks and into the cave, ready to collapse and sleep for a very long time.

Stepping inside, a fire was already lit and eleven jubilant men were waiting for us. They eagerly greeted Vidar and Anders before forming a circle around Vidar and dropping to one knee, facing him.

"Rise," Vidar commanded. "Kaia, welcome to the Order of the Krigers. I'd like you to meet everyone. This is Einar, Geir, Harald, Jorgen, Marius, Gunner, Reidar, Henrik, Oddvar, Tor, and Stein. Everyone, this is Kaia—the most powerful Kriger I've ever met. With her help, we will defeat Morlet." A chorus of cheers rang out.

Everyone bent and retrieved their weapons. As soon as they stood, I felt my bo staff hum with an energy I'd never experienced before. Suddenly, I was no longer exhausted but eager to begin working with these men.

"Tomorrow, you will begin training together. You will learn how to link your power. And when the time is right, we will attack and defeat Morlet."

Vidar wanted to help the Krigers kill Morlet in order to end the curse and avenge his parents' deaths. As excited as I was to link with my fellow Krigers and harness my full power, I felt torn about killing Morlet. Would I be able to when the time came?

My father had died today so that I could live to fulfill my duty as a Kriger. He wanted me to end our family's curse so that the next female born wouldn't face the same fate as all the women before me had. He'd taught me how to fight and defend myself. Now, here I was, standing with the Order of the Krigers, ready to make my father's dream come true. I had to carry on for him, and for my mother.

"We all have a choice, Kaia," Anders whispered in my ear. "Morlet made his. Now it's time for you to make yours."

"Before we start training," Vidar said, "I think a celebration is in order!"

Everyone cheered and stomped on the ground. Someone

found a lute among the supplies and began playing a lively tune. Mugs of ale were passed around to everyone. Vidar grabbed my hand and pulled me to him, spinning me around.

"I don't know how to dance," I admitted, trying not to step on his toes.

"Just follow my lead." He danced around the cave, passing me from one partner to another. As the night wore on, exhaustion overtook me and I sat down, leaning against the wall. Everyone was either drinking or dancing by the fire. The sound of men laughing echoed in the cave.

"What are you doing over here all alone?" Anders asked, sitting next to me.

"It's been a long day," I said, yawning.

"Yes, it has. How are you holding up?"

I leaned my head on his shoulder. "With you by my side," I said feeling bold, "I'm holding up just fine."

He smiled and squeezed my hand. "You're engaged to my best friend."

In all the chaos, I'd forgotten about that.

"Grei Heks said your bloodlines are destined." He released my hand.

I sat up straight, my eyes wide. Had Grei Heks said bloodlines? Or had she specifically mentioned Vidar? If she said bloodlines, she might not have been referring to Vidar, but his brother, Morlet. Unable to voice my concern, I laid my head back on Anders's shoulder, trying to calm my raging heart.

"And you'll make a beautiful queen."

"What?" I asked.

"Vidar is the heir. When we kill Morlet, Vidar will retake the throne. Since you'll be married to him, that will make you the queen."

There was no way I was queen material. A warrior—yes. Royalty—no. "I don't want to be queen." All I ever wanted was a simple life.

"And I don't want to be an assassin." He sighed. "Another time, another life perhaps."

"Perhaps."

"You look exhausted. Go to sleep."

Leaning on Anders's shoulder, my eyes grew heavy and I drifted off to sleep.

*Morlet laughed—the menacing sound making my body turn cold. I stood in the middle of an empty cabin I'd never seen before.*

*"You didn't think it'd be that easy, did you?" He sauntered closer to me, his black cape billowing around his legs. "Oh, my dear Kaia," he purred, tilting his head to the side, so I could see his mouth. "I will kill the eleven Krigers, and there's nothing you can do to stop me."*

*I took a step away from him, searching the cabin for my bo staff.*

*"Then, when I'm done with them, you will watch as I destroy Vidar and that pathetic assassin. Mark my words—they will burn." He smiled as he curled his fingers, making a fist and placing it over his heart, sealing his promise.*

*"I think you overestimate your magic."*

*He laughed. "While I do appreciate your bravado, I know you better than that. And Kaia, I'm coming for you."*

## End of Book 1

# Order of the Krigers Word Guide

*Kriger* = warrior
*Soldat* = soldier
*Heks* = witch/warlock
*Ulv* = wolf
*Brubjorn* = bear
*Fugl* = large bird

# ACKNOWLEDGEMENTS

I'm not even sure where to begin. As I sit here composing my seventh, yes SEVENTH, set of acknowledgments, I am truly stunned. Seven books. What an accomplishment. When I first started out, all I wanted to do was write a book I wanted to read. And here I am.

None of this would be possible without my best friend and husband. His endless support has allowed me to embark on this wild dream of mine. I am so thankful to have him by my side every step of the way.

To my three kids who inspire and challenge me every single day. They are my biggest fans and always want to know what's going to happen next in my stories. I love talking about my books with them. Their enthusiasm is absolutely priceless.

To my one and only sister. She is simply amazing. She works so hard, is fiercely passionate, and is a fantastic mother. I'm lucky to have her as my sister and friend.

To my mom who is my rock. She is always helping me out whether it is running the kids to and from school, soccer, or MMA. I'd be a mess without her love and support.

To my first reader, Jessica. I wrote five chapters of a new story just to see what would happen. Then I gave Jessica those five chapters. The next thing I knew, she wanted five more. My characters came to life, and she became my biggest cheerleader. I don't think this story would have been written if it wasn't for her.

To Allyssa, Stacie, Debi, and Rebecca. These girls are my extraordinary beta readers. I honestly don't know what I'd do without them. From the incredibly disastrous first draft, they read and critiqued my manuscript countless times until I had something that exceeded my expectations.

To Neil. I am thankful we met all those years ago at a SCBWI meeting and became critique partners. He was instrumental in polishing this manuscript and is truly one of the most talented writers I know.

To Sarah. Where would I be without our Panera writing stints? She makes writing fun, engaging, and forces me out of my writing cave to be social. At least as social as I can be.

To Georgia McBride. I can't thank her enough for taking a chance on me. Not only that, but she pushed me to be a better writer, and I am eternally grateful. I've never had someone take such interest in me, teach me so much, and do it with grace and professionalism. I am truly blessed to work with her.

To my fabulous editor, Cameron, and everyone at Month9Books. They worked endlessly to take my manuscript and turn it into the beautiful book it is today. I am lucky to work with these amazing people.

To Jaime my publicist extraordinaire. She has a love for books that rivals my own. I am honored she works so hard to put this book into the hands of readers.

To Damaris. She is always promoting my books and helping to spread the word about them.

To my Davis Divas. Best street team ever. I love working with each and every one of them. Writing is such a solitary thing. However, when I share a cover or a synopsis with them, it is a privilege to obtain their feedback. I don't know where I'd be without their unending support and enthusiasm.

Lastly, to my readers. I certainly wouldn't be a writer without you. It brings me such joy to hear how excited people are for my stories, to hear how they love or hate one of my characters, and that they can't wait for more books! Sometimes I pinch myself to make sure I'm not dreaming. THANK YOU!

JENNIFER ANNE DAVIS

**Jennifer Anne Davis** is the bestselling author of the True Reign Series. She graduated from the University of San Diego with a degree in English and a teaching credential. She currently lives in Southern California with her husband and three highly energetic children.

# OTHER MONTH9BOOKS TITLES YOU MIGHT LIKE

THE MISSING
NAMELESS
IN THE SHADOW OF THE DRAGON KING

Find more books like this at http://www.Month9Books.com

Connect with Month9Books online:

Facebook: www.Facebook.com/Month9Books
Twitter: https://twitter.com/Month9Books
You Tube: www.youtube.com/user/Month9Books
Blog: www.month9booksblog.com

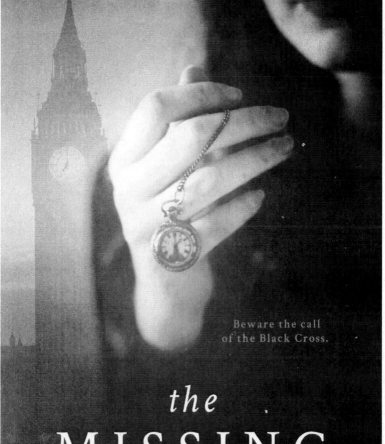

Beware the call
of the Black Cross.

*the*
# MISSING

*J.R. LENK*

# NAMELESS

## JENNIFER JENKINS

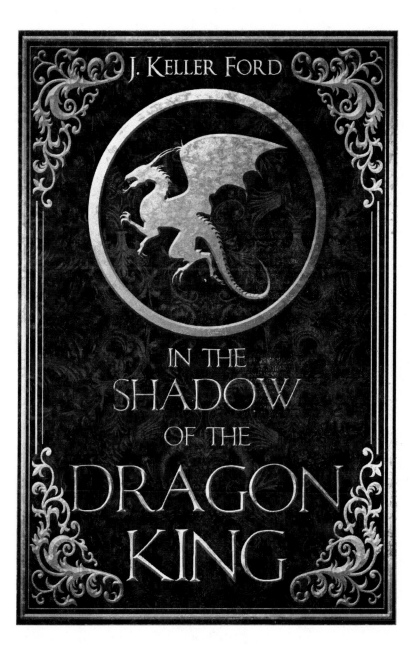

J. KELLER FORD

IN THE
SHADOW
OF THE
DRAGON
KING